COMING HOME TO MAPLE TREE LODGE

ALISON SHERLOCK

B
Boldwood

First published in Great Britain in 2025 by Boldwood Books Ltd.

Copyright © Alison Sherlock, 2025

Cover Design by Alice Moore Design

Cover Images: Shutterstock and iStock

The moral right of Alison Sherlock to be identified as the author of this work has been asserted in accordance with the Copyright, Designs and Patents Act 1988.

All rights reserved. No part of this book may be reproduced in any form or by any electronic or mechanical means, including information storage and retrieval systems, without written permission from the author, except for the use of brief quotations in a book review. This book is a work of fiction and, except in the case of historical fact, any resemblance to actual persons, living or dead, is purely coincidental.

Every effort has been made to obtain the necessary permissions with reference to copyright material, both illustrative and quoted. We apologise for any omissions in this respect and will be pleased to make the appropriate acknowledgements in any future edition.

A CIP catalogue record for this book is available from the British Library.

Paperback ISBN 978-1-83617-695-4

Large Print ISBN 978-1-83617-696-1

Hardback ISBN 978-1-83617-694-7

Ebook ISBN 978-1-83617-697-8

Kindle ISBN 978-1-83617-698-5

Audio CD ISBN 978-1-83617-689-3

MP3 CD ISBN 978-1-83617-690-9

Digital audio download ISBN 978-1-83617-693-0

This book is printed on certified sustainable paper. Boldwood Books is dedicated to putting sustainability at the heart of our business. For more information please visit https://www.boldwoodbooks.com/about-us/sustainability/

Boldwood Books Ltd, 23 Bowerdean Street, London, SW6 3TN

www.boldwoodbooks.com

1

'Turn left here,' announced the satnav. 'You have arrived at your destination.'

Lily Wilson turned off the country lane and immediately slammed on the brakes. She peered through the car windscreen at the locked wooden gate in front of her, barely visible through the heavy rain.

She pressed the button to wind down the window and stuck her head out before sighing as she stared at the vast overgrown and empty field beyond the gate. This most certainly was not Maple Tree Lodge.

The rain was running down her face so she quickly wound the window back up. Lily glanced at the Google Maps screen on her mobile. But her phone had no signal at all and was still under the impression that she was back in the small village of Cranley which she had driven through ten minutes ago.

So she switched off the satnav screen in the hire car and set off once more, hoping blind luck would help her find the hotel. She flicked the windscreen wipers to double time but could still see hardly anything on the road in front of her, such was the intensity of the downpour. It was the end of September and autumn was arriving with an extremely soggy fanfare.

She had to face facts. She was completely and utterly lost in the middle of the English countryside on a rainy Friday afternoon. And there wasn't a single person around to ask for directions.

It felt as if the universe was sending her a clear signal. *You're lost and it's pouring down with rain. Are you sure you don't just want to turn around and go home to London instead?*

She shook her head at the idea, telling herself that there were three problems with giving up on this journey despite the odds seemingly stacked against her.

First of all, her current home wasn't really somewhere that she wanted to go at any time of day or night. She had rented the small double room in a shared house in Wimbledon for six months and that was over five months too long to live with the three strangers that were her current housemates. Between Wayne starting up his thumping music every afternoon and leaving it on until midnight, Moira saying that she wasn't 'borrowing' Lily's make-up every time she went out and Jason with his dubious plantation growing in the attic, Lily couldn't wait to leave the following week when the lease ran out.

She had lived in various grim places in the capital city over the past decade and each seemed to be worse than the previous one. It was all a stark contrast to the fancy upmarket residences that she had grown up in.

Lily had been born in England but the family hadn't remained in the country for very long and had left when she was only two years old. Her father was a diplomat and, as far back as Lily could remember, they had moved every two years or so from country to country, being sent wherever the current government at that time decided to post them. Her mother was an English teacher and thus was able, most of the time, to continue teaching in each new country whilst also supporting her husband.

Lily had spent her entire childhood starting a new school every year or so in a different country and sometimes a different continent as well. She was barely given enough time to make friends before leaving and having to start all over again. It was extremely unsettling.

As the years went on, Lily began to hold back from making friends, getting used to the feeling of nothing ever feeling permanent as it always, inevitably, changed – schools, friends and homes. As such, and being an only child, she only had her parents for company most of the time and the feeling of loneliness never really went away.

At the age of twelve, she was sent away to boarding school in England and hated it as soon as she had arrived. Almost immediately, she had begged her parents to let her return to them but they had refused, telling her that it would get better. But it hadn't. The feeling of not being accepted by the tight-knit groups of girls only exacerbated her loneliness and feelings of abandonment. So Lily withdrew into her shell, deciding that she didn't need anyone. That she was stronger on her own and that life would be easier that way.

When she went to stay with her parents during the school holidays, they didn't seem to sense how much she was missing out by not having friends, merely encouraging her to focus on her schoolwork so that her own career would be as stellar as theirs.

But Lily had never been overly ambitious. In fact, it sometimes felt as if the only things she had inherited from her parents were her mother's thick red hair and green eyes. She only ever wanted attention from her parents but with their hectic social calendar, they didn't have a great deal of time for her. However, her bright mind ensured that her exam results were always satisfactory and pleased them.

One Christmas when she was growing up, her parents had gifted her a large doll's house. It wasn't very big, with only two floors, but she loved it. For Lily, it represented a permanent home, the one thing she had always dreamt of.

At the age of ten, she was too old to play with dolls but the empty rooms sparked something else inside of her. She would redecorate them over and over, playing with different styles and ideas for each room and becoming excited when a new idea formed for the next design. She knew from that moment onwards that she wanted to be an interior designer, despite her parents' reservations. They wanted her to follow in her father's footsteps, telling her that it was a more steady career, but Lily's mind was made up.

At sixth-form college, she studied graphic and textile design. Once she had left school, she had moved to London to start her apprenticeship in interior design.

She knew that her parents were disappointed in her choice of career. They knew how little money she earned each month as an apprentice but her creative side was too strong to resist. She refused all offers of money from them, determined to prove that their reservations were wrong. So she had worked endless weekends and overtime to get ahead of her competition.

The goal had always been to have her own interior design company, a dream that had always been just out of reach. But she had to make it. Had to make that ambition come true. Because then she knew that her parents would finally approve of her choice of career.

However, the hard work had meant that she had put her ambition above almost everything else, including the small group of people in her life who meant the most to her.

Which was reason number two why she couldn't turn the car around despite feeling ever more lost in the unfamiliar Cotswolds countryside.

When she had arrived in London fourteen years ago, Lily didn't know anyone. She had managed to secure rent on a room without first viewing it. London rental prices were ridiculously expensive so her choices had been limited to a shared house in an extremely undesirable area. But despite the shabbiness of both the location and the house itself, it turned out to be one of the best things to ever happen to Lily.

The house was a brand-new listing and had attracted three other women of the same age: Hannah, Beth and Ella. Despite Lily's reluctance to get close to anyone, she couldn't help herself from slowly bonding with her housemates over their first weeks of living together. They were all fresh out of college and eager to commence what they hoped would be long and glittering careers in their chosen fields. Hannah was training to be a pastry chef at a popular restaurant in the West End, Beth was an aspiring astronomer and so was thrilled to be working at the Royal Observatory in Greenwich and Ella was a social media assistant in Canary Wharf.

Coming from different areas in England, it was the first time living in London for all of them and after a hard day's work, they enjoyed nights out in wine bars and even cheaper nights in gossiping over pizza whilst *Desperate Housewives* and *The Big Bang Theory* played in the background.

They were all different in their personalities, as well as choices of career, but had remained best friends ever since. After being so lonely for much of her life so far, Lily instantly felt comforted by their love and friendship. However, she still never really opened up fully to any of them about her innermost feelings. The legacy from being sent away to boarding school meant that she would always fear rejection and getting hurt. And yet Hannah, Beth and Ella had become her family when her parents had always been so distant.

After a couple of years living together, however, things in the house began to change. Beth had been the first to move out with a once-in-a-lifetime offer of a two-year sabbatical at the South African Astronomical Observatory. Ella followed soon afterwards, heading to Manchester to work for a tech start-up company.

Only Lily and Hannah remained in the house, and the two new housemates did nothing to endear themselves to the firm friends, so they kept to themselves for another two years with intermittent meet-ups with Beth and Ella whenever they could.

Four years after arriving in London, Lily was still a lowly junior in an interior design firm, not having progressed at all, and Hannah was far too shy and unconfident to make a name for herself in the cut-throat world of catering.

Then Hannah had unexpectedly fallen in love. Lily had hated Sean on sight and couldn't see what on earth Hannah saw in him. He was moody and completely opposite to kind, soft Hannah. But her friend was bewitched and when Sean suggested they move into their own place a couple of months later, Hannah had willingly gone with him.

Lily found that she suddenly couldn't bear to be in the house where once she had been so happy with her three best friends. So she had quickly handed in her notice and moved on, sharing other houses and large flats ever since but never getting close to any of her new housemates.

Apart from her best friends, Lily's social circle hadn't grown at all, such was her reluctance to grow close to anyone else. Due to her shyness, Hannah didn't have too many friends either and Lily had a feeling that it wasn't a particularly healthy relationship with Sean. She was proven correct a year later when Hannah let her know that she had left Sean and had moved back to stay with her family in Cranley for a while. Ten years later, she was still there.

The four best friends continued to meet up over the years, although recently, as she finally began to receive recognition for her skills and achieve greater responsibilities at work, Lily had found that her time was more limited and often reluctantly cancelled, due to deadlines. She was still pursuing her career, still trying to prove her parents wrong and make them proud of her choice of being an interior designer. However, the friends still talked every week and texted nearly every day. Now in their early thirties, the friends' lives continued on different trajectories, although none of them had found happiness in their dating lives. They had all had various relationships; however, despite a few boyfriends over the years, Lily had stopped dating entirely to concentrate on her career.

Lily knew all about Hannah's family, of course, having heard so much about them over the years despite never meeting them. But the fact that they owned a hotel hadn't felt that significant until their last conversation a few days earlier.

'It's all so different since Ben took over,' Hannah had told her. Hannah's brother had taken over the running of the hotel since their father had unexpectedly passed away six months ago. 'The whole place is a complete mess as everything needs to be updated apparently. Anyway, when all the work's finished, it will need redecorating so I've suggested to him that you're just the person to come and help us out!'

Lily had taken a deep intake of breath. 'Me?' she said.

'Of course!' said Hannah, laughing. 'Who else? After all, you're the talented designer at that fancy firm!'

Lily's thrill of delight was short lived as she gulped away the shame of not being honest with her best friend.

Which was the third reason that she couldn't turn around the car, despite still being lost. She needed this commission more than she had ever needed anything before in her life.

From the beginning, Lily had slowly built up her career from being an apprentice to a junior position. She had made many sacrifices, including her own personal life or lack thereof, until finally she had accepted a job as an assistant to a flourishing modern interior designer two years ago. Hans Haubermann was considered a genius and after a couple of recent high-profile commissions by the London elite, he was *the* hot designer of modern times.

Lily had been thrilled to get a job with such an exclusive designer. Finally, her sacrifices had been worth it. She was almost there. With a few commissions of her own, she could finally be her own boss. Even her parents were impressed by Hans' exclusive customer list.

But the job came at a heavy price. Hans' designs were minimalistic and highly modern, in total contrast to Lily's own style, which was to ensure a space was warm and comfortable. But she decided it was a sacrifice worth making if she had Hans' name on her CV.

However, to her horror, she had quickly discovered that Hans was a fraud. He had no talent. It was a company secret that he used all of his assistants' talent and hid behind their creativity, passing it off as his own. And Lily had been no different, only discovering the truth three months ago thanks to an unhappy colleague who had blabbed at her leaving drinks.

It was all so unfair. Hans had promised so much in the beginning, including making her partner in the interior design firm. But it turned out that they were the same promises that he had made many times to many different designers over the years.

Then, a week ago, he had dropped the huge bombshell that he was giving her notice. Hans had stated that they were downsizing and letting staff go but Lily knew that it was just her who had lost her job. Hans had been sneaky enough to terminate her job just days before her two-year anniversary, meaning that she wasn't eligible for statutory redundancy pay either.

Since her immediate dismissal, Lily had spent the past few days in a mess, crying in her room over the unfairness of it all. But what could she do? Nobody would believe her, even if she could tell them. Because it turned out that there was a small clause in her original employment contract which prevented her from spilling the secrets of the company to anyone.

All she wanted was the chance to prove that she had made the right career choice, to show her parents that she could make it on her own. She had the skills and the experience. However, she now had no recommendations and the client base that she had built up was gone, tied to Hans' business instead.

She knew that she was good enough to have her own company. But where to even start? She just needed a bit of luck.

And then lovely Hannah had called her up about the hotel and it was as if fate had given her a second chance. Hannah still believed that Lily worked at the firm and Lily hadn't told her the truth. In fact, she hadn't told anyone, not her best friends or her parents who were currently based in Canberra. The truth was that she was embarrassed. A failure. After so many years of hard work, she had absolutely nothing to show for it. However, if the commission for the hotel worked out then she would reveal the truth to her friends in time, just as soon as her future was sorted out.

But she also knew that the Jackson family wouldn't give the

hotel commission to someone without the backup of a slick company behind her so it was best to keep it a secret for now. Lily also knew that to work on a prestigious project such as a countryside hotel was the perfect place for her, a stepping stone to starting her own business and, hopefully, success. If only she could find the hotel, that is!

The rain had eased now and she could see that autumn was showing signs along the hedgerows that flanked the country lane and across the faraway green hills. The dark green of the countryside was now scattered with touches of amber and ochre as the seasons began to change. It was a stark contrast to the urban streets that she was used to but the view was all the more pleasurable because of it.

Finally, just as the rain stopped, she saw what appeared to be a shiny new sign by the side of the lane for Maple Tree Lodge.

With a whoop of relief, she turned the car onto a narrow track and found herself enveloped into a shaded woodland almost immediately. Instantly, the light was much darker but as she headed around a corner, she could see a glimmer of water in the distance through the trees.

She could now also make out part of a substantial building as well. Hannah had told her it was a small hotel but it was much larger than Lily had anticipated. She felt a thrill rush through her. What a start it would be to have this hotel as her very own commission.

Not used to driving, having lived in London for so long, Lily accidentally pressed the accelerator, not the brake pedal as intended, and the hire car leapt forward so quickly that she almost crashed into an oncoming vehicle which had just appeared around a bend.

In order to avoid a head-on collision, she grabbed the steering wheel and pulled the car hard left. With the crash avoided, Lily found that the car was heading sharply down a bank instead and straight into what appeared to be a small pond.

The engine stalled and finally she was at a halt. She felt relieved, despite the car being surrounded by water. She took a deep breath and checked that she was OK. Thankfully she had been wearing her seat belt which had protected her from anything worse than a stiff neck.

Seeing movement nearby, she looked over to the other car and saw a man climbing out of his vehicle. Feeling a little sheepish, she wound down the window.

'Are you OK?' she shouted over, realising her voice sounded a little breathless from the shock.

He ran a hand through his dark hair and looked dazed. 'I'm fine. You?' he shouted back.

'I'm OK,' she replied, despite the car being stranded in the middle of the pond.

The stranger puffed out a sigh before looking annoyed. 'Although if you had been driving properly and not like Lewis Hamilton then this wouldn't have happened,' he told her.

Feeling embarrassed, she was about to reply when she realised that water was beginning to trickle inside at the bottom of each of the car doors.

Grimacing, she pushed her door open, anxious to get out in case it sank any further.

'Wait!' she heard the man call out.

But she was in no mood to listen. She was panicking about the water coming in and, after pushing the door against what felt like a mound of earth, Lily jumped out of the car and straight into what appeared to be a bog.

Her favourite white trainers were quickly submerged into a brown ooze which at least only went up to her ankles. She stared down in disbelief at the pond which appeared to be more mud than water.

'I did say wait,' called out the man, walking towards her.

'You could have elaborated on that a little,' she told him, her humiliation growing by the second.

'I'll give you a hand,' he said, coming to the edge of the bank to stretch out his arm towards her.

'I can manage just fine,' she muttered, waving his arm away with her hand. She wasn't some damsel in distress. The embarrassment at her predicament made her words sound harsher than usual. 'I don't need saving!'

He looked surprised but withdrew his hand and leant against a nearby tree. 'Go ahead,' he told her. 'I haven't had my daily laugh yet.'

What was this man's problem? she wondered. He was about the same age as her, dressed casually in jeans and jumper. But his admittedly attractive face was currently looking extremely smug and she couldn't figure out why.

And then she realised. Because she couldn't move her feet. At all. She tried and tried until she was red in the face and yet no matter how much she tugged at her feet, they wouldn't move. It was as if they were stuck in glue.

With a howl of frustration, she finally and reluctantly looked at the man, who was smiling down at her from the nearby bank.

'It's the combination of sand and soil mixed together,' he told her. 'Makes for the stickiest of muds. The trees love it. Holds on to all the moisture and makes them grow big and strong.'

'Great,' she murmured, trying one last tug of her foot to no avail. 'Lucky trees.'

'So, are you going to accept my help now?' he asked.

'Yes, please,' she muttered.

He reached out both of his hands to take her outstretched

ones. They locked fingers and she tried not to feel even more mortified.

'Ready?' he said, before bracing himself. 'In one, two, three...'

At the count of three, he gave her one almighty tug. But as she registered that she was finally free from the mud, Lily also realised that her feet were now bare as she flew through the air. Her trainers had been left behind.

However, that was nothing compared to the utmost problem in her mind and that was, thanks to his extremely strong pull, she was catapulted not only out of the muddy pond but straight into the stranger's chest instead. Hearing him exclaim 'ooof' upon impact, the momentum carried her forward and they both crashed to the floor.

For a moment, Lily felt somewhat stunned. And then finally, the realisation that she was now lying directly on top of a stranger in the middle of the forest came rushing into her consciousness.

She looked down into his face and found him staring up at her with dark brown eyes. For a moment there was nothing but the sound of the drops of water dripping down from the trees onto the ground.

Then his handsome face broke into a grin.

'Welcome to Maple Tree Lodge,' he said.

2

Ben Jackson had been having a bad day until he unexpectedly ended up with a gorgeous redhead lying on top of him.

It was just a shame that she was scowling down at him, her green eyes inches from his. And, of course, that she was a perfect stranger. Which begged the question, who on earth was she?

He was just about to introduce himself when she abruptly stood up, leaving him to slowly sit up on the forest floor. Ben took a moment to try and come to terms with what had just happened, all in a very short space of time.

It had been a whirlwind five minutes since he had left the hotel in a fit of temper. He hadn't even known where he was driving except that it had to be anywhere but the hotel. Anywhere but Maple Tree Lodge. And yet he had only made it yards from the hotel car park when he had found himself avoiding a head-on collision with another car.

He glanced over at his car, which thankfully was unscathed. But with the other car appearing to be fully embedded in the pond, it looked as if it could be a write-off. Thus he knew that his much-needed getaway was over as quickly as it had begun.

Now he had to go back to the hotel and face his grandad once more, despite having left in a fit of pique only a short while ago after yet another argument. Ben loved his grandad very much. He just didn't think that they could live together for too much longer.

He looked over at the stranger and saw that she was brushing off pine needles and wet leaves from her jeans and jumper. As she bent down, her long red hair wafted around her shoulders, reminding him of the leaves that the chestnut trees had turned in the autumn already, glossy, warm and vibrant.

'Are you hurt?' he asked, standing up.

'Only my pride,' she replied, giving him a sheepish smile which lit up her pretty face.

He couldn't help but look at her incredible hair, then the long dark eyelashes and pale skin highlighted by freckles and a rosy blush of embarrassment across her cheeks.

He gave himself a little shake and looked away. Had it been so long since he had last been on a date that the first attractive woman who came into view would render him temporarily speechless?

'So before getting rerouted into our pond, what were you doing out here in the middle of nowhere?' he asked, finally finding his voice.

She looked surprised. 'I was heading to the hotel. I'm staying there tonight.'

Now it was Ben's turn to feel surprised. 'Stay? At Maple Tree Lodge?' he asked, unable to betray his shocked tone of voice.

She nodded before frowning. 'Yes.'

He found himself even more amazed. He wasn't going to admit that there weren't any bookings that evening. And that there hadn't been any bookings for the past month either, he added to himself. The state of the hotel at the moment didn't help, of course. There were workmen and mess everywhere. And that had been the cause of the argument with his grandad that morning. The cause of every argument since he had returned home earlier that year.

Back then, he had been a partner in a successful architectural firm in London. It had been the job that he had always dreamed about and studied hard for. But it hadn't quite panned out as he had hoped. Where Ben had been hoping to design glorious buildings of architectural interest, he had ended up doing more generic work on shopping centres and malls around the world. It had supplied a very nice paycheque into his bank account every month but not the creative satisfaction that he found himself craving.

However, with a decent flat and business, life hadn't been so bad in the capital city. He'd had a great social life with his friends along with many frequent dates. Everything was fine until the phone call one evening that spring from his mum that had changed everything and brought him home.

Home had always been Maple Tree Lodge to Ben. In fact, it had been home to five generations of the Jackson family. His great-great-grandfather, desperate to leave the horrors of the First World War far behind him in 1918, had ventured far into the English countryside to find some much-needed peace and quiet.

On the outskirts of a tiny village called Cranley, he had discovered a large lake and 50 acres of woodland up for sale. Once purchased, he had begun to build himself and his new bride a home to bring up their family in.

Each generation of the Jackson family had added more rooms and space to the lodge, using a mixture of the warm-coloured brick that was popular in the area, as well as the endless amount of timber that the Jackson family now owned, thanks to the surrounding woodland.

These days it was a two-storey building with long wings that extended along the sandy bank of the lake. Too large a building for just his parents, his wife and two children to live in, Ben's father Tony had decided to open up the place as a hotel in the early 1980s. He had altered the top floor to accommodate twenty guest bedrooms with en suites, leaving the family to live in private staff quarters at the end of the west wing.

But whilst he was a brilliant carpenter, Tony had never had many business skills and although they received some guests over the years, along with glowing reviews, the hotel had never been the success that he had dreamed of. It didn't help that the place was tucked away in the middle of nowhere and before the days of the internet, trying to get the word out that they even existed was almost impossible.

There had been some guests in recent years but had the hotel ever been truly successful? Ben didn't think so. Growing up, all he could remember was the odd group of guests arriving but other than that, he and his sister had the run of the hotel in which to play hide and seek with their friends.

His dad had often been depressed that his dream of running a successful hotel hadn't come to fruition and the strain of the business had probably put an additional stress on his heart that had taken his dad from them so suddenly that spring.

Ben had rushed home to be with his family in their shared grief. But during his prolonged stay, he had discovered the source of his dad's stress. The hotel accounts did not make for pleasant reading and the family's home was perilously close to financial ruin. Tony had taken out a large bank loan to try to keep the place afloat but, along with some much-needed renovations, the debt was enormous.

And then there was the bombshell letter he had found in the drawer of the desk. It was from a large conglomerate of hotels offering to buy Maple Tree Lodge which would then be turned into one of their modern spa hotels. The sum of money they were offering was eye watering and, to Ben, highly tempting, and yet he had found a file where his father had already drafted a reply to refuse the offer. With a heavy heart, Ben knew he too would have to decline the offer and try to act upon his late father's wishes by keeping the hotel in the family. Selling to the multinational corporation would ensure that his family would have to leave their beloved home and nobody wanted that.

So the only solution was to try to update the hotel instead to secure its future. With his grandparents almost into their eighties and his mum still grief-stricken, it was up to Ben to take charge. He had sold his share of the architectural firm and had remained at Maple Tree Lodge ever since, desperately trying to think up ways to keep it from foreclosure. Despite the overwhelming amount of updating that the old building required, he had thought the job would be relatively easy. Surely Maple Tree Lodge had to have something to offer if the large multinational company wanted their hotel? But as the months had passed, and the renovations became ever more extensive, it had been a heavy weight on his shoulders with the burden of the family's happiness and security all resting on him.

He suddenly realised that the woman was looking at him with a question in her eyes and decided to introduce himself.

'Hi, I'm Ben Jackson,' he told her. 'The hotel manager.'

'I'm Lily Wilson,' she replied. 'Hannah's friend.'

'Oh, yes,' he said, suddenly recalling what his sister had told him over breakfast that morning. 'Of course.'

He had heard all about Hannah's best friends over the years but had only met Beth and Ella since he had moved back home. Lily, according to his sister, was the busy career woman and seemingly never appeared to have any spare time to see her friends.

Hannah had also reminded him that her friend was an interior designer and his sister was hoping that they could use her to redecorate the hotel. Ben had googled the interior design firm where Lily worked and found himself impressed. Their style was minimalistic and modern, just what he wanted for the hotel. The hotel needed a new updated look that was sleek and stylish and would match their competitors' décor exactly. He just hoped the bill wouldn't be too expensive as his funds were seriously depleted.

He was about to ask her about her work when there was an ominous rumble of thunder overhead and he realised that the sky was becoming darker once more with the threat of yet more rain.

'I think we'd better get indoors into the dry,' he told her.

'I agree,' she replied, walking over to her stricken car to gracefully lean forward to grab her handbag from the front passenger seat and then a larger overnight bag.

As she straightened up, Ben was about to offer her a lift in his car but she had already strode away from him towards the clearing of the hotel car park.

Ben decided to leave his car behind and walked swiftly to keep up with her. She didn't seem to mind being in bare feet in the forest which he found himself surprised at. Most of the women he had dated over the years would have shrieked at the muddy floor and possibility of insects crawling around on the ground. This woman appeared to not worry about anything as trivial as that, he noted.

As soon as they reached the car park, Lily stopped to stare at the view. He couldn't blame her. It was the most spectacular setting, he thought, staring across the lake. Even on a dark and rainy day, the wide expanse of sky was reflected in the large body of water. There were gentle rolling hills surrounding the lake, as if hugging it and keeping it safe from any outside foes. Then there was the lake itself, sparkling even on such a dull day. It was surrounded by trees and large swathes of forest, all of which was owned by his family.

He then watched as Lily turned to stare up at the hotel with wide eyes. He followed her stare to the large building in front of them. His great-great-grandfather had felled many trees to build the original lodge and the future generations had followed suit so that the outside walls of the hotel were layers of huge logs, giving the place a solid but warm look. Vast brick chimneys hugged the outside walls all the way up to the slate-tiled roof, where spires of smoke were trailing upwards into the air.

Despite the beauty of the hotel, as usual these days, Ben could only see the sheer amount of money that it had cost him so far with the renovations. He had used the majority of his profits from selling his business to underpin the hotel which had been revealed early on to be in danger of subsiding into the lake. That expensive building work, along with new double-glazed windows, doors and an entire new roof had pretty much emptied out his bank account.

With the plumbing and electrics still being brought up to date, Ben still had no idea whether the hotel would survive even when everything was completed. But he had to try for the sake of his family.

However, the changes had caused him to butt up against his grandad every step of the way. His stubborn grandad was set on leaving things as they were. But Ben knew that couldn't be an option, otherwise the place would fail and they'd lose their home anyway.

He looked over to where his sister had just appeared at the oak-porched front door and rushed towards them.

'You made it!' said Hannah, a wide smile lighting up her face.

Ben realised that it had been a while since he had seen his younger sister so happy to see anyone and found himself smiling as he watched her embrace Lily in a hug.

Sweet Hannah, he thought. It was good to see her smile again after such a sad time following the loss of their father.

She was always such a quiet but calming presence. Unlike Ben, she had failed spectacularly with her studies at school, never finding anything academic easy. She had cracked under the pressure during her exams and had never returned.

With no qualifications, she had taken a job in a local restaurant at sixteen until finally, at Ben's urging, she had taken the plunge and headed to London. She was an extremely skilled baker but he had since realised that placing Hannah in the cutthroat world of the capital city was like placing a country mouse on an African savannah. He still felt guilty that he had put her under so much pressure, especially when neither the job nor her romantic relationship worked out and she rushed back to the sanctity of Cranley four years later. And she had remained there ever since.

Hannah was always happiest in the kitchen, behind the scenes. Baking was her favourite thing in the world. She was currently working in a local pub restaurant in the evenings to make money whilst the hotel restaurant lay empty during its renovations.

'It's been too long but you look gorgeous as usual,' Hannah told Lily as she stepped back from their hug. Then Hannah frowned as she looked her friend up and down. 'Except you have a leaf in your hair and where are your shoes?' She looked wide-eyed from Lily to Ben.

'I had a small accident,' said Lily, with a laugh. 'I ended up driving into a pond on the way in!'

'What?' Hannah didn't laugh, merely looking horrified instead. 'Are you OK? Are you hurt?'

'I'm fine,' Lily told her. 'But I could probably do with washing my feet!'

Hannah looked relieved and put her arm around Lily to take her inside. 'You'd better tell me all about it,' she said.

Ben was about to follow them when his grandad appeared from around the side of the hotel. Even from that distance, Ben could sense his grandad's scowl after yet another argument that afternoon.

Walter Jackson was stubborn but still filled with great determination and spirit, despite his seventy-nine years. Ben knew that his grandad only wanted the best for the hotel but at the same time, any new ideas were met with resistance and another battle would begin. So Ben's idea that each of the bedrooms had wireless internet, as well as new flat-screen televisions and LED lighting in each room, had been met by yet more grumbling about losing the soul of the place.

At one time, Ben and his grandad had had a good relationship but ever since his father had died, it felt to Ben as if he were a constant disappointment to Walter. That nothing he had done to the hotel met with his grandad's approval.

Ben had been left the hotel in his father's will but it was a constant stress hanging over him. The finances just didn't add up and hadn't done for a very long time. It was a mess which he was desperately trying to keep from his family, who were still grieving his father's sudden death.

He knew he had to keep trying to save the place, not only to appease his grandad but because it was their home. Ben was trying everything he could think of to keep Maple Tree Lodge afloat, but he still didn't know if it would be enough.

3

As Lily let Hannah lead her towards the hotel, her mind was still reeling, mainly from utter mortification.

It had been a crazy ten minutes, from crashing her car into a pond, getting stuck in the mud and then finding herself lying on top of Hannah's brother.

Hannah had shown her photos of Ben over the years. But somehow she hadn't made the connection between Hannah's big brother and the good-looking man she had ended up on top of. She hadn't expected him to be so attractive, for his eyes to be such a dark brown or for him to be strong enough to pull her free of the mud.

She glanced at him once more. He didn't look at all like his younger sister. Where Hannah's hair was golden blonde, Ben's was dark and still a bit spiky from being out in the rain. Hannah was slim and petite where Ben was far taller and more muscular. She briefly found herself wondering whether he had a girlfriend before she pulled herself together.

She had hardly made the right professional first impression

she had been hoping to give, especially as he had told her that he was the hotel manager. After all, this was a make-or-break job for her career so it hadn't been a great start so far.

Lily was thrilled to see Hannah though. It had been too long since they had last seen each other face to face and she was grateful to see her friend looking well. She couldn't wait until they had a proper catch-up, although she knew she had to keep quiet about the loss of her job.

But what a commission Maple Tree Lodge could be, she told herself, looking up at the hotel. It was so warm and rustic looking, and so much larger than she had imagined.

As they drew nearer to the entrance, Hannah called over to an elderly man who had appeared from around the corner.

'Grandad! Come and meet my friend Lily,' said Hannah.

Her grandad nodded and held out his hand. 'I'm Walter Jackson,' he said.

'Lily Wilson,' she replied. She remembered Hannah telling her that they had celebrated his seventy-ninth birthday earlier that year but despite that, he had a surprisingly firm handshake and the blue eyes that studied her were still sharp above the bushy grey eyebrows.

'Welcome to Maple Tree Lodge,' said Walter. 'What do you think of our home?'

He turned with what appeared to be pride on his face as he looked up at the building in front of them.

'It's lovely,' she told him. 'Really spectacular.'

The warmth of the wood panelling along with the sandy-coloured stone seemed right at home in the middle of the forest. Hannah had invited her to the hotel many times to stay and yet Lily had always been so busy with work that she had never found the time. Now she was regretting not staying before as it was so beautiful.

Walter's smile faded. 'Shame you won't see it at its best inside,' he muttered, shooting his grandson a piercing look as Ben came over to join them.

'Let's go inside and get you cleaned up, shall we?' said Hannah in an overly bright tone.

Lily wondered whether she was imagining the tension in the atmosphere that had suddenly developed.

She followed Hannah through the oak-framed porch and into a large reception hall. It was a long room, flanked by an ornately carved oak staircase which rose in an arc up to the upper floor.

The whole place was filled with wooden beams along the walls and a grey flagstone floor. It felt cosy and warm, despite the lack of decoration, she realised. There were no pictures, no furnishings of any kind, in fact. But it was in the middle of a renovation as a large scaffolding tower took up most of the room.

'This is Frankie, our receptionist,' said Hannah, gesturing at a dark-haired woman in her late fifties who had just come out of a nearby room at the sound of their voices. 'This is my friend Lily who's staying here this weekend.'

'Nice to meet you,' said Frankie, with a warm smile.

'And don't mind the mess,' added Walter, from behind them as he stepped over some trailing wires to turn and go through a doorway on their right. 'We're just having what I've been told is yet another update.'

'A necessary one,' she heard Ben mutter under his breath.

'It's hardly necessary,' grumbled Walter, before turning to head towards a nearby doorway with Ben in pursuit.

At the sound of their muted but definitely tense voices, Lily hesitated about what to do or say next.

Frankie, the receptionist, looked at her. 'Don't mind them,' she said, with a cheerful smile. 'They're just having their daily argument.'

'The usual one,' added Hannah, rolling her eyes.

Lily remained silent. This was obviously a problem between family members and nothing to do with her.

'So you're the interior designer,' said Frankie, eyeing Lily up and down. 'Heard all about you, of course.'

'None of it good,' joked Hannah, nudging Lily with her elbows.

'Apparently you're the creative one of Hannah's group,' carried on Frankie. 'Let me see, Beth's the brainy one and Ella's the trendy one always on her phone.'

'That's about right,' said Lily, laughing.

'Hang on. What does that make me?' asked Hannah in a mock-hurt tone.

'The only one that can bake given your friends' attempts recently,' Frankie told her, with a wink.

'Beth and Ella came here?' asked Lily, somewhat surprised.

'Over the summer,' confirmed Frankie. 'They came, sunbathed, drank a lot and laughed even more, from what I remember.'

'Thanks to your cocktails,' replied Hannah. Her smile faded and she looked a little awkwardly at Lily. 'It was Beth's birthday over August bank holiday. When you had that deadline...' Her voice trailed off.

'Haven't I always?' said Lily, in a breezy tone. She had seen the photographs, of course, but she still felt a small pang at the thought of her friends being there together without her. Thankfully she knew that they understood how important her career was and why she couldn't always meet up with them.

In any case, at least this weekend would give her a chance to catch up with Hannah properly.

Hannah glanced at her watch and gave a shout of exclamation. 'I've got to get a cake out of the oven before it burns. Frankie, would you show Lily up to her room? She desperately needs to wash her feet.' She looked at her friend. 'You're staying in one of the guest rooms.'

'There's no need,' said Lily, thinking that she didn't want any of the guests to be inconvenienced. 'I'm happy to bunk in your room.'

'It's fine. Anyway, it's not like we haven't got the space,' said Hannah, rolling her eyes. 'Get yourself sorted and then come and find me in the kitchen. Mum's desperate to finally meet you after all this time.'

As Hannah walked off, Lily realised something as she glanced around. 'Where are all the hotel guests, by the way?' she asked.

'I'm looking at 'em,' drawled Frankie, giving her a pointed look.

'Oh.' Lily blinked. 'It's only me staying here?'

She couldn't believe it. Especially as it was a Friday night. Given that it was the weekend, shouldn't a thriving hotel be even a little bit busy? She wondered whether the renovation work was putting off potential guests.

But Frankie just sighed. 'Just think of yourself as a very VIP.' As she came around the desk, she glanced at Lily's bare, grubby feet. 'Are you some kind of tree hugger?' she asked.

Lily shook her head. 'I had a small accident and had to leave my trainers behind.'

Frankie's eyebrows shot up but she didn't reply.

'So how many rooms do you have?' asked Lily, still wondering about the state of the business.

'Twenty,' replied Frankie, reaching under the counter to pick up a No. 1 key. 'So I understand you're going to give the place a makeover?'

Lily nodded, before picking up her overnight bag and following Frankie up the wide staircase. 'Yup,' she replied. 'I've come to help out.'

'Well, the Jackson family need all the friends and help they can get at the moment, I reckon,' said Frankie as they reached the landing.

Lily took a sharp intake of breath. Was the business in trouble? She made a note to ask Hannah later. After all, this was the important commission that she was pinning the start of her own business on. Perhaps it was just a quiet weekend now that the summer rush was over, she told herself.

Lily glanced across the entrance hall before Frankie led her down a hallway and opened up the door to Room 1.

Lily was surprised to find a pleasingly large double room with a large picture window looking out across the lake.

'How lovely,' she said.

Frankie glanced around. 'You'll be the first one to try out the new bed. Updated plumbing and a fancy new en suite as well. Looks good, eh?'

Lily nodded. 'It does,' she lied.

Because although the king-size bed looked extremely comfortable, it seemed to be the only thing in the room that was. She couldn't work out why.

'Well, I'll leave you in peace,' said Frankie. 'The kitchen's just off the main hall. Come and find us whenever you're ready. Dinner will be in a while.'

After she had left, Lily took another look around once more, trying to work out what the room was missing. After all, it was a good size with two out of the four walls made out of wooden logs, the other two newly plastered. Also, the downlighters and polished floorboards might look in place in a fancy hotel in a city, but out here in the forest, it felt a little barren. A little too severe for the softness of the spectacular setting outside. The only furniture was a divan bed which was steel grey and again felt a little too modern. The bedroom didn't feel like a place to relax in, which was crazy because the outside view was mesmerising.

She wandered over to stand next to the huge window. The lake stretched out in front of the hotel, almost lapping at the bottom of the veranda on the floor below. The water sparkled, even on a dull afternoon. At its edges was lush tall grass and reeds swaying in the breeze. The forest surrounded everything, making the whole place feel private, protected and special.

Of course, somewhere in the forest was her abandoned hire car. She grimaced to herself. She was already regretting not taking out the full insurance. That would probably be the last of her meagre savings gone, she realised. After all, there was no way she was going to get her deposit back on it, seeing as how it was currently stuck in a muddy pond!

She turned around and looked at the room once more, wondering what kind of budget she would have to work with. Then she frowned to herself, once more asking herself whether there was trouble regarding the finances given the odd comments that she had picked up on. She hadn't even worked out what commission she would receive yet.

But putting the money issues aside for a moment, she let her mind wander, imagining how she would redecorate it and make it warmer and more cosy. Her imagination immediately ran riot, thinking up a style of cosy warmth and soft muted colours which would work perfectly, she thought, with a thrill of excitement.

She would keep the wooden wall behind the bed as a feature. The rest of the room she would freshen and lighten up to bring in some much-needed colour to the room. It also needed warm rugs to make it cosy, soft furnishings too. But also a touch of elegance here and there, such as lamps and perhaps even a desk with some books.

With a satisfied nod, she smiled to herself. Oh, yes. Doing up Maple Tree Lodge was going to be so easy, she decided. Just perfect for her new portfolio of her very own company.

With a little dance of excitement, she headed over to her bag to get showered and ready for dinner.

4

Ben was still getting over the last, somewhat eventful, hour. First of all, he had argued with his grandad. Storming out ready to go somewhere, anywhere, other than Maple Tree Lodge, he had managed to narrowly avoid a head-on collision. Finally he had ended up with a gorgeous redhead in his arms!

But even that unexpected treat didn't make him feel any better as he followed his grandad into the large kitchen, their earlier disagreement still weighing heavily on him. He hated that they couldn't get along at the moment when they had always been so close, until the past six months.

At least the kitchen had a cheery atmosphere. It was the beating heart of the whole place and where the family had gathered as usual for dinner. The aroma of home cooking filled the air as his mum Faye was taking a freshly baked loaf of bread out of the oven to accompany the pie she had made. Nearby, his sister Hannah was drizzling water icing over a cherry cake. His grandmother Dotty was knitting by the fire and his grandad had just sat down at the head of the long oak table that filled the other side of the room.

Only one person was missing from the family. Ben glanced at the empty chair at the other end of the long table and walked straight past it. He couldn't sit there. It was his dad's chair. Perhaps in time but it was still too early, still too strange a time for them all.

It had been almost six months since the family had lost his dad and yet, deep in their grief, they were all still struggling to find a path forward without his presence among them. Earlier on, Ben had suggested a family meeting before dinner to try and move the business in the right direction but between the knitting, baking and home cooking, he didn't think the Ritz was going to be worried about the competition for hotel reservations.

Ben tried to find some positivity from somewhere as he sat down. He still had his mum and Ben was grateful for her quiet strength, although the unexpected loss of her husband had undoubtedly taken its toll.

He watched her as she chopped up some herbs at the large island in the middle of the work area. She had always been softly spoken, happy to be in the background, but these days Faye was even more withdrawn, her smile not quite so frequent as it had once been. Now fifty-seven, her short blonde hair was tinged with a few grey hairs but despite keeping her slim figure with frequent walks around the lake, she was a little slower and sadder these days.

'Shall we try and hold this meeting before our guest comes downstairs?' said Ben. 'Frankie's just showing Lily to her room so now's a good time to discuss the business whilst it's just us family.'

'Business meeting,' Ben heard his grandad mutter from the other end of the long oak table. 'Never needed business meetings in the old days.'

'Was that before or after we stopped receiving bookings?' asked Dotty, his grandmother, in a mild tone.

Dotty was an exuberant character, or had been until the loss of her son. Suddenly her zest for life had become far more muted, so much so that she had even let her hair dye grow out and now that her hair was grey, she appeared much older all of a sudden. And yet, once in a while, she showed a steely glint in her soft blue eyes and even sharper observations.

Faye placed a jug of water on the table and sat down at the table.

'What's all this about Lily's car?' she asked, looking concerned as she looked across at her son.

'It's pretty much embedded in the small pond, from what I could see. It's going to need towing to get it out of there,' Ben told her. 'I'll try the winch on it in the morning.'

He looked around the table and realised that his sister had not yet sat down. Hannah was still fussing over her cake but glanced up when she felt her brother looking at her.

'What?' said Hannah, with a shrug. 'You don't want a dry cake for dessert, do you?'

She was trying to avoid any kind of responsibility as usual but he desperately needed her support. Ben sent her a beseeching look of desperation which she must have felt as she finally joined the family at the table and sat down with a huff.

'So,' said Ben, trying to drag some semblance of order to the meeting as his grandmother continued with her knitting and his mother topped and tailed runner beans into a bowl. 'Now that the plumbing is done and the electrics are underway, we need to come up with some kind of marketing plan for when the renovations are finished.'

It had been a major undertaking during the past six months. Ben hadn't realised quite how run-down the place had become before he had inherited it from his dad. Perhaps he hadn't wanted to see, he had often wondered. But the fact of the matter was that the renovations had been necessary in order for them to comply with all the modern rules and regulations for hotels. Updating all the electrical wiring and then replastering were the last two major jobs before decorating. And a good job too, he knew, as he had almost run out of money.

His eyes drifted towards the window and the small gamekeeper's lodge beyond where his grandparents now lived. He'd managed to persuade his grandmother that it had also needed updating. Dotty was happy to go along with it, especially with a new stove and walk-in shower. Meanwhile Walter had mumbled and muttered about the unnecessary cost but had never denied that it needed doing for ease of living.

Ben glanced at his grandad. Walter had retained his tough, can-do attitude despite his advanced years and nothing Ben had done to the place had been good enough for his grandad, or so it felt to him. He'd complained about the new en suites as being 'too fancy' and the roof slates not being the same shade as before. That morning he had grumbled at the new silver light switches in the reception hall being 'a bit flash' which had led to Ben walking out, feeling that it was the last straw.

Ben daydreamed about what he would be doing now if he hadn't needed to come home. Being his own boss and building a great reputation in business. At the beginning of the year, he had had an efficient work team around him, hanging on his every word. And now? He caught the scowl on his grandad's face. Everything had changed in his life. And not for the better.

'What's a marketing plan?' asked Walter, his grey eyebrows knitted into a frown. 'And why do we need one of those?'

'Because we're not receiving any bookings so something's amiss,' replied Ben.

'How would you know?' retorted Walter. 'You're not in the hotel business. You even wanted to turn it into a conference centre! Pah!'

Ben blanched at the reminder. It hadn't been his finest idea, he knew. And thankfully it hadn't met with planners' approval. But, as always, his first instinct had been to try to find any source of income to keep them from losing the hotel. He had thought that if he copied the competition it would work but it had been a bad idea from the outset, he knew. Worst of all, it had built mistrust into his grandad's view of him.

'It's a family inn,' carried on Walter, on his favourite topic. 'People like that. Not some bland resort that looks the same whichever town you're in.'

Which was exactly what Maple Tree Lodge would become if they had to sell, thought Ben with a heavy heart. The letter from the conglomerate with its large offer of money felt as if it were burning a hole in his pocket. He hadn't wanted to burden his family with any more pressure so it was his secret to keep. His millstone to carry around with him until he finally found a solution to all their problems.

'People don't want a fancy place with a spa,' said Walter, warming to his theme. 'That's not why they come here.'

'They're not coming here at all at the moment,' muttered Ben.

'That's because of all these ridiculous updates you've got going on. The hotel will run just fine when it's all finished,' said Walter, with a huff.

No, it's not, Ben wanted to shout at the top of his voice. But he didn't. He loved his grandad and didn't want to upset him any more than he seemed to with every conversation.

'I stayed on to help,' he said, trying to remain calm.

'You didn't need to,' muttered Walter. 'This place was working fine before you got here and it will work just fine once you leave.'

No, it won't, thought Ben. Because it was only his own money that was keeping them afloat.

'You're not leaving, are you?' asked Faye, turning to look at her son. He could see the tears in her eyes across the table.

He shook his head. 'I hadn't planned on it yet, Mum,' he said.

'Good,' interjected Dotty before turning to look at her husband. 'We need Ben and his young blood around here.'

'Humph,' said Walter. 'I think I do just fine.'

'Is that why the doctor had to up your blood pressure medication?' asked Dotty in a mild tone.

'Doctors,' muttered Walter. 'What do they know?'

'Only what all their years of medical training has taught them, Grandad,' said Hannah. 'Now is that it? I want to check on Lily.'

Still needing his sister's solidarity, Ben gave Hannah a despairing look. 'We haven't even started to talk about a marketing plan yet. This meeting isn't over.'

'I reckon it is,' said Walter, reaching over to pour himself a glass of water. 'He keeps going on about us not making money and then all he does is spend it.'

Ben rubbed his forehead, which was beginning to ache. It was the same battle over and over. Nothing needed to change according to his grandad.

He had gone from being the successful partner in his own company to feeling like a teenager once more. He had no control. No new ideas were allowed to flourish. He had a permanent mark on his tongue from biting it so much. And everyone's stress levels were through the roof from the tension between them.

Ben was beginning to lose his temper. 'Well, all the money I've spent has come from my own savings, Grandad. Not yours because…'

Because there was no money, he added in his head. But he

didn't need to say it out loud. Everyone around the table knew just how dire things were. Even his grandad and yet, for some reason, the eternal struggle with trying to change things went on and on.

His temper died as quickly as it had flared up as he saw the pain in his grandad's eyes. Walter was a tough man but he was still grieving for his son. It was as if changing the hotel meant eradicating Tony's memory and that wasn't Ben's idea at all. But if nothing changed then they would lose their home.

At that moment, Frankie walked into the kitchen and Ben was grateful for the interruption. 'Our very VIP is all settled in,' she said.

Frankie had moved into the hotel soon after Faye was widowed. She had just split up from her husband and needed a place to stay. Frankie and Faye were old friends and she had helped them get through their grief with her wry humour and plain speaking. And on days like today, it was much needed.

'Is it all right if I get these beans on?' asked Faye, looking across the table to her son. 'Otherwise the pie will burn.'

He nodded, suppressing the heavy sigh deep within.

It looked as if the marketing plan was going to have to wait for another day. Or at least until Lily had given them her plan for the interior design.

He just hoped whatever she came up with, it would be good enough to entice some new bookings and save the hotel.

5

After a much-needed shower, Lily headed downstairs, grateful to be wearing the spare pair of trainers that she had packed, along with clean jeans and a jumper.

At some point she was going to have to figure out what to do with the hire car and face up to the loss of her deposit and possibly worse. She also needed to retrieve her favourite trainers, now stuck in the mud next to the car. But, for that evening, she decided to focus on the positive and that was seeing one of her best friends.

She had just reached the bottom of the staircase when Hannah appeared at a nearby doorway, just off the hall.

'There you are,' she said, with a wide smile. 'No more mud?'

'Nope,' said Lily, shaking her head. 'That power shower is amazing.'

Hannah studied her before saying, 'Wow, your hair is so much longer now I've seen it properly.'

Lily touched a strand of red hair which she'd just washed. She hadn't had it cut for almost six months so it now hung right past her shoulders. 'No, it's been this long for ages.'

'Yeah but I haven't seen you for three months.'

Lily gave a start. 'I didn't think it was as long as that,' she replied, feeling surprised. Hannah must have got her dates wrong.

But Hannah shook her head. 'I last saw you in July when I went into London for Beth's talk at the Greenwich planetarium. We had lunch by the river.'

'What about Ella's birthday meal?' Lily reminded her. 'That fancy place with the awful food.'

'You were only with Beth and Ella, remember?' Hannah told her. 'I couldn't get away because there was some solicitors' stuff that needed going through because of my dad...'

Her voice trailed off and Lily took a sharp intake of breath. How stupid of her to forget, she told herself, stepping forward to give her friend a huge hug. The texts and calls had worried her enough about Hannah so it was good to finally be there to support her face to face.

'How are you doing?' she asked softly.

Hannah shrugged her shoulders under her friend's embrace. 'You know,' she muttered, leaning into her briefly. 'It's been pretty awful around here.' She gave herself a little shake as she stepped away. 'Thank goodness you're here at last. Come on. Come and meet everyone properly. Dinner's almost ready.'

Lily felt her friend's grief and pain and was glad that she was around that weekend to finally lend some support.

She followed Hannah into a large kitchen and was pleasantly surprised. In contrast to the empty interiors in the rest of the hotel, the kitchen felt warm and welcoming.

The cupboards along one side of the wall were all oak, weathered and used over many years, she suspected. Open shelves were filled with every conceivable dish and bowl required, all mismatched and well used. Stainless-steel pots and pans hung from a cast-iron rail in the ceiling. Herbs filled small terracotta pots along the windowsill and the view of the trees outside made it feel as if the woods were inside instead. It was a busy room but instantly Lily felt relaxed.

Walter gave her a wave from the end of a long oak table.

'This is my mum, Faye,' said Hannah, introducing the woman in her late fifties who was wearing an apron and stirring a pot of some kind of delicious-smelling sauce on the stove.

Faye turned around and smiled as she headed across the tiled floor, wiping her hands on her apron as she came over.

'Hello,' she said, with a warm smile before drawing her into an unexpected hug. 'Lovely to meet you at long last. Hannah talks non-stop about you.'

'Hi,' replied Lily, stepping back from the embrace and smiling at her. 'Lovely to finally meet you too.'

Faye looked like an older version of Hannah, tall with blonde hair, albeit with wisps of grey mixed in. There was also a similar softness to her, of a gentleness of character.

'This is Grandma,' announced Hannah, leading Lily over to the table to introduce a grey-haired lady who was standing nearby. She was petite but Lily was surprised by the strength of the woman who then engulfed her in a hug.

'You must call me Dotty,' she said, when she had stepped back. 'Gosh, your red hair is gorgeous.' She reached up to touch her grey hair and frowned for a moment before letting her hand drop. Lily was surprised to see how many rings she was wearing on each hand, all of different styles. 'Come and sit down with me and warm yourself up by the fire.'

'It's such a lovely room,' said Lily as she sat down.

'We've got our own small kitchen,' Dotty told her. 'Walter and I live in the gamekeeper's lodge just over there, you see.' She pointed through a window to where Lily could just see a tiny oak-framed lodge in the semi-darkness. 'But everyone ends up gathering in here.'

Lily nodded. She understood. It was a family kitchen, something she didn't know too much about. There had been the odd time growing up when she and her parents had snuggled up on the sofa to watch a movie but most of their time had been spent entertaining or going out for official functions.

'So you're not working at that pub tonight?' she asked Hannah.

'I took the weekend off because you were coming here,' replied Hannah, laying out some knives and forks.

'Good job too,' said Walter, creasing his grey fluffy eyebrows into a frown. 'They work her all hours at that place and the pay is rubbish.'

Lily looked at her friend with concern. Hannah's good nature meant that people were always taking advantage of her.

'It's fine, Grandad,' said Hannah, with a wave of her hand. 'And the pay isn't that bad.'

'Great,' said Ben as he came into the room. 'Lend me a fiver, I'm broke.'

Hannah shot her brother a grin. 'Me too, bro,' she replied.

Lily still felt embarrassed about how they had met but thankfully Ben seemed quite at ease as he grabbed the bread basket from the side and brought it over to the table.

Faye placed a large pie topped with golden pastry into the middle of the table, ready for serving up, alongside vegetables, mash and gravy. As the family all helped themselves and chatted away, Lily felt touched by how close they all were.

The chicken pie was delicious and the first taste of home cooking that Lily could remember having for a very long time.

'This is fantastic,' she said before thanking Faye.

Faye smiled at her. 'It's an old recipe,' she said. 'Easy to put together.'

Lily thought that she was very much like her daughter. Gentle in nature and happy to sit back and let the others chat on. Perhaps she too lacked confidence, much like Hannah.

Even though the pie had been warm and filling, there was still room for cake afterwards. Hannah placed a tray of still-warm brownies in the middle of the table which were delicious and Lily found herself also asking for a small slice of cherry cake as well.

'Yum,' she said, looking across the table at her friend. 'I've missed your cakes.'

'I keep telling her that she should open up her own bakery instead of wasting her talents at that pub,' said Walter. 'You've got a real skill there.'

Hannah rolled her eyes. 'I'm doing fine, Grandad,' she muttered, blushing.

It was always the same with Hannah, thought Lily. Dismissing her incredible skills all too quickly. What little confidence she had in her baking in the early days when they had first met seemed to have been eroded over the years. But perhaps she was happiest at home, just baking for her family.

Dotty suddenly turned to ask Lily, 'So tell us about yourself. Where did you grow up?'

With the whole family listening in, Lily was suddenly embarrassed at the attention. She shifted in her seat, always uncomfortable talking about herself.

She blushed as she replied, 'Pretty much everywhere.' She then went on to give a very quick history of how her father's job meant that they had travelled the world when she had been growing up.

'So where have you been?' asked Ben, sounding intrigued.

'Most places until I went to boarding school,' she told him. 'Africa, South America, India, and then finally the Far East.'

'How marvellous,' said Dotty, her eyes gleaming. 'India was one of my favourite countries,' she added, looking down at her ornate rings. 'These gold ones were from a market in Kolkata. I treated myself when I was working there.'

'What did you used to do?' asked Lily.

'I was a photographer for *National Geographic*,' Dotty told her. 'Used to do a little bit of journalism too, in my time. Remind me to show you all the treasures I picked up on my travels. We can compare notes on the places we've both been to.'

'Replace the word treasures with junk and it would be about right,' murmured Walter, giving his wife a wink.

Dotty brushed his teasing aside with a wave of her hand. 'I'm sure Lily would appreciate it.'

'So you've also travelled around the world?' asked Lily, grateful for the change of conversation direction so that the spotlight wasn't on her.

'Oh, yes,' said Dotty, nodding in memory. 'I went everywhere. And then I went to London to photograph the mods and rockers in the mid-sixties and got a puncture on my motorbike. Some guy who was visiting for the bank holiday weekend ended up helping me...' Her voice trailed off and she looked across at her husband. 'I married him a week later.'

Lily watched as Dotty exchanged a smile with Walter before turning back to look at her.

'So you decided to settle in England?' she asked.

Lily nodded. 'I moved to London after college.' She shot Hannah a grin across the table. 'Which is where I met your granddaughter.'

'In that awful house,' replied Hannah, laughing.

'It was terrible,' agreed Lily, joining in her laughter. 'The windows were so rotten that they eventually got stuck and wouldn't even open.'

'And then one night Ella pushed the bathroom window open and the whole thing fell out into the garden!' added Hannah.

Lily smiled at the memory, still hearing the laughter shared with her friends over the disaster. 'And trust me, the places I've rented since haven't been any better,' she found herself saying.

'Is that why you keep moving about?' asked Faye. 'Hannah tells me that you have a new address every year or so.'

Lily instantly felt the need to shut down again, even under Faye's gentle questioning.

'Well, they've all been pretty awful,' she said. 'Not lovely like this.'

She looked around the kitchen once more, hoping they picked up on the change of topic. The truth was that she had deliberately kept moving around. She was still wary of getting too close to anyone other than her best friends.

To distract anyone from asking her anything else, she reached forward to pick up another brownie from the plate, even though she was full. 'They're just too delicious,' she said.

'I agree,' said Walter, with a rare smile. 'They're my favourite.'

'Hannah's got such a talent for baking,' said Faye, looking proud.

'I inherited it from you but it's really not anything special,' said Hannah automatically. She had always had no confidence in her abilities.

'Rubbish,' said Ben, helping himself to a large piece of cherry cake and shooting his younger sister a smile.

Lily found herself warming to this close-knit family. She wondered again about the lack of hotel guests but decided that after the renovations, and with a great new interior that she would design for them, the hotel would be full once again all year round.

Then maybe they could all help each other become a success, she thought.

6

Once dinner was over and the plates had been cleared, Ben leant back in his chair, feeling exhausted. He hadn't had a day off in months and was willing to let the family concentrate on Lily and the conversation washed over him.

'I still can't believe your family built all of this,' Lily was saying to Hannah, as she looked around the room.

'Well, to be fair, it was already built,' Dotty told her. 'Walter and Tony, our son, just added a few more rooms, as well as the veranda.' She shot Lily a grin. 'I did help with that though. I'm great with a hammer and a bunch of nails.'

Ben smiled to himself. His grandmother had always had a passion for life, although the loss of her son had taken its toll. She seemed a little older these days, not wanting to socialise with her friends and staying in most of the time despite encouragement from everyone else.

'Thankfully we've always had plenty of trees to use,' added Walter. 'Our very own builders' merchants here on our doorstep.'

'The wood certainly adds a lovely warmth to the place,' replied Lily.

Walter nodded. 'It does. I like to think that's what my grandfather thought all those years ago.'

Ben waited in anticipation for the familiar story to be told.

'Five generations of the Jackson family have lived here,' began Walter. 'In 1918, my grandfather bought the land. We've got fifty acres of woodland and a fifty-acre lake as well, you know. So he had lots of materials to start building himself a home for his family.'

'Amazing,' murmured Lily. 'Which bit of the building was the original part?'

'This here kitchen,' Walter told her. 'The reception hall was the sitting room in those days. Then he added the stairs and added the bedrooms upstairs.' Walter pointed at the ceiling. 'Then my father and me added the other wing, the lounge downstairs and more bedrooms.'

'That must have taken a lot of work,' Lily told him with a soft smile.

'I was younger and fitter back then,' he admitted.

Ben found himself surprised at his grandad's admission that age had taken its toll.

'I'm still cutting logs and doing my bit,' he carried on quickly, with a glance at Ben. It was as if he didn't want to admit that he couldn't cope any more, thought Ben. That he needed to be helpful and necessary to the hotel.

'I'm sure you are,' said Lily.

'But it was always about the trees and the lake for me,' carried on Walter. 'Tony, our son, loved working with wood, like me. Made this table and chairs, didn't he, Ben?'

Ben nodded in response, taking a sip of his beer instead of looking at his grandad. He'd practically grown up with a chisel in his hand, it felt. And yet it had been years since he had cut down trees or worked with the wood to create anything. Growing up, it had been his grandad, his dad and Ben busy in the outside workshop, chatting and laughing as they worked. It had been a happy childhood spent mostly outside. Now it was just him and his grandad and the gulf between them felt huge.

Feeling uncomfortable, Ben drained his beer and pushed his chair away from the table. 'Well, I've got some admin to do in the office,' he lied. But he stayed in his seat, reluctant to face up to the paperwork.

Most of the time he spent in the office was looking at the invoices for all the expensive work that had been carried out over the summer and worrying about the next payments.

Dotty yawned. 'Time for us to wander back home, Walter,' she said, looking weary.

They wished everyone goodnight and left soon afterwards to head back to the small lodge a few yards away.

'How about a nightcap in the lounge?' Hannah asked Lily.

'I'd love it,' replied Lily.

'Great,' said Hannah, standing up. 'Just let me go and get a sweater. It's colder tonight, isn't it?'

Lily stood up, looking a little awkward as Hannah suddenly left the room. Frankie was helping Faye in the kitchen loading the dishwasher and setting up some breakfast things in the kitchen, which left Lily alone with Ben at the table.

'Have you seen the lounge yet?' Ben asked her.

She shook her head in response.

'Oh, yes, show her the view across the lake,' said Faye with an encouraging smile. 'It's a full moon.'

So Ben led Lily out of the kitchen, across the hallway and into the large lounge where he switched on the overhead lights.

The lounge had always been one of his favourite rooms. Perhaps it was the happy memories growing up of Christmas days spent in front of the tree or lively games of Monopoly which the whole family participated in.

The room hadn't changed at all since he had grown up. It always felt light and airy, with its high ceiling and oak beams. The large windows and new French doors framed the glorious view outside when it was daytime. The huge chimney breast had been made with the same sandy brick stone used elsewhere and the fire that had been lit before dinner had begun to run low.

Ben went over to place another couple of logs on the fire before turning around. In deference to the many workmen who had come and gone over the past few months, any decorations had been taken down with only the large brown leather sofas and oak coffee table remaining, positioned near the fireplace.

He then headed over to the French doors to open them up and show Lily the view.

And what a view it was, he thought, especially on a night like this.

The rest of the place might feel like a building site with wires hanging out the walls and scaffolding in the hallway but the view from the lounge offered nothing but serenity and calm. The stars were magnified in the black sky above and, where the rain clouds had finally cleared, were mirrored on the still water. As his mother had promised, the full moon shone down onto the lake, its reflection rippled from the gentle breeze that came across from the hills beyond. Everything else, from the trees in the forest to the boathouse nearby, was in inky darkness.

For a moment, Ben and Lily remained silent as they looked at the view.

But when Lily went to step forward onto the veranda, Ben stuck out his arm to stop her.

'Careful,' he advised. 'It's pretty rotten down this end.'

She looked down and even in the semi-darkness, they could

both see the gaps where the wood had disintegrated into the lapping water below.

'Yet another job on my list to do,' he said. Although his grandad was insisting that they replaced the long balcony in its original design of solid wood, whereas Ben's instinct was to add some large glass panes to show off even more of the view from inside.

He felt Lily turn to look at him and, realising he was still holding on to her, quickly let go of her arm.

'Have you always run the hotel?' she asked.

He shook his head. 'No, I became an architect instead,' he replied.

She looked impressed but he knew that it hadn't become the dream job he had been hoping for.

'So you're home for a while?' she asked. 'You're taking a career break?'

He nodded. 'The family needed me,' he said simply.

'Of course,' she replied in a softer tone. 'I'm sorry to hear you lost your dad this year.'

He nodded. 'Thank you.'

The truth was that he hadn't really had time to grieve for his dad. He had come home to support his family and that support, overwhelming as it felt at times, had given him no time for emotions or to show weakness. He had to stay strong for the rest of the family. But sometimes he just felt exhausted by it all.

The responsibility for the family home and the livelihoods of everyone who depended on Maple Tree Lodge was all-encompassing. He was trying to protect both the past and the future for everyone and he still wasn't sure it was enough.

'Erm, I couldn't help but notice that I'm the only one staying here,' she carried on.

'We've been having some major renovations,' he told her.

'They're almost done and when they are, hopefully the guests will begin to return pretty soon.'

He had decided a while ago that he needed to treat the hotel like a business. It was the only way to deal with the mess and insecurity hanging over his family. He remained detached from it all, businesslike in all matters.

There was no time for play, women or otherwise. Even his best friends had been moaning about not seeing him. He had met Jake and Alex at university and they had remained close ever since, despite their hectic schedules. Three months had now passed since he had seen them. But whilst his single friends talked about their busy lives, Ben's own life felt as if it were on hold.

Ben glanced at Lily once more and as she looked up, her green eyes locked with his.

He found, to his surprise, that he felt a jolt deep within. A spark of something new and exciting. The romance of the stars and the lake obviously helped, he reminded himself. Besides, romance seemed like something from a long time ago in his life. Even his best friends teased him about his lack of dates these days. All work and no play makes Ben a dull boy. But he had no time for any of that.

He looked away as he stared down at the water once more. So Lily was attractive, so what? He'd met pretty women before without having this kind of effect on him. Besides, this was someone who was there in a professional capacity as well as her friendship with Hannah.

'I have to confess that I don't know much about interior design,' he told her, dragging his mind back to business. 'Can we have a chat tomorrow morning about your design ideas and where they might fit in with my own plans for the hotel?' He looked back into the lounge as Hannah wandered in. 'I'll leave you and Hannah to catch up tonight.'

Lily nodded. 'Of course,' she said, giving him a smile before heading inside.

He glanced briefly at her long legs, shown off by her slim fitted jeans, before turning to close and lock the French doors.

As he crossed the lounge, he heard Hannah say, 'Frankie's made us a couple of her special cocktails. Cheers!'

Then he left the room and headed towards the office. His life suddenly felt very empty, devoid of dates and the life that had been full before he had returned home. He wanted that life back but with his partnership sold, there was nothing for him to return to.

So he was stuck here at the hotel but even then he wasn't really in charge. It just felt like a terrible burden that he wanted to be rid of. But he couldn't because he needed to take care of his family. He wanted to live his life and yet what life could he possibly have in the middle of nowhere?

He wanted freedom to make his own decisions and the lure of taking work away from there was tempting. But the thought of abandoning his family was too much to bear.

It surprised him to feel this stressed because he had always thrived under pressure, unlike Hannah.

But he knew that it was because this time, the project as he viewed it, was personal. Personal for him, for his family's future.

He was trying to please his family but everyone still seemed extremely unhappy. He was failing, feeling trapped and out of control.

And he couldn't see how on earth anything could change for the better, no matter how many new ideas he tried to come up with.

It felt as if time was running out for Maple Tree Lodge.

7

Lily woke up the following morning after a great night's sleep.

Being used to the constant traffic noise outside her bedroom window, as well as her boisterous flatmates who didn't need an excuse for a party, meant that she wasn't used to the quiet hotel. So it had taken her some time to fall asleep in the peaceful surroundings.

But after a solid seven hours' sleep, she felt invigorated, feeling as if she could take on the world that day. Which was good because she was going to talk to Ben that morning with her interior design pitch for the hotel and, fingers crossed, it would lead to a whole new business of her very own.

Before getting into bed the previous night, she had spotted a new tag on the end of the bed and she remembered Frankie telling her that all the beds were new. Well, she thought, whoever had updated the mattresses could at least know that it was money well spent. It had been like floating on a cloud, she said to herself with a smile, running her hand across the soft material beneath her.

However, the bed was one of the few high points in the

bedroom, she thought, sitting up once more. Despite the amazing mattress, the room was too stark. The bare floors and plain white linen on the bed seemed at odds with the cosy, charming hotel and its countryside setting.

She thought back to Walter's story the previous evening and how he had told her that it had been in the Jackson family for five generations. It seemed to her quite unbelievable for a family to stay in one place for so long. She couldn't imagine living anywhere for any length of time.

And yet, she thought, as she rose to open the bedroom curtains, she could certainly see the appeal of the place. She was instantly enveloped in the wonderful view in front of her, both visually and, opening the window a little to let in some fresh air, with the sound of birdsong filling the bedroom as well.

Along with the chorus of birds chattering and singing amongst the trees, there was also the call of the coots and ducks on the sparkling water of the lake. A soft breeze rustled the leaves of the nearby trees and fluffy white clouds drifted lazily around the cobalt-blue sky before disappearing behind the green rolling hills surrounding them. The sun was beginning to climb its way into the sky and Lily felt herself yearning to be outside which, for a city dweller, was something of a surprise.

She saw movement beyond the trees in the far distance and realised that it was a steam train puffing its way through the countryside. How wonderful, she thought.

It was a completely magical setting. Like being in a Disney movie or something. She wondered what it would be like to wake up with that view each morning. How could anyone be tense living here?

And yet she had picked up on a strained atmosphere the previous evening. Despite the family chatter full of small talk and the delicious meal, Ben and his grandfather had seemed at odds.

Unable to even look each other in the eye, she had realised afterwards when she had thought back over the evening.

It saddened her to see a rift in an otherwise loving family. Especially as there was a warmth between them all, such a contrast to her own parents who merely seemed interested in her work whenever she spoke to them. Hannah's family had seemed interested in Lily as a whole person. Although that caused other problems, with Lily at pains not to try and get too close to them all. After all, if she received the commission for the hotel then the job would be finished and she would leave once more. Relationships, apart from with her three best friends, were fleeting. So it was always best not to get too close, regardless of how charming the family were.

She focused her mind back on Maple Tree Lodge and spun around to face the bedroom once more. Instantly the ideas rushed forward and she could see exactly how she would decorate the place. It needed soft colours everywhere, she decided, looking around. Perhaps some warm colours on a couple of the walls, keeping the logs on show as well. Then she would add a lamp, pictures, rugs and cushions. Definitely carpet as well, soft and luxurious under the feet.

She always got a tingle inside her stomach when she hit upon the right idea for a place and this time was no different. Everything she had in mind would make it feel more comfortable and cosy but luxurious and modern as well. It would be perfect, she decided with a determined nod. She couldn't wait to tell Ben.

She got dressed and, thanks to her amazing night's sleep, she felt a spring in her step as she headed downstairs to the hotel reception.

Her stomach rumbling, she hesitated for a moment, wondering where to go for breakfast. She went into the lounge where she had shared a drink with Hannah the night before but there was no one there. She peeped through an open doorway into what appeared to be a large dining room but that was dark and obviously not used at the moment.

Finally, and feeling a little embarrassed, she went into the family kitchen where she had enjoyed dinner the previous evening. Faye looked up from behind the island in the middle of the work area and smiled.

'Good morning!' she said. 'How did you sleep?'

'Good morning,' replied Lily. 'I had a great night's sleep, thank you. It's so quiet here compared to the all the noise I get outside my bedroom window back in London.' She made a face. 'My room overlooks a busy railway junction.'

'Poor you. Sit down and I'll rustle you up some breakfast,' Faye told her.

'I'm sorry. I didn't know where to go,' Lily told her, feeling a little embarrassed. 'The dining room was empty.'

'Nonsense,' replied Faye. 'You ended up in exactly the right place. Now, what can I get you? Fruit? Eggs? Toast?'

'Toast would be lovely, thank you,' said Lily. 'Can I help?'

'Oh, this is easy compared to the old days,' Faye told her, with a wave of her hand. 'I used to prepare breakfast for all the guests on the odd occasion when we were full.'

She sounded a little wistful and Lily guessed that perhaps Faye was thinking of her late husband. Perhaps it was a lot busier in those days.

'I was thinking that it must be a beautiful place to wake up here every day,' said Lily.

Faye nodded. 'I thought so from the moment Tony brought me here. Ben and Hannah seemed to thrive growing up here as well. They were always messing about in the woods and on the lake.'

Gradually the family wandered in over the next half an hour to join them at the table for breakfast.

Frankie was first, heading straight for the coffee pot which had already percolated and was ready to be drunk.

Dotty followed almost immediately afterwards, greeting everyone with a warm smile. 'Good morning, all,' she announced, pouring herself a glass of cranberry juice before sitting down at the table. 'I looked out of the window this morning and the maples are finally beginning to turn.' She sighed happily. 'What's that quote? The leaves are changing and poetry is in the air.'

Frankie sat down with a large mug. 'I don't need an inspirational quote in the morning,' she said. 'I just need coffee.'

'You should switch to rose tea,' Dotty told her. 'It's a great anti-inflammatory.'

Frankie shook her head. 'Caffeine helps maintain my sunny personality.'

'Is that what we're calling it?' murmured Faye, giving her friend a smile.

Walter also wasn't feeling particularly sunny when he joined them.

'Nearly tripped over that damn scaffold in the hall,' he said, with a scowl.

'Did you hurt yourself?' asked Faye, looking concerned.

'Course not,' said Walter. 'I'll be glad when the thing's taken down though.'

Ben, who had followed his grandad into the kitchen, remained quiet as he helped himself to a mug of coffee.

Soon everyone was sitting down to eat their breakfast. Only Hannah was missing, obviously taking advantage of a lie-in after all the late nights at work recently. She had told Lily that she was exhausted, often staying late after closing time at the pub to help out with tidying up.

'So how long is the hotel closed for?' asked Lily, who had been wondering what extensive works had occurred so far.

The family turned to look at her as one.

'It's not actually closed to guests,' said Faye in a faltering voice, flicking a nervous look between Walter and Ben.

'Oh. Sorry,' said Lily, feeling aghast at her error. 'I just assumed with the building works...'

Her voice trailed off.

'And that's the problem,' said Walter, with a frown. 'Our guests agree. All this unnecessary building stuff is keeping them away.'

Ben said nothing but Lily noticed there was a slight shake of his head as if to himself. She could have kicked herself for creating more tension in the air before she talked to Ben about the commission.

Breakfast continued in a stilted silence as everyone finished their meal.

'I need to go check on the sluices,' said Walter, getting up from the table.

'And I'm heading into Aldwych,' said Frankie. 'I need to go to the bank and see if they can lend me a million pounds.'

'I'll join you,' said Faye. 'I need some bits from the supermarket. What about you, Dotty?'

Dotty nodded. 'I might come in and see what the charity shops have got in recently,' she replied.

'You can join us if you'd like?' suggested Frankie, looking down at Lily.

'Thanks but I'm busy this morning,' said Lily, before looking across at Ben. 'We're going to discuss design ideas for the bedrooms.'

'No time like the present,' he replied, reaching out to top up his coffee mug from the pot.

'We'll leave you to it then,' said Frankie, shooting Lily a grin and crossing two fingers behind Ben's back before she walked away.

Once everyone else had left and she was alone in the kitchen with Ben, Lily still felt bad about her blunder.

'I'm sorry about what I said earlier about the building works. I didn't mean to cause an argument,' she said quickly.

'You didn't,' replied Ben, with a soft sigh. 'The original argument never finished so it's just a continuation of the same one over and over.'

Lily looked at him. 'But I'm sure it'll all be worthwhile when the renovations are complete. Then the guests will return again.'

He smiled without humour. 'You're assuming we had any guests in the first place,' he told her.

'I don't understand,' she told him, feeling puzzled. 'This place is amazing. What happened?'

'Tastes change, I guess,' he replied. 'And my father didn't keep up with them. He and my grandfather thought that the hotel should remain the same as it had always been. The trouble was that the regular guests began to stay away for longer or, worse, not return here at all.' He appeared to deliberately brighten himself up. 'Anyway, with your skills with design, I'm sure the guests will be returning in droves.'

'Let's hope so,' replied Lily. 'I have had some ideas for the bedrooms, if you want to hear them.'

'Of course,' nodded Ben, suddenly looking concerned. 'We just don't have the budget for anything fancy, if you haven't noticed.'

'I understand,' she told him. 'I'm used to working on a tight budget.'

'Thank goodness for that,' he said, looking relieved. 'Well, that's great news. I must say, I was thrilled when I looked up your firm. It's just the aesthetic that I think we need. Minimal, sharp and modern.'

Lily found she was trying hard not to let her jaw drop open in shock. Minimal? Modern?

'Really?' she said, her voice a little high. She cleared her throat. 'My own ideas were more inspired by the outdoors. All those soft greens and blues of the lake and sky. Other touches of colour, such as pale yellows and pinks, that would really smarten up the place but also keep it cosy.'

'Cosy?' Ben shook his head. 'No. That's definitely not the vibe we're going for.' He looked at her with piercing brown eyes. 'I'm amazed that this is your idea. I looked up your portfolio last week when Hannah mentioned you. Your company is an exact match for what I wanted. If not, then perhaps I should look elsewhere...'

'No!' Lily almost shouted the word, such was her horror that her dream project would slip away from her before it had even begun. 'I mean, you're the customer. Of course, if it's stark minimalism you want then I can provide that.'

'Good,' said Ben, standing up, not catching on to her sarcastic tone. 'So where do we go from here?'

'I can get you some rough sketches by the end of the day,' she told him. 'I've got my laptop with me so I can show you my vision. If you can give me some kind of timeline and budget then we can exchange ideas and hopefully get started.'

'Excellent,' he told her, with a smile. 'I'm glad we're on the same page.'

As he left the kitchen, Lily sank back in her chair with a groan. It was an utter disaster. On the same page? They were at total odds with both taste and ideas.

If she agreed to do the work on his terms, it went against every instinct of her creative soul. If she walked out instead, then she was left with no work at all.

What on earth was she going to do?

8

Lily was still sitting at the kitchen table in shock when Hannah came into the room.

'Morning,' she said, with a yawn. 'I totally overslept. Must have been Frankie's strong gin measures.'

Lily smiled, despite feeling wretched after her conversation with Ben. 'Morning,' she replied. 'Frankie does pour a strong drink, that's for sure.'

'She used to be a barmaid so I guess she's got the knack for it.' Hannah headed over to the warm coffee pot on the side and poured herself a large mugful. Then she joined Lily at the table, still yawning.

'What have I missed?' she asked, before taking a sip of her hot drink.

'Your mum, Frankie and Dotty have headed into town to do some shopping,' Lily told her. 'Walter's around somewhere. And Ben and I have shared our ideas for decorating the hotel.'

Hannah's pretty face lit up. 'Great! So he's going to hire you?' she asked.

'I think so,' began Lily tentatively.

She thought back to Ben's ideas. All minimalism and no charm. Totally wrong, in her mind. It was the complete antithesis of what she had been creating in her mind. But if it got the job done and that was what the customer wanted, what else could she do?

'But we still need to agree exact budgets, timelines and the rest of it,' she carried on. 'I'm going to show Ben some sketches on my laptop later. So I've got a bit of work to do before then.'

'Oh, you'll be fine,' said Hannah, still beaming. 'I'm so glad it's going to be you helping us. It'll be such a great help to everyone knowing that you've got the right skills for it. It's going to look wonderful, I'm sure.'

Lily really wasn't so sure and was feeling more and more disheartened about her first solo project before it had even begun.

After breakfast, Lily walked outside with Hannah, hoping the fresh air and wonderful view would enliven her mood. She was feeling a little despondent despite the possibility that she might just have her first solo commission.

Walking around the back of the hotel led them to the shoreline of the lake where there was a long stretch of sand onto which the water gently lapped.

As they stood next to the lake in the sunshine, Walter came along the path towards them.

'Lovely day,' he said, by way of greeting.

'Been for your walk?' asked Hannah.

Walter nodded. 'Oh, yes,' he replied. 'My morning walk around Dragonfly Lake always makes the day a little better.'

'Dragonfly Lake?' Lily looked back at the water. 'What a wonderful name!'

Walter smiled. 'My grandmother's idea, apparently,' he said. 'She thought the lake should have a proper name.'

'It's lovely,' said Lily. 'Not that I know much about them.'

Walter came over to stand next to her before pointing at the nearby bank. 'See there? That blue on the tallest reed.'

Lily squinted at the bunch of reeds until she saw it. 'There!' she exclaimed. 'I can see one!'

In the rays of the early-morning sun, a double set of gossamer wings glinted.

'It's so pretty,' she said, entranced by the bright blue body and sparkling wings. Now she was looking more closely she could see a couple more amongst the reeds.

'They can't take off until their wings are dry,' Walter told her. 'Watch now. They'll slowly climb up as the sun warms everything up.'

They watched in peaceful silence for a while until the dragonflies began to flap their wings. As Walter had promised, they edged upwards on the reeds until finally taking flight.

Lily watched in amazement as the blue dragonflies darted around the reed beds and across the water.

'That was amazing,' she said, before grimacing. 'My daily commute is a little more crushed on the tube in rush hour. No room for dragonflies or even space to breathe normally.'

'You're still going into the office?' asked Hannah.

Lily shrugged. 'My current bedroom isn't big enough to set up as a work from home environment,' she replied. 'So I have to sit on the bed. I mean, I can work anywhere but the office helps. Especially as one of my housemates seems to run an all-day party club.' She rolled her eyes.

As she spoke, she realised that now that she had lost her job, wherever she was going to work and live in the future, she would need a little more space in her next home.

'Poor you,' said Hannah, wrinkling up her nose. 'I don't miss housemates like that. Apart from you, Beth and Ella, that is. They were the best of times.'

Lily smiled and nodded. 'They were,' she agreed, finding herself wistful at the time spent with her best friends. 'Thankfully I won't miss my ghastly housemates after next week when the lease runs out. I'm outta there!'

'Where are you moving to next?' asked Hannah.

'I've been so busy that I haven't worked it out yet,' she confessed. 'That's a job for Monday when I get a free moment.'

'You're such a workaholic,' said Hannah, shaking her head. 'You work so hard. No wonder you've got such a great career whilst mine didn't even begin.'

A great career? Lily tried not to baulk in front of her friend.

'What about this, er, what did my grandson call it? Interior design, was it?' asked Walter. 'Aren't you going to be decorating the hotel?'

Lily held up her crossed fingers. 'I hope so,' she replied. 'We just need to finalise plans later today.'

'You'll be fine,' Hannah assured her.

'I agree,' said Walter. 'So why don't you move in here whilst you work on the place?'

Lily looked at him in amazement. 'Here?' she stammered.

'Why not?' he told her.

'Grandad, that's a great idea,' said Hannah, her face lighting up as she looked at Lily. 'It'll be so lovely! You can get all the peace and quiet here whilst you sort out the interiors. Then it'll give you time to find your next home.'

Lily immediately felt wary. Mixing work and home life was never a good idea, she reminded herself. Before wondering what on earth home life actually looked like as she had no idea.

'Best of all, we'll get to see each other every day,' added Hannah, her eyes gleaming.

Lily desperately didn't want to hurt her friend's feelings but it was hardly a professional set-up. 'I don't know,' she began.

But, for once, Hannah was being quite forceful. 'I do,' she said, in a stern voice. 'You can keep your room here. It's not like we're going to be full any time soon. I think it's a brilliant idea. Let me grab my phone. I'm going to ring the girls! They can come and visit and we'll all be together at last!'

As Hannah dashed off, Lily was left frowning to herself, deep in thought.

'It's not the worst idea I've had,' said Walter, breaking into her muddled thoughts. 'After all, if you're here then Ben won't be able to turn the hotel into some monochromatic soulless conference place, will he?' He gave her a pointed look.

'Conference?' she stammered.

'One of his worst ideas,' said Walter, his mouth going into a thin line. 'I mean, can you imagine? Thankfully that was a no-go from the start.'

Lily thought back to Ben's decorating plans and realised that he hadn't strayed too far from the soulless conference hotel idea, contrary to what Walter was thinking.

Walter was still studying her. 'So what do you think about the place?' he asked.

'Me?' She tried to look on the positive side of things. 'Well, I think that if I knew this amazing lake was here then it would be nice if other people could enjoy it as well. Not just the hotel occupants. Hopefully all the work we'll be putting in will do that.'

Walter frowned. 'You think you can help with all that with just some paint and curtains?' he said, before raising his eyebrows.

Lily smiled. 'Interior design is a bit more than that,' she told him. 'It's about space and light. How a room is going to be used. The feel of the place. Textures and layers.' She stopped and looked at Walter in earnest. 'But yes, I can do all of that with my designs. They can make a real difference. I wouldn't lie to you. It's too important.'

He raised up his chin. 'You get it. The importance of the place. I like that.' He gave her a nod. 'So what did you have in mind?'

For a moment, Lily let her mind wander. 'A feature wall of wood in each bedroom. Then against a backdrop of the warm oak and neutral tones, I would add hints of colour in the soft furnishings. Greens, taupe and blues to reflect the outside. Bring it indoors. With touches of character as well.'

Then she realised in horror that she had been speaking out loud and, worse than that, she had given Walter her true ideas for the design.

'Maybe you'll do an all right job after all, if you can make all that happen,' Walter said, giving her an approving nod. 'I warn you though. If you stay here for too long, you'll never want to leave.'

She smiled at him. 'I promise you, Walter, that I will be able to leave at the end of the project.'

'We'll see,' he told her, with a knowing smile. 'Anyway, sounds as if you've got a busy day ahead so you'd best get started.'

As he walked away, Lily realised that both Walter and Ben had completely different visions for the hotel and that she was firmly stuck in the middle of their ongoing argument.

Whatever happened in the future, someone was going to have to give way and it wouldn't help mend an already fractured relationship between the two men.

Despite all of her worries, she allowed herself a small shake of the head. Walter might have been right to agree with her design ideas but he was completely wrong with the notion that she would be staying once the project was complete.

She might be staying at Maple Tree Lodge for a little while

longer. But whilst the thought of getting any closer to the family unsettled her, for a brief moment she was surprised to find herself almost relishing the thought.

She also found herself hovering outside for a few more moments to enjoy the glorious view before turning away and heading indoors to get started on her designs.

9

Ben was feeling a little more optimistic about the hotel's chances of survival as the morning went on.

The electrician had told him that the rewiring of the entire lodge was almost complete. The plasterers had completed the ceiling of the reception hall so at least his grandad could stop grumbling over the scaffold as it would be taken down the following day.

Last and perhaps best of all, Lily seemed entirely on board with his vision for the hotel.

Although he was a little unsettled by the fact that his sister had invited her to stay whilst the redecoration was carried out.

'I don't understand what the problem is,' said Hannah, when he mentioned it to her when they met in the lounge later in the morning.

'I'm not sure Mum will want to keep catering for one more person every day,' he told her.

Hannah laughed. 'Are you kidding? Mum's thrilled.'

'OK,' carried on Ben. 'How about the fact that she's here to work and that we've got an awful lot to do? I'm not sure she's going to have time to chat and gossip with you every day.'

Hannah raised her eyebrows. 'Can't she do both?' she said in a sarcastic tone. 'She's very gifted.'

Ben blew out a long sigh. 'I'm not sure she needed to move in here, whatever the circumstances,' he replied.

Hannah made a face. 'She's living in a rubbish place and the lease is about to run out.'

He shrugged his shoulders. 'So why can't she just find somewhere else to live?' he snapped.

'Because she's my friend and it's my home too,' Hannah told him, with a glare.

'I know,' he said.

'So I've invited Beth and Ella to stay next weekend as well, not that I need your permission for that either, big bro,' she carried on.

He was surprised but actually pleased to find his sister sounding a little stronger, a little more self-confident. Perhaps having her friend to stay would do her good and she would begin to break out of her shell a bit, he thought.

Working in that grotty pub in Aldwych didn't help, of course. Staff turnover was always high there for a reason, because the manager was so awful. He knew Hannah downplayed how miserable she was there but he had always tried to protect her from any school bullies, always tried to look out for her, even though they were both now in their early thirties.

Perhaps he could have a quiet word with Lily whilst she was around. See if they could both work on Hannah to find another job, at least until the hotel reopened. After all, she had known Lily for many years and obviously trusted her.

'OK.' He held up his hands in submission. 'Point taken.'

'Can't you just be a little nicer these days?' asked Hannah, shaking her head.

'I'm always nice,' he told her, offended.

'You used to be until you became hotel manager.'

Hannah gave him a wink to offset her jibe before she walked out of the room.

Ben's shoulders sagged as he leant back on the sofa. He knew he ended up borderline nagging each day. He felt permanently miserable and just couldn't see a way out. Perhaps when the hotel was finally finished, he could take a step back and begin to enjoy himself again. But if they didn't receive any guests, he couldn't see what the future was.

When he wandered into the kitchen a short while later and found everyone but Lily making themselves lunch, Ben braced himself for the worst before speaking.

'There's a company coming tomorrow to install the wireless internet,' he announced. 'It should be accessible from every room in the hotel.'

'At last,' said Hannah, clapping her hands. 'It'll be so nice not to wait until I go to work to download stuff.'

'Pah!' Walter, who was sitting at the table, gave a shrug. 'Folks should come here to switch off, not look at their phones.'

'Good thing too with the lack of wi-fi,' drawled Frankie, pouring herself a glass of water. 'There's absolutely no signal out here which is no good for all my suitors lining up to ask me for a date.'

'Well, after tomorrow, that might just be sorted,' Ben told her.

Frankie laughed. 'The dates or the wi-fi?' she asked.

He smiled at the small joke because it was so rare to hear Frankie laugh these days. They had known her all their lives as she was their mum's best friend. But she had had a chequered love life and her last husband had turned out to be abusive. She had gotten out of the marriage but not before an air of sadness had descended upon her.

Faye had offered her the spare room in the staff quarters a couple of months ago and she had stayed with them ever since as a receptionist-cum-girl-Friday-cum-anything.

Her biggest role most of the time, along with Ben's mum, was as peacemaker, it felt.

'Anyway,' he said, dragging the conversation back to more pressing matters. 'That company with the solar panels are coming on Tuesday so at least things are moving forward at last.'

Walter nodded. 'That's the first good idea you've had. Use the sun for our energy.'

'If we ever get any,' quipped Frankie.

'We've got to do something,' Ben told her. 'The electricity bills are still way too high. I'm hoping once the electrician's finished, the new circuit board will get the costs down a bit.'

'You could always ask Del for ideas,' said Frankie.

Ben immediately shook his head. Del was Frankie's godson. He had been the local coach driver until that business had begun to dry up and he had turned his hand to becoming a taxi driver instead. Del was a nice guy, always trying to be helpful around the local villages. It was just that his dubious ideas to help out his friends and himself had earned him the nickname Dodgy Del a long time ago. Trouble followed Del everywhere he went, despite his generous nature.

Thankfully Ben was saved by the phone ringing in the main reception and Frankie went to answer it. He sat down next to his grandad at the table.

'So now that things are moving forward,' said Ben, 'we need to decide on a date to reopen properly.'

'And then you'll go?' asked Walter.

Ben baulked. Was his grandad so desperate for him to leave already? 'I thought I'd stay on a bit longer to help,' he said slowly.

'We don't need your help,' said Walter, his mouth set in a firm line.

For a moment, he looked every bit of his seventy-nine years of age and Ben's heart ached. This was the man who had taught him how to fish. About the trees and the land. About the lake and the nature surrounding it.

Nobody wanted this place to be sold. It was their home. Their bolt-hole. And he was needed, however bad it made the atmosphere.

'This land has been in our family for five generations,' said Walter, sticking to an old, familiar routine.

'And I'm trying to make sure it stays in the family for another five,' Ben told him.

'Why? Have you got some great-grandchildren for me hidden away somewhere?' asked Walter, with a rare twinkle in his eye.

'Not given the state of my love life at the present time,' muttered Ben.

'Even Dodgy Del's had more dates than you, from what Frankie tells me,' said Walter.

They exchanged a small smile. 'I pity those poor women,' said Ben.

Walter nodded. 'Me too. You're not going to let him near our new, entirely safe electrics, are you?'

Ben shook his head. 'Absolutely not,' he replied. 'I've said that he can do a few of the odd jobs around here to save money on the main contractors but he's not touching anything that compromises safety. With his track record? Definitely not.'

Ben glanced at his phone and saw that he had received a notification from the bank that morning. Funds were definitely beginning to run low.

The hotel had been an albatross around their necks all of their lives. Would the hotel survive another year? And the year after that as well? He just didn't know.

But it was still home. Where they always returned to.

And where would he go to anyway? If he could get the hotel back up and running then surely he could design his own buildings for the future. He missed designing and building something with his own hands though.

But that all felt a very long way away. Frankie came back in, chatting about the phone call she'd just received which was from the local newsagents. She still needed a safe place to stay. Then there was his sister, who had declared that she was never moving away from Maple Tree Lodge ever again. His mum was still grieving, still trying to work out her place in the world without her beloved husband. She hadn't worked out what to do with the rest of her life either. They had all just about managed to get through the first six months without Ben's dad, but then what?

His grandparents had just lost their only son and they too were rudderless and uneasy about the future. Dotty spent her time knitting and worrying about Walter. Walter was just cross about everything and seemingly unhappy.

For Ben, the worst feeling was what if his business skills were actually rubbish? What if he couldn't save the hotel for his family, what then?

So many people dependent on him and sometimes it felt overwhelming. Frankie had once referred to herself as a waif and stray. Now even Lily appeared to be joining them for a while. Another person to be responsible for.

They were all desperate for the security of Maple Tree Lodge but the trouble was, he couldn't tell them that it wasn't secure at all.

10

After her discussion with Ben, Lily had been holed up in her bedroom all day, working on the interior designs for the hotel.

First she updated the measurements that Ben had given her for the bedrooms so she could upload them into the software she always used. Instantly, she had a 3D scale of each bedroom, including the windows and doors, to work from.

She left her room briefly to wander into each bedroom, noting which way they were facing, whether into the forest or at the lake, which would affect the natural light. She also marked how many plastered walls each room had and how many were made up of the log timbers.

Finally, she had her blank canvas with which to start work. Going along with Ben's wishes, she created a pale palette for each room. The log timbers were covered up with plasterboard and painted white, the floorboards were given a soft grey tint and all the furniture was pale ash. It was modern and stark, exactly what Ben had asked for.

But her heart sank as she flicked through each bedroom. It

was wrong, so very wrong, she told herself. But it was what the client wanted, wasn't it?

Feeling despondent, she wandered downstairs to make herself a coffee. For once, she found the kitchen empty and so, after making herself a drink, headed into the lounge. There were various wires hanging out of sockets, waiting for the electrician to fix them up, but it still felt like a room needing more.

It was just a little barren at the moment, thought Lily. She knew that Ben had enlisted her to decorate just the bedrooms but the rest of the place could certainly do with a makeover as well. For instance, the lounge wasn't an inviting space to settle down in, despite the obvious amount of money that had been spent on the expensive sofas which were covered with clear plastic to save them from getting ruined. Even the stone chimney and oak mantelpiece were bare. It was crying out for some decoration and a little bit of magic.

As she turned to look at the glorious view outside, she spotted a door on the opposite wall which she hadn't noticed before. She walked over and pulled it tentatively open.

'That's the snug,' Frankie told her, suddenly appearing and making her jump.

'What's that?' asked Lily.

'Pretty much a dumping ground,' said Frankie. 'It used to be a bar from what I remember. But that was a long time ago.'

As Frankie joined her in the doorway, Lily peered into the space. It too had a French door that led onto the veranda but only the one, making it more cosy. But it was still a large space, if you could look beyond the plethora of goods piled up everywhere. There were coat racks and vases jostling for space alongside a snooker table and candlesticks, hurricane lanterns and piles of old books.

'This lot was left over from when Walter and Dotty moved out into their lodge,' said Frankie. 'Dotty's a known hoarder. She was always picking up trinkets and other stuff from car boot sales and charity shops. Then you've got Walter who has never thrown anything out in his life. But the lodge was so much smaller that anything spare was left in here and has never been retrieved,' Frankie told her.

'Shame it's not used,' said Lily. 'It's a really good space for people to enjoy.'

'Gotta clear it out first,' said Frankie. 'And find some guests too.'

As Frankie wandered away, Lily took one last look at the snug before turning to look out across the lake once more.

The trees were now tinged with pale yellow and orange as the greens of the summer began to turn with the imminent arrival of autumn. She turned her back on the view and looked at the room once more. That would be her choice of colours in this room, she thought. Soft yellows, taupe and some burnt umber would be perfect. Soft rugs, blankets and cushions. Fairy lights and soft candles in the evenings to mix with the firelight.

She took a sharp intake of breath. In that moment, she knew that she couldn't follow Ben's desire for the minimalistic design that he wanted. It was totally wrong for the place. She knew that with every fibre of her being.

She would have to be careful, she realised. This contract was make-or-break for her future career. So she decided to keep two different design portfolios going forward. One would be for Ben, showcasing his own ideas. But there would be another secret one for herself. The real one. The one that she knew was just right for the place.

She knew he would disagree but she was determined to prove him wrong.

* * *

Sitting down later in the lounge with Ben to discuss her ideas for the design, Lily had butterflies in her stomach.

She had spent all afternoon working on her own designs and her heart was singing with the thought of decorating the hotel in her own style.

But first there was Ben to contend with.

She flicked on the first file on her laptop to show him what she had created.

He peered at the design on the screen before nodding his head in approval. 'Looks great,' he told her, looking once more at the almost white palette of the bedroom. 'Just the vibe we were going for.'

She just managed to stop herself from rolling her eyes in time. She had blocked out every log, every piece of wood. It hardly even looked like a lodge any more.

'So your USP when you open it is for the whole place to look like this?' she asked.

'Absolutely,' said Ben in a firm tone. 'Sharp. Modern. Slick. That's totally the in-look at the moment. A lot of the hotels in the area are going the same way.'

Slick and modern? thought Lily. Was the man insane? He seemed bright enough but Ben was insistent that he wanted some kind of urban take on a modern hotel. It was totally at odds with both the people who ran the hotel and the place itself.

'So about the budget,' she began.

Ben's face fell into a frown. 'It's got to be pretty tight, I'm afraid.'

She nodded. 'I understand. You know, as I've been invited to stay on by Hannah for a while, I can do a lot of the decorating myself. I'm very good so there wouldn't be a problem about the quality of the finish.'

He looked surprised but pleased. 'That's great,' he said, relief filling his voice.

'Obviously I'll cost up all the materials for you but I'll get going on the bedrooms in the morning, if that's OK.'

'Sooner the better,' he replied.

'When's our deadline?' she asked.

He leant back on the sofa. 'I was thinking about that. We need some kind of grand reopening, I guess.'

'That would be good in getting the word out,' Lily told him.

He nodded. 'I agree.'

'Obviously there's still the bedroom furniture to be ordered, curtains and the rest,' Lily reminded him. 'As well as the actual decorating.'

'And the plasterers haven't finished yet. And it's already October,' said Ben. 'OK. How about 1 December?'

'Sounds good,' said Lily, thinking that the extra time might just be enough for her to decorate a few extra rooms. 'And what about the lounge and dining room?'

'Oh, I think we can make do as we are,' said Ben. 'Like I said, the budget's pretty thin.'

Not wanting to push her luck at this stage, Lily merely nodded. 'OK,' she told him.

'Well, this is great,' said Ben, looking at the screen once more. 'I'll leave you to it.'

'See you later,' she replied, as he got up from the sofa and headed out of the lounge.

As soon as she was sure that he wasn't in sight, Lily flicked the screen onto the secret plan that she had been working on that afternoon.

Immediately she found herself nodding at her own design.

This was much better. They were the same bedrooms but in a completely different colour scheme. It was still modern but it was also cosy, warm and comfortable. The wall of wooden logs behind the bed glowed against the soft green of the walls. Touches of pale pink came from a blanket and cushions that she had placed on the bed. In addition, she had added some more homely touches such as candlesticks and a pile of books on a small wooden table.

She knew that it was going to be tricky. That she would have to work fast to complete the room before someone saw what she had done. She planned to put up a 'wet paint' sign once she was done to keep everyone out. Hopefully it would sustain her for long enough to persuade Ben that she was right with her ideas.

She felt bad about misleading him but she was the designer, wasn't she? This was what she was being paid to do. Design the best room and that was what she was going to create.

She had wondered briefly about sharing her secret with Hannah before deciding that her friend wasn't the greatest actress and she didn't want to cause a rift between brother and sister. Besides, she was used to working by herself.

Lily knew she was ignoring Ben's wishes and that he was the client but she knew in her heart that she was right. With a determined nod, she felt ready to get started.

After all, the future of the hotel depended on this. And so did her future as well.

11

Before she was able to implement her secret design plan, Lily first had to head back into London to retrieve the remaining items left in her rental room before the lease ran out in a couple of days' time.

Also, she didn't trust her flatmates not to help themselves to her belongings if they found out that she was leaving.

Early in the morning, Hannah had organised a local taxi to take Lily into London. Del, the taxi driver, seemed nice enough. He was a skinny man with dark hair and a motor mouth which didn't stop running for the whole journey.

She quickly found out that he was Frankie's godson and he filled in a few more details about Frankie's life as well.

'That husband of hers was the worst,' he said, carving up a lorry as they whizzed down the motorway. 'A rotter through and through.'

'Poor Frankie,' replied Lily.

'She's not as tough as she makes out,' said Del.

But before Lily could ask him to explain, his mobile rang and he spent the rest of the journey chatting on a call.

Once they had arrived outside the house, Del quickly plugged his electric car into the hallway socket to top up the battery before the journey home. Lily had been told by Hannah that Del's heart was generous, even if his methods were somewhat questionable.

She didn't much care about the electricity bill for charging Del's car. She was just glad to be getting out of there. Having been away only for a short while, the house looked even shabbier on her return.

Even Del seemed unimpressed. He made a face as he looked around the bedroom. 'What a dump,' he muttered, looking at the cracked walls and peeling paint on the ceiling. 'Who would want to live in a place like this?'

'Sometimes people have no choice,' Lily told him, laying the last of her clothes into a suitcase before zipping it up.

Del looked at the three suitcases and a couple more large bags of stuff in the middle of her bed. 'Is that it?' he asked, sounding surprised.

She nodded, glancing over at the carefully wrapped doll's house that she would take down the stairs herself.

'Never known a woman not to have too much stuff,' Del told her, frowning.

She shrugged her shoulders. 'This is everything I own. I travel light.'

'What about your folks?' he asked. 'I guess you've kept some stuff with them?'

She laughed. 'It wouldn't be terribly convenient. They're stationed in Canberra at the moment.'

His eyes widened. 'Wow,' he said. 'I've never been to India.'

She was going to correct him on the right continent but thankfully at that moment he picked up a suitcase and carried it downstairs.

Coming Home to Maple Tree Lodge

After the room was cleared, Lily made one last double check before picking up the doll's house and heading out. She left the spare key on the side before closing the front door behind her.

Even in Del's small taxi, her belongings didn't take up much room.

'Glad I didn't bother to bring my van,' he said, switching on the engine before driving out of the road.

Lily looked out of the car window. Would she miss the hectic streets of London for a while? Perhaps not, she thought. Especially when the urban sprawl fell away a while later and the view out of her window changed for the better. Suddenly they were in the countryside and she could see even Del relaxing at the change of view as the grey streets were replaced with a kaleidoscope of autumnal colours.

'This is better,' said Del, nodding his approval. 'Can't stand all those noisy city streets. Can't hear yourself think in them, can you?'

Lily had to admit that the peace and quiet of Maple Tree Lodge would certainly be a welcome change. Perhaps it would even give her time to work out what her next step would be. After she'd completed her commission for the hotel, that was.

As Del turned the taxi onto the narrow track leading to the hotel, she saw that a tow truck was slowly winching out the stranded hire car out of the pond at last.

'You won't get your deposit back on that one,' he muttered.

Lily nodded, having already received notice from the hire company.

Once back at the hotel, Del helped her carry the boxes and suitcases up to her bedroom. After thanking him, she headed downstairs to make herself a coffee.

Having sat down on one of the stools at the large island, she was just checking her phone when Ben wandered in.

'Hey,' he said, heading over to flick on the kettle once more. 'You're back.'

She nodded. 'It didn't take as long as Del expected.'

'Thought the traffic would slow you up.'

She shook her head. 'It was pretty quiet out there so early in the morning.'

'I used to get stuck on that motorway all the time when I used to come home from working in London,' he said, making a face. 'Used to take hours on a Friday night.'

'Do you miss it?' she found herself asking, wondering how he had fitted into the big city coming from this kind of landscape.

'It's certainly different than here,' he replied. She noticed that he avoided answering the question.

'Well, I'm sure once the place is up and running after all the renovations, it'll be as busy as the streets of London around here, full of guests,' she said.

'Let's hope so,' he told her, stirring the contents of his mug slowly round and around.

But his voice didn't sound full of hope.

He looked up with a start, as if he had forgotten she was even there. 'Well,' he said quickly. 'I'd better go and see what the builders are going to achieve today.'

With that, he walked out, leaving Lily with the feeling that there was something wrong at Maple Tree Lodge. Was business really that bad? And what did it mean for the Jackson family if it was?

That thought made her even more determined to ensure that the rooms had the very best designs that she could think of. And any doubts she had harboured about her secret plan vanished into thin air.

12

A couple of days later, Ben was feeling decidedly grumpy due to a couple of emails he had received that morning.

One was expected. It was the invoice for the rewiring of the whole hotel from the electrician. The high number at the bottom of the invoice made him feel ill, especially as he wasn't sure how they would ever be able to get back into the black but at least the hotel was safe for a while longer. Pretty soon it would be fully renovated and redecorated. But would it be full of guests? He just didn't know.

Another email was the latest electricity bill, which seemed unnecessarily high, considering they had just updated the circuit board. He couldn't understand it and tried to ask around at lunchtime when the family had found themselves all in the kitchen at the same time. But the family couldn't think of any reason for the higher bills.

'Where's Lily?' asked Faye, stirring some apple chutney on the hob. 'I've made her a sandwich.'

'She said she was going to work through lunch today as she was halfway through painting the ceiling,' replied Hannah, sitting down on one of the stools at the middle island. 'I'll take it up to her just as soon as I've finished mine.' She yawned. 'I can't wait to have some time off at the weekend when Beth and Ella get here. I'm so tired.'

'You girls work too hard,' said Dotty, shaking her head in disapproval.

'Well, that will all change this weekend,' said Hannah with a wide grin.

Ben felt pleased that Hannah was enjoying having her friend around. She had been badly bullied at school, having not fallen in with the 'in' crowd, and despite him trying to protect her from the worst of it, the bullies had dented her confidence.

Walter came into the kitchen, his jumper covered in tiny pieces of wood.

Faye raised her eyebrows at him. 'Have you been chopping wood all this time?' she asked.

'Nights are beginning to turn colder now,' he muttered, sinking down at the table with a heavy sigh. He looked tired, thought Ben.

Frankie placed a plate and sandwich in front of him. 'I should have thought that at your age you should be slowing down, not speeding up,' she told him.

Walter gave her a pointed look. 'I'm not a feet up kind of guy,' he replied before taking a bite of the sandwich.

'Well, those afternoon naps you take on the quiet don't exactly affirm your point there,' Dotty told him with a knowing smile.

Dodgy Del walked into the kitchen. 'Afternoon, all,' he said. 'Oooh, am I in time for lunch?'

'A free lunch, you mean,' muttered Walter.

'I've been working hard actually,' Del told him, trying and

failing to look hurt. 'Those bathrooms won't kit themselves out. I've got ten more towel rails to put up.'

'Actually I've got a bone to pick with you regarding that,' said Ben. He had always regretted allowing Frankie to talk him into letting her godson help out with the bathroom renovations. Cheap didn't always mean better, he had begun to realise. There was a reason why Dodgy Del's handyman skills didn't come highly recommended.

'Wassup?' said Del, his mouth full of sandwich. 'I put those loo seats on as you asked.'

'Yes, but you've wired them the wrong way,' Ben told him. 'The idea is that with that sensor they go up when you go near them. But you've wired them up so that the lid closes when you stand next to them.'

'I'm sure you're wrong,' said Del, shaking his head. 'I checked them all out.'

'Electric loo seats,' muttered Walter.

'This place needs a touch of luxury,' said Ben. 'If they want rustic, there's a new glamping site just down the road in Cranfield they can book into instead.'

'Humph,' said Walter.

Ben found that he had lost his appetite and stood up. His endless fights with his grandad weren't doing either of them any good.

'Aren't you going to finish your lunch?' asked Faye, looking concerned.

'Not hungry.' He picked up the plate with the sandwich on for Lily. 'I'll take it up for her,' he said. 'I want to check on the progress of the bedrooms anyway.'

He walked out of the kitchen feeling despondent. More than anything, he longed to escape out of there. To have life back as it had been before, without responsibility and with a loving relationship with his grandad. But he couldn't see them ever getting along again.

Feeling wretched, he noticed that his hands were smeared in mayonnaise. Leaving the plate on the reception desk, he headed into the downstairs bathroom to wash his hands before he went to see Lily.

But as he went through the door, he almost tripped over a long electrical lead. He looked around and realised that it was trailing out of the small open window above the double sink.

What on earth was it for? Had one of the workmen left it behind? He turned around and headed back out of the washroom to find that it was plugged into the wall behind the reception desk. Still bemused, he walked out through the front door and into the car park. He turned right and went around the side of the hotel to find the open window from the bathroom and the same lead dangling down and across to a nearby vehicle.

He came to an abrupt halt and stared, spluttering out a shocked exclamation. In front of him was Dodgy Del's new taxi. Having been a coach driver, Del had decided to increase his earnings by becoming a local taxi driver, although without any guests at the hotel, the pickings weren't rich at Maple Tree Lodge.

However, the hotel did come with an added bonus. Because the taxi was a second-hand electric vehicle, Dodgy Del was obviously using the hotel's electricity to charge his car!

Ben turned around, feeling enraged. But at least he knew why the electricity bills were so high now!

13

Lily wandered downstairs when she finally couldn't ignore the hungry rumble in her stomach any longer, especially as the aroma of home cooking was wafting up the stairs.

She found all the family except Ben in the kitchen.

'I thought Ben was taking you the sandwich that I made,' said Faye, frowning when she realised that Lily was hungry.

Lily shook her head. 'I haven't seen him.'

Faye looked bemused. 'How odd. I wonder where he went?'

'No worries,' said Lily. 'I can make another.'

'You've been working hard enough,' said Faye, in a firm tone. 'Which is more than I've been doing this morning, picking flowers and making chutney.'

Lily looked at the autumnal arrangement in a nearby vase. 'It's so pretty,' she said, admiring the twigs full of berries, the orange chrysanthemums and a couple of red roses.

'Most came from the garden but the berries are from the woods,' said Faye. 'I love wandering around week to week and seeing the changes.'

'I've been admiring the view out of the window most of the

morning,' said Lily, before thanking Faye as she placed a sandwich on a plate for her to eat.

'I can waste away many hours staring out of the window,' said Faye in a wistful tone.

'Especially when it's framed like that,' replied Lily.

'So are you looking forward to your friends arriving tomorrow?' asked Faye.

Lily nodded. 'It's been so long since I saw them. There's so much to catch up on.'

'Beth's new boyfriend, for a start,' said Hannah.

Lily sighed. 'Another one,' she replied, rolling her eyes.

'What's wrong with him?' asked Frankie.

'Everything, probably,' muttered Lily.

Frankie and Faye exchanged a confused look. 'Then why is she dating him?' asked Faye.

'Because Beth is so desperate for her very own happy ever after she doesn't seem to have any kind of filter where men are concerned,' Hannah told her. 'She falls in love so easily, thinking the next guy is the one. She can't think badly of any of them.'

'When they're mostly awful,' finished Lily, with a shudder. 'Do you remember that one that tried it on with me a few years ago? Ugh!'

'Poor Beth,' said Faye, shaking her head. 'And she's so sweet as well.'

'I know,' said Frankie, making a face. 'She's so sunny and happy it's positively sickening.'

Everyone giggled.

'Ella's more like me,' added Frankie, with a nod of approval. 'She knows that men are to be toyed with and then discarded as soon as they've moved beyond usefulness into annoying.'

'But you must believe in love,' said Hannah, looking shocked. 'I mean, you've been married two times!'

'Oh, I never make the same mistake twice,' Frankie told her, smiling. 'I make it four or five times just to make sure.'

'So what are you girls up to this weekend?' asked Faye, after shaking her head at her friend.

'Chilling out,' Hannah told her. 'With lovely autumnal walks, silly movies...'

'And plenty of alcohol!' finished Lily, with a grin.

'Glad to hear that,' said Frankie. 'That's true BFFs, that is. After all, a best friend reaches for your hand – and puts a wine glass into it.'

'I'd better get back to work before all this talk of alcohol makes me thirsty for cocktail hour,' said Lily, standing up.

'Do you need a hand?' asked Hannah.

Lily quickly shook her head. 'You save your energy for work later,' she told her.

She was still smiling to herself though as she headed back upstairs. She was trying to hold back from getting too close to the family whilst she was staying there. But she had to admit that she was enjoying the company of all the Jackson family.

She went back into the bedroom she had been working on. The ceiling was finished and three of the walls had a fresh coat of white paint as a base. Behind the bed, she had carefully removed the large wall panels, exposing the traditional logs behind. At once it had felt warmer and more cosy, which was just the vibe she had been looking for. However, she had painted the plasterboards white and kept them up in front of the exposed wall so that Ben didn't ask too many questions.

She was just getting her paintbrush ready when there was a knock on the door. To stop anyone from wandering in, she had put a 'No Entry' notice outside, with the excuse that the paint was wet around the door.

'Come in,' she called out.

The door opened to reveal Ben holding a sandwich. 'I brought you lunch,' he said. 'Sorry it's a little late.'

'That would be my second,' she told him. 'I went downstairs a little while ago and your mum made me a sandwich.'

'Oh.' He frowned. 'It must have been when I was having a go at Dodgy Del for charging up his bloomin' electric taxi using our mains!'

Lily laughed. 'He does seem like a character.'

'Hmm,' said Ben, stepping further into the room. 'That's one word for him.' He looked around, nodding as if pleased. 'It's looking good, isn't it? What happened to that wall?' He pointed at the small amount of exposed logs behind the bed.

'I had to remove the panel to get right into the corner. But I'll fix it back when I'm done,' she said.

'Good, good,' he said. 'This white really brightens it up, doesn't it? The modern look is much better, don't you think?'

'Yes,' she lied.

'Well, I'll leave you to it,' he told her, heading out of the bedroom and closing the door behind him.

Lily puffed out a sigh of relief. It was going to get a bit tricky from here on in but she knew that she was right. In time, hopefully Ben would agree with her, she told herself before turning to open up a brand-new pot of green paint that she had kept hidden.

14

It had been a laughter-filled evening and one which Lily couldn't remember enjoying more for a very long time.

She had just managed to complete painting the whole of the first bedroom before her best friends had arrived to stay until Sunday night.

'I can't believe you're here!' she said, giving Beth a huge hug when she and Ella arrived in a taxi late in the afternoon. She hadn't realised how much she had truly missed her friends until she saw them face to face.

'Right back at you,' replied Beth, giving her a tight squeeze before finally letting go. 'Look at you! You've got paint on your ear!'

Lily grimaced. 'Occupational hazard,' she said, touching her earlobe and hoping that it was white and not the soft green that she had been using that day.

Whilst Lily was dressed casually in jeans and a sweatshirt, as usual Beth was dressed in her vintage style. Beth often scoured the charity shops in search of retro fashion and that day's outfit was no exception. She was wearing a pale pink beret and matching sweater, matched by a glamorous black winter coat and flower-patterned A-line skirt.

Her long dark hair was braided into two plaits and her dark eyes were lined with heavy eyeliner, as well as wearing deep red lipstick.

However, beneath her slightly kooky fashion and happy-go-lucky personality lay the sharp intelligent mind of an astronomer. 'I'm a total nerd,' Beth would often tell her friends. 'People expect me to look a bit weird.'

In stark contrast to Beth's individual style, Ella was always dressed more conservatively. That day she was wearing a long camel coat over white jeans and a classic white shirt. Around her neck was a Hermès scarf which Lily knew that Ella had saved up for months to buy.

'Hello!' she said, giving Lily a hug. 'Wow, it's so good to finally see you.'

Lily stepped back and smiled at her friend. 'You too,' she replied.

As always, Ella's blonde hair lay in a perfect straight curtain to her shoulders and her discreet make-up was immaculate, despite having journeyed on the train for the best part of three hours.

'Come in!' Hannah urged everyone. 'Let's get this party started!'

'And this is one night you can't miss because you're already here!' said Ella, giving Lily a nudge before heading indoors.

As she followed her friend indoors, Lily mulled over Ella's words. She wasn't that bad a friend, was she? She shook her head. It was just one of Ella's bad jokes, that was all, she decided.

After a noisy dinner with the family, the group of friends decided to leave the rest of the family in peace and had an impromptu pyjama party in Hannah's bedroom.

'This is great,' said Beth, jumping onto the bed. 'I've been stuck in a bland meeting room all week and now look, we've got a real fire, chocolate cake and, well, whatever's in this cocktail!' She held up the glass and took a sip. 'My, that's even stronger than the one Frankie made last summer.'

She put it down and curled her feet up underneath her legs. She had changed into old-fashioned blue-striped men's pyjamas, fluffy socks and her long black hair was in bunches.

'In which case, I'm going to take it slow,' said Ella, putting hers down carefully on the rug.

She had changed into maroon silk pyjamas with a matching dressing gown.

'Why?' asked Hannah, shrugging on an oversized hoodie. 'You like Frankie's cocktails.'

'I've got a Zoom call tomorrow and my face is going to be enlarged fifteen times onto a screen for a work meeting, I can't look haggard,' Ella told her, reaching out to smooth on some night cream onto her perfect pale skin. Her shiny blonde hair was held back in a ponytail.

'Here, eat some chocolate cake,' said Lily, holding out the plate. 'You're making me feel dishevelled.'

Ella gave her a slow look up and down. 'You look fine, as always. That green really brings out your eyes.'

Lily glanced down at her hoodie before shrugging. She knew she would never be anywhere near as stylish as Ella.

'Well, despite us not meeting up in some glamorous gin cocktail place,' began Ella, 'the most important thing is that we're all together for once. Cheers.'

They all chinked their glasses together before taking a tentative sip.

'How long has it been since us four were together?' asked Bella, wrinkling up her freckled nose in thought.

'Too long,' said Hannah.

'Well, we all made it to see Taylor Swift, didn't we?' said Lily.

That had been a night to remember at Wembley, when they had all dressed up and covered themselves in glitter to sing and dance along to all the music.

'Well, the main thing is that we're all together now,' said Beth, reaching to her neck to fiddle with her necklace. It was a simple silver star pendant. She had given each of them one before she had left the shared house all those years ago. It had been given with the promise that they would always look out for each other wherever they were in the world.

Lily felt bad, as she reached up to touch her own necklace which she had deliberately worn that evening. She hadn't done that, she found herself thinking. She'd broken her promise, especially with Hannah these past few months. Realising how grief-stricken the family still were had made her feel guilty that she hadn't made more time to be with her friend.

'Shame you never made it to Wicked,' Ella told Lily. 'You should have seen Beth's pink fairy dress that she wore. It was outstanding.'

'It was amazing,' agreed Hannah.

'And extremely short,' added Ella. 'All the men in the cinema were just looking at her legs rather than the screen most of the time.'

'They were not,' laughed Beth.

'See for yourself,' said Ella, scrolling through her mobile to find the photo.

She handed her phone to Lily who looked at the picture of her friends who were relaxed and smiling in the selfie.

'You should have been there,' said Hannah. 'It was such a fun night.'

Once more, Lily felt a little rattled. As if she was the spare wheel in the friendship more and more these days.

'I was on a deadline,' she said, shuffling awkwardly on her corner of the bed.

'Aren't you always?' murmured Ella before holding up her hand in defence. 'I know! It's your career, after all. And I can't talk as I've got that Zoom call tomorrow.'

Beth shook her head. 'Take it from me,' she said. 'The stars have been here forever. In the vastness of space, we're just a tiny piece. So if you look at it that way, in the scheme of things, work's not that important.'

Lily knew that they were teasing her but she felt a little upset. These were supposed to be her best friends. Supposed to understand why she worked so hard all the time. She had to prove it to her parents, didn't she?

And yet, when she listened to her friends and the fun she had been missing out on, she wondered what pursuing her career was costing her. And, as it had turned out, all that hard work had been for nothing as she had been fired anyway.

But a tiny part of her wondered whether there was a small truth in what they were trying to tell her. Could it be that her friends were right and maybe she was wrong after all?

15

Having spent a busy Saturday with her friends, shopping and then going to the local cinema, Sunday morning was a more low-key affair. Especially as Beth and Ella had to catch a train later that afternoon to head home in time for work in the morning.

Lily felt better for the break away from work, despite the pressures of the deadline beginning to creep up on her. She had managed to catch up properly with all her friends and was even beginning to relax for the first time in a long time, she felt.

'How are you getting to the train station?' asked Faye when they all gathered around the long table for breakfast.

'Frankie says her godson has offered us a free lift,' replied Ella.

'Wow.' Hannah blinked a few times, appearing surprised. 'What did he want in return?'

Lily laughed. 'You sound just like your brother, all suspicious!' she said.

Hannah smiled. 'Rightly so, where Del is concerned.' She looked at Ella. 'Don't tell me, he wants you to sort out some marketing or some such thing.'

'Well...' Ella's voice trailed off as she realised it was true. 'Actually, he did mention something about his taxi service website needing a makeover.'

'Ha! Told you so,' said Hannah, sinking onto a stool and sipping her coffee. 'He means well but if Del gives you a favour he expects one in return. Unless he wants a date instead?'

'Eww, no!' Ella made a face. 'I mean, he's a nice guy but no! Not my type. Besides, I only like a man if he's like my weekends: gone by Monday morning.'

Lily smiled at her friend. Ella had long since declared that she would never find Mr Right but was happy to consider quite a few Mr Wrongs instead.

Ella looked at Hannah. 'Maybe he's your type instead?' she teased.

Hannah shook her head so strongly her blonde hair swung about her face. 'Oh, no. Not Del. He's almost family! Anyway, I'm sworn off all men for the foreseeable future.'

'I'm sorry to hear that,' said Walter, coming into the kitchen. 'So I won't be getting any great-grandchildren any time soon?'

'Ha!' laughed Hannah. 'You'd better have a word with Ben instead, Grandad.'

'Humph,' said Walter. 'No chance there either.' He shook his head. 'You youngsters have no idea about love and romance.'

'Not much chance of that around here,' said Frankie, following him into the kitchen to place a shopping bag on the counter.

'And on that note, I'm going to get dressed.' Hannah stood up and stretched. 'I'm so sleepy today.'

'A bit of fresh air would wake you up,' said Walter.

'I think it might,' replied Hannah. 'Do you know, we still haven't shown Lily around the lake. Good as time as any, I reckon.'

Ella and Beth nodded their approval.

'What do you say, Lily?' asked Hannah.

'Sounds like a plan,' replied Lily.

'Great!' Hannah looked pleased. 'Meet you in the entrance hall in a while.'

As Lily was the only one who had got dressed for breakfast, she was able to quickly grab her wellies and coat from upstairs before heading outside.

It was such a beautiful day, she thought, taking a deep breath in. The early gloom had disappeared and there was nothing but a wide-open blue sky mirrored in the water across the lake. There was no sound of traffic, no congestion, no people, she realised. Just her and nature.

'Not bad, is it?' said Walter, coming to stand next to her.

'It's lovely,' said Lily. 'The colours are amazing.'

She looked across once more to where the maples were now wearing their autumnal splendour, coloured deep shades of red and gold scattered all around the surrounding forest.

'I think it's my favourite season when it's like this,' said Walter. 'But then again, I say that about every season here.'

'How long have you lived here?' asked Lily.

'All my life,' he replied. 'Never wanted to be anywhere else, to be honest.'

'I can see why,' she told him.

'Which makes me all the more puzzled as to why folks don't want to come here,' carried on Walter. 'I mean, look at it.'

He had a point, thought Lily. 'I agree,' she said. 'But perhaps Ben's new ideas will help bring in the guests once more.'

Walter's good mood faded. 'He shouldn't be here. He should be off living his life,' he muttered.

Lily was surprised at the fierceness of his tone. 'Maybe he wants to be here,' she told him. 'After all, this is his home too.

Some of us don't have one of those, not a permanent one in any case.'

Walter looked at her with piercing blue eyes. 'I guess not.' He turned back to look at the lake. 'Maybe you're right. This place is certainly in his blood. When he was young, he loved working with the timber. He understood the importance of taking care of the land. That we're just caretakers. You don't own it. It belongs to nature.' He sighed. 'He and I used to spend hours together in my workshop.'

'Maybe that's where he got his love of architecture from,' she told him.

Walter huffed. 'He's got a rare talent,' he said, with a proud look on his face. 'Hate to see him wasting it out here in the middle of nowhere.'

'But as you said, it's his home,' Lily reminded him.

Walter sighed heavily but didn't reply.

Before she could ask him any more, she saw Hannah, Beth and Ella walking towards them and, after a short greeting, Hannah's grandad walked away.

'What was that about?' asked Hannah, as they all began to walk the circuit of the lake.

'He was telling me how much Ben used to love helping in his workshop,' replied Lily.

'Oh, yes,' said Hannah, nodding and smiling in memory. 'You could only lure him out of there with food sometimes.' She took in a deep breath of the crisp cold air. 'Hate to see him and Grandad so far apart after everything that's happened this year.'

Beth reached out and linked arms with Hannah, giving her a squeeze.

'You must miss your dad very much,' said Beth.

Hannah nodded. 'Oh, yes,' she said, breathing out a sigh. 'I miss his hearty laugh and the way he was always there with a warm hug. But most of all,' she hesitated before carrying on, 'most of all, I miss how we all were so much happier back then.'

'How has it changed?' asked Lily.

'Take Grandad and Grandma for a start,' Hannah told her. 'Grandad tries so hard to prove that he's up to running the hotel when he clearly isn't because he's nearly eighty and allowed to be tired some of the time. Grandma seems to have lost her spirit as well. Mum's so sad too. And Ben? Well, he's so busy I'm not sure he's even had time to grieve these past few months.'

'And what about you?' asked Ella. 'You're important as well.'

'Me?' Hannah gave her a small smile. 'I just try and help in my own small way. Cake helps, I've been told.' Her face dropped. 'Not that it's any use, I'm sure.'

Lily looked at her friend, hearing the pain in her voice. 'I'm so sorry I didn't come and see you sooner. I should have made the time to come and see you when you were hurting so bad.'

'Thanks but it's fine,' said Hannah with a small shrug. 'We all know how busy you are.'

They carried on walking but still Lily felt guilty that she'd been so busy with work that she hadn't seen quite how much Hannah was struggling with her grief.

'Maybe I should start wild swimming again,' said Hannah, looking out across the water. 'Grandma always used to as well when the weather was warmer but it's been a few years now since we bothered, to be honest.'

Ella shuddered. 'Isn't it a little cold for that at the moment?'

'It clears the mind,' Hannah told her. 'And it's probably better for me than baking all the time.'

'Are you kidding?' said Beth, giving her a nudge with her elbow. 'I've tasted your chocolate cake and it's amazing.'

As usual, Hannah shrugged off the compliment and led them over a narrow wooden bridge.

They carried on around the lake and Lily found there was a beautiful view whichever way she looked. Out across the lake, the bullrushes nodded gently in the soft breeze with the call of the moorhens as they bobbed about on the water. In the forest that hugged the path all the way around, squirrels leapt from tree to tree, gathering up the acorns that were scattered across the leaf-strewn floor. Underneath the horse chestnut trees, glossy conkers lay amongst the amber leaves that had already fallen from its branches.

They crossed another wooden bridge on the opposite side of the lake as they headed towards the boathouse. It was another building made up of layers of logs but this time it was set over the water on large timber stilts. Underneath the floor of the boathouse, Lily could see a rowing boat tied up in one of the three docks underneath.

'I can show you my boating skills, if you like,' said Hannah, with a laugh.

'I'm staying with my feet firmly on terra firma, thank you very much,' Ella told her with a shudder.

'I spent those three weeks in the Antarctic studying the southern skies,' said Beth. 'I'm pretty good in a canoe. You know, with someone else helping.'

'Don't look at me!' said Lily, laughing.

They were all giggling and linking arms as they walked back towards the hotel. It had been an absolute tonic to see her friends again, thought Lily. How much stronger she felt for being together with them once more.

She just wished that she could share the secret plans she had for the hotel with them all. But perhaps it was better this way for the time being, she told herself.

16

The following afternoon, Ben was trying and failing to talk to one of his best friends on the phone.

'What?' he heard Jake shout for the second time in less than a minute. 'I can't hear you!'

Ben wasn't surprised. He could barely hear himself talk above the hammering and endless noise from the renovations all around him. At least the new oak skirting boards were looking good, he thought, as he looked around the entrance hall.

They would be painted white once they were finished, sticking with the pale scheme of the bedrooms. He was pleased that Lily had agreed with his ideas to copy a more corporate hotel theme. He had yet to see the results but was looking forward to the first viewing.

He couldn't continue his conversation outside as there was no phone signal out of the hotel. So in the end, he shouted to Jake that he would call him later and hung up. Almost immediately, his mobile rang once more.

Figuring it was Jake trying with another number, Ben picked up. But it wasn't his friend this time.

'Mr Jackson?' said the man on the end of the line. 'I'm Hans Haubermann. I'm so sorry it's taken so long for me to get back to you but we've had a cancellation so I would be happy to discuss your ideas for the hotel redesign at some point in the near future, if you would still like to use my services.'

Ben was nonplussed. 'I don't understand,' he replied, thinking that he had misheard. 'Your designer is already here and working on the project.'

Now it was Mr Haubermann's turn to sound shocked. 'Our designer? Who exactly is there, might I ask?'

'Lily Wilson,' he replied. They didn't seem a particularly efficient company if they couldn't even keep tabs on their own staff, he surmised, less than impressed.

'There must be some mistake. Miss Wilson was fired from this company two weeks ago.'

Ben was shocked. 'Fired?' he repeated.

Mr Haubermann confirmed the details and Ben hung up, feeling puzzled and extremely concerned.

He rushed up the stairs two at a time, determined to get to the bottom of the problem. He strode down the hallway towards Bedroom No. 2 and hesitated, seeing the 'Fresh Paint' sign on the door. In the end, he decided one splodge of paint wasn't going to stop him getting to the bottom of the matter. So he turned the handle and went inside.

Lily wasn't in the room but that didn't stop him staring around in shock. What had happened to the white design that they had discussed? Three of the walls were now painted a delicate but quite strong shade of green. The wall behind the bed had had its plasterboard removed and the thick logs were exposed from floor to ceiling. On the floor was a soft pale pink rug, which matched a cushion on the bed as well as a blanket that hung over a leather chair that he didn't recall seeing before.

However, it was the use of the colour that was a shock. Where he had been expecting white and cool, it was completely different. The colours were warm but vibrant and the use of wood helped as well. He had to admit that it felt modern, warm and comfortable. And deep down, he liked it.

But that wasn't the point, he reminded himself. That wasn't what she had been hired to do!

Incensed, he spun around on his heel and stalked out of the bedroom, determined to get to the bottom of the issue.

'Where's Lily?' he barked at Frankie, whose eyebrows raised in surprise at his harsh tone.

'She went out for a walk around the lake with your mum,' said Frankie.

She opened her mouth to ask him what the problem was but it was too late. Ben was already striding out of the hotel.

With each step, he was feeling more and more annoyed. By the time he came across his mum walking on her own, his temper had risen even more.

'Where's Lily?' he snapped.

She looked shocked. 'She's in the boathouse, having a look around,' said Faye. 'I had to leave her because I'm taking your grandmother into the village. What's the problem? Hey!'

Ben heard her call out but he was too busy walking towards the boathouse, determined to get to the bottom of the problem.

* * *

Lily was walking around the interior of the boathouse, feeling in awe. It was beautiful, she thought. She hadn't been inside it before but after seeing it on her walk around the lake, she had been desperate to peek at the interior. Now she was standing in the middle of the floor, she could appreciate how large a room it was with its double-height oak-framed ceiling. There was even a wide balcony along the whole of the first floor, although it looked a bit rickety so she wasn't going anywhere near it.

In the far corner, there was an opening in the floor where the top of a ladder could be seen peeping above the gap. It led down to the three docks below where she could hear the water lapping against the ancient boat that Faye had just shown her.

Faye needed to leave for an appointment but Lily had found that she wanted to loiter in the space for a while longer. There were no windows but the openings in the wall out onto the water made her feel as if she was floating above the lake itself.

The air was cool, coming in from the shutters through to the open front door. It still needed a complete renovation as all the floorboards were a little rickety and even the front door itself had to be wedged open with a heavy lump of wood that they had found.

'There's no handle on here,' Faye had said, showing her the smooth door. 'You won't be able to get out otherwise!'

Not that Lily was in a hurry to leave. The peace after the endless noise and hammering of the workmen in the hotel was blissful. And for all its run-down state, the boathouse felt a warm and welcoming place.

She suddenly heard footsteps outside and figured it was Faye coming back.

But it wasn't Faye at all, she realised, turning to look at the open doorway. It was Ben and he was looking extremely cross.

'There you are!' he said, standing in the doorway and filling the space with his wide shoulders.

'Yup. Here I am,' she said, somewhat worried about his tense expression.

'I've had a *very* interesting time this afternoon,' he carried on.

'How nice,' she said, wondering where this was leading.

'Not really,' he replied. 'I thought I'd see progress on the decorating. So I've just been into Bedroom No 2!'

She took a sharp intake of breath. He had seen the room! The truth was finally out on her secret design.

'You totally disregarded all of my ideas,' he told her.

'Only because they were awful,' she replied, finally feeling relieved enough to tell the truth.

'That's only your opinion and besides, that's not the point!' he wailed, before checking himself. 'I wanted the minimal look.'

'Which was completely wrong for the place!' she told him. 'Look, I know design and trust me when I say that I was on the right track. You've got to admit that the room looks much better.'

'They were my ideas! Mine! I'm in charge around here, although heaven knows nobody seems to realise that!' he shouted.

'Listen,' she began.

But he was in no mood to hear her ideas.

'But why should I be surprised that you ignored everything that I hired you to do,' he carried on. 'I mean, if your own design company can sack you then you're not exactly the most professional person at this, are you?'

Lily gasped, as a chill ran through her. 'You've talked to Hans?' she asked, with a gulp.

It was her worse nightmare coming true. Her dream job, her future, now coming apart at the seams. Worse still, she wouldn't have anywhere to live either when he threw her out. She would be both homeless and jobless. Her career wasn't just on a temporary hold, it was at a complete and utter end.

'I spoke to your ex-boss just half an hour ago,' he told her. 'So, do you want to tell me exactly what's going on around here? Why have I hired someone who's been given the sack? Why have you lied to me? To my family? To Hannah?'

On the last word, he gave the lump of rotten wood keeping the door open a kick in anger. It slid across the floorboards and the front door swiftly closed with a click.

'Well?' he asked.

But despite everything that he had just accused her of, Lily suddenly had a more pressing problem on her mind. 'You've just closed the door,' she told him, peering around him to double check the horrible thought that she now had.

'Yes, I'm aware of that, thank you,' he replied in a cool tone. 'Don't you think we've got bigger things to discuss?'

'Bigger than being stuck in here, you mean?' she asked.

'Stuck?' Ben's eyes widened before he spun around to reach out to the door. Lily watched as he felt around where the door handle would normally be and slowly realised what Faye had already told her. That there wasn't one.

He turned back around. 'Well, that really isn't an issue, is it?' he said, patting the back pockets of his jeans. And then his front pockets. Before patting the back pockets once more.

'I haven't got my phone either,' Lily told him, with a heavy sigh, thinking of her mobile, which she had left in the kitchen on charge. 'I mean, with no signal outside of the hotel there was no point taking it out for a walk, was there?'

Ben's mouth turned into a flat line as he pressed his lips together. 'So we're trapped in here, are we?' he asked, sounding as if she were the last person that he wanted to be with at that moment.

She nodded slowly. 'Yup.'

She didn't know what was worse. Being stuck in the boathouse alone or with Ben. Although one glance at his scowling face and she had the answer to that question. She would much rather have been stuck in there by herself!

17

Lily watched as Ben tried once more to open up the door by pressing his fingertips into the door frame. But with the door being completely smooth and having no handle, it was an impossible task.

'Believe me, I'm not thrilled about being stuck in here either,' Lily told him, sinking down to perch on a nearby table.

Ben turned around to scowl at her. 'I'm not sure I can believe anything that you say any more,' he replied.

She gulped, the guilt of her lies made her feel sick to her stomach. 'Look, I understand why you're upset,' she told him in a small voice. 'But can you let me at least try and explain why I lied about still being employed by Haubermann?'

Ben looked at her for a long time before coming over to sit down on a nearby crate, crossing his arms in front of his chest.

'Go on then,' he said, piercing her with his brown eyes.

She took a deep breath, trying to find the right words to convince him that she wasn't a bad person. She had thought that by lying she could safeguard her future career but she had only ended up making everything worse.

'I'm sorry,' she began, finally speaking the truth from her heart. 'I thought I was protecting you and your family by lying about my job but the truth is that I was only thinking of myself. I've been fighting for so long to be recognised for my talent as an interior designer. It's been incredibly frustrating, to be honest. I did all the work but Hans took all the credit for everything.'

Ben frowned but didn't say anything.

'Then two weeks ago it all came to a head,' she said, forcing herself to carry on into the silence. 'He had promised me a partner position and I thought that all the sacrifices would be worth it. But Hans announced that he had changed his mind and made me redundant instead. With less than two years at the company, the pay-off was almost worthless.' She dragged a hand through her hair. 'I was devastated. All those years of hard work. All that effort, all those years of wasted opportunity and for nothing.'

She was still so incredibly disappointed with what had happened.

'What do you mean he took all the credit for your work?' asked Ben.

'Hans has no creative talent,' she replied. 'None at all. So he gets us junior assistants to create the designs and then steps forward right at the end to tell the customer that it was all his own work.'

'That's awful,' said Ben, looking aghast. 'You should sue him.'

'Apparently there's a tiny clause in our contracts that doesn't allow for that,' she told him, with a shrug. 'Which is another lesson learned – always read your contracts from start to finish.' She tried and failed to raise a smile.

'So why did he sack you?' he asked.

'Apparently it always happens whenever anyone gets too close to being promoted.' Lily ran a hand through her hair before letting it fall. 'I was an idiot to ever believe him.'

Ben shuffled on the crate but remained silent.

Lily forced herself to look at him, meeting his dark eyes with hers. 'And then Hannah rang,' she carried on, her voice a little shaky with emotion. 'Lovely Hannah with her kind heart had thought of me and suddenly I saw a way to keep everyone happy. The hotel could receive its makeover, I'd help out my best friend and I would have a stepping stone towards setting up my own interior design company.'

'Is that what you want?' he asked. 'To have your own company?'

As the silence stretched out once more, suddenly she had an urge to speak from the heart. To reveal a little more about her dream, something she had never shared with anyone.

'You don't understand,' she told him softly. 'You see, I don't have anything else in my life but my career. I spent my childhood following my parents around from country to country and that wasn't the best way to make friends. So I buried myself in my career. I thought that owning my own company would be the pinnacle of success. It would be the absolute proof to my parents that it was the right decision to choose this path.'

He looked at her thoughtfully. 'Hannah told me how creative you've always been. Decorating the house you all shared and other stuff. I'm surprised there was any doubt that you would have chosen being an interior designer, given your obvious talent.'

Lily gulped. 'My parents weren't always supportive,' she told him. 'My dad's a diplomat and they were both hoping that I would follow their footsteps into a similar career. To be creative was always viewed as frivolous, where they're concerned.'

Ben raised his eyebrows in surprise.

'They love me and I know how much they care for me,' she told him, rushing on. 'And yet there's always this underlying feeling that they're disappointed in my choice of career. So I have to succeed to prove them wrong. And that means having my own company, whatever the sacrifices.'

'But you said that they loved you.'

She nodded.

'So they would support your career anyway?' he carried on.

'I just know it's not their choice for me,' she said.

'But you made that decision for yourself anyway. Have they ever said anything?' he asked.

'No.' She gave him a rueful smile. 'Except to nag me that I don't have a social life.'

He looked surprised. 'You don't?'

She shook her head. 'Only the girls and even then I don't see enough of them. You know how it is, working in London. Everyone's chasing their dream and working overtime.'

'I disagree,' he told her. 'When I was working, I still went out and had fun each weekend.'

'Yes but you must also understand about the pressures of deadlines,' she said.

'I had all of those things too,' he replied. 'But work is just work.'

She leaned back against the wall and blew out a sigh. 'I think that's what your sister's been trying to tell me for a while. And Beth and Ella too.'

'Well, we can't all be wrong, can we?' He gave her a small smile. 'Look, I understand about your career but is it really more important than being honest to your friends? To my sister?'

She shook her head. 'No.' She felt guilty. And upset. She'd lied to Hannah. When had she started doing that? 'I love my friends, of course.' Lily hesitated, looking down at the floorboards beneath her Converse trainers instead of him. 'Hannah doesn't know that I lost my job, by the way. None of them do. I was too embarrassed to tell them that I was a failure.'

Finally she looked up at him.

'I'd already guessed that she didn't know,' he replied before giving her a warm smile. 'Hannah's always been terrible at keeping secrets.'

Suddenly Lily saw herself through his eyes and was embarrassed. 'What's wrong with me?' she asked, rolling her eyes at herself. 'Why can't I trust people? I mean, Hannah's one of my best friends and I still can't be honest with her. I've let her down. I've let you all down. I'm so sorry.'

She heard the shaky note in her voice and stopped speaking, worried she might actually start to cry in front of Ben. The truth was, she realised in that moment, that despite moving around and not letting anyone close, she had actually always daydreamed of a permanent home and to have that daily connection with others. The closeness of the Jackson family had highlighted just how lonely she had become by cutting herself off from her friends.

'Being ambitious isn't a crime,' he told her, giving her a crooked smile. 'But you've isolated yourself away from your friends and that's never a good idea. Especially when it sounds like you need them more than ever. I mean, Alex and Jake are a pain in the neck but I couldn't do without their support. Nor my family.'

'Lucky you to be so happy in both your work and home life,' she blurted out. 'I haven't been happy in either for a long time.'

Expecting him to agree with her, she was shocked when he looked at her with haunted eyes. 'What? What's the matter?' she asked.

'You're not the only one that's been lying,' he told her.

She was shocked by what he had just said. 'You?' she asked. 'You've been lying as well? To the family?'

He sighed and nodded. 'Me too,' he said softly.

She waited for him to speak on.

Finally, he did. 'When my father died, I came back here to help my mother. I thought I'd give the family some support and then head back to my own life, my own career. But then I looked at the finances and discovered things had gotten bad. Really bad. And so I never left.' He looked up at her with a bleak expression. 'Dad had secretly remortgaged the place and then there was the fact that the whole hotel was in danger of slipping into the lake unless it was underpinned. It went pretty much downhill from there, almost literally in fact.'

'But surely once the renovations are complete...?' she began to ask, but her voice drifted off as she saw him shake his head once more. Lily was shocked and dismayed. She had had no idea that things were truly that bad.

'I honestly don't think it'll be enough to save Maple Tree Lodge,' he told her.

18

Ben was a little surprised to find himself blurting out the truth about the future of the hotel. Especially to Lily, of all people, after all of her secrecy and lies.

And yet he had found himself touched when she had confessed about her lonely childhood to him. It had touched a nerve, certainly in stark contrast to the large family environment that he had grown up in. Whenever there had been a problem, his family had always gathered around.

Until now, of course. Since coming back after his father's death, it had felt different. He was so unhappy fighting Walter when they should be uniting under the shared goal of trying to save the hotel. He had been closed off instead, not telling them the truth.

Just like Lily, he found himself thinking. Everything that he had accused her of, he realised he was equally guilty of acting that way.

'The hotel's in that much trouble?' she asked, breaking into his thoughts.

He nodded, the reality hitting home.

'I can't believe it,' she said, getting up and walking across to look out of the open window at the lake beyond. 'I mean, I knew that with the renovations bookings were down but I thought it would be OK when it was all finished.'

'We didn't have any guests to begin with,' he told her. 'Well, not enough, anyhow.'

She spun around. 'But your grandad always spoke about how busy the place had been.'

'Maybe in the early days but that was an awful long time ago,' he replied. 'Before I can remember.'

'I see.' She puffed out a sigh. 'Do they know? The family? How bad it is?'

He shook his head. 'You're not the only one who's been keeping secrets from them.'

She frowned. 'But why not tell them the truth?' she asked.

'I needed to see if I could save the place first,' he told her. 'Before the worst-case scenario plays out. You see, we've received a very large offer from a firm that wants to buy us out. They want to turn us into yet another chain hotel.'

He was mollified to see her grimace. 'You can't!' she stammered. 'Maple Tree Lodge is unique, special, a one-off.'

He nodded. 'I agree, which is why I'm trying to think of every reason not to sell.'

'So that's why Hannah says you've been so stressed,' said Lily, running a hand through her long red hair. 'It's not just the grief.'

'I had to close myself off from all the family stuff,' he said. 'I've been trying to think logically, trying to treat it like a business.'

'Yes, but it's also a home,' she told him. 'Your home. Your family's home.'

'Which makes it a thousand times worse,' he replied, with a heavy sigh. 'Especially after losing Dad. But what do I know about the hotel business? All I know is architecture and even then...'

His voice trailed off.

'Even then?' she prompted after a short silence.

He figured, what the hell, and decided that it was a time for confessions. The fact that it was to Lily of all people amazed him.

'My dream never worked out either,' he told her, with a wry smile. 'I ended up designing these dull box-like structures for shopping malls and offices. Never what I wanted to design. Never anything from the heart.'

She looked at him for a long moment before asking, 'What was it you liked about architecture in the first place?'

He picked up a nearby block of wood and held it in his hands. 'I guess I've always liked building and designing things that can last, ever since those early days messing around with Dad and Grandad in the workshop. I thought that I would be creating buildings that would be around for generations to come.'

'You mean, like Maple Tree Lodge?'

He felt startled. 'Yeah, I guess,' he said, frowning in thought. He had never thought of it like that.

'So you've got more in common with your grandad than you thought you had,' she said softly.

He smiled ruefully. 'Not sure he'd see it that way.'

'Don't sell yourself short,' she told him. 'He's proud of what you achieved by qualifying as an architect. I know he is because he's told me so.'

'Much use that will be if the place goes bankrupt,' he muttered.

But even so, a small part of him felt touched that his grandad might just be proud of him.

'I should have come home sooner,' he said out loud. 'Dad was a great father but not a good businessman.'

'You're here now,' she told him. 'That's all that matters. And you could still have your dream if the hotel makes it.'

He looked up at her. 'How?'

'Look at all the land you've got around here,' she said, pointing out of the window. 'Why can't you design and build something amazing right here on the lakeside?'

'I did have this one idea,' he began to say.

'What was it?' she asked, leaning forward and looking interested.

'Lodges. Private accommodation,' he told her. 'Oak-framed cottages dotted about on the edge of the lake.'

'That sounds wonderful.' She paused before carrying on. 'And not very minimalistic.'

He looked at her and saw a smile in her eyes.

'I got sidetracked,' he confessed. 'I thought we should turn into this bland place, just like the competition. I thought if we completely changed it from top to bottom then it would survive. That my family could keep their home.' He gulped before carrying on. 'I also wondered whether I should stick to what I already know, in other words modern buildings. I think I was trying to prove to myself that I wasn't my dad. That if I was completely different then the place might make it.'

He knew deep down that was true. He didn't actually like the minimal look. It wasn't him. He had just been proving a point.

He looked at Lily.

'I'll let you into a secret,' she said, in a soft tone. 'The first rule of design is that there are no mistakes. Sometimes it's a lucky accident and the thing that really shouldn't work is the thing that's actually really cool. Look, you could have something special here,' she told him. 'Stop pretending to be what you're not and embrace what you are, what you've always been. This place has a charm. Use it. Don't decorate for your guests. Decorate for your family and for you.'

'You were right,' he told her. 'You are right. Your design in that bedroom was great, by the way. I admit I was totally wrong.'

She smiled. 'If we decorate the whole place like that, people will want to check in, cosy up, unplug and enjoy the seasons. Snuggle up in front of the fire or look at the amazing view. They want peaceful afternoons with a book on a comfy chair in front of the fire. They want bracing walks around the lake before coming back to warm up. Hot chocolate. Fairy lights. A big piece of cake. Back to basics but make them luxurious.'

He tried to imagine how that would look. 'And you think redecorating can do all that?' he wondered aloud.

'Of course,' Lily told him, sounding certain. 'Choose décor that exudes cosy charm. Guests want to get away from all the dreadful daily news, busy lives and relax. Your ideas for the bland and corporate weren't relaxing. It just felt as if I should be on a Zoom call at some awful online meeting.'

He smiled ruefully to himself.

'This place needs to reflect you and your family,' she carried on. 'It's not just a hotel, it's your home. Along with the lake and the woods too. It doesn't need to be expensive either. We can add a lot of texture with all the stuff your grandmother's bought over the years. There's loads of stuff in there. There's even a few things in here too.'

He looked around and saw that she was pointing at some old crates and lamps.

'Your ideas were better than mine,' he finally said.

'I know,' she said with a soft smile. 'I might be rubbish at relationships but I'm a very good interior designer.'

But he found he couldn't smile back. 'I really don't want to have to sell up,' he confessed. 'This is our home. I think it would break Grandad's heart to leave here. Mine too, if I'm honest.'

'I understand.'

He looked into her green eyes and found that he believed her. But the reality was still burrowing its way through to his heart.

'Yes, but will it be enough?' he wondered out loud.

She reached out to take his hand in hers. 'I think so but we'll make sure of it.'

He stared down, feeling the warmth of her hand on his. 'We?' he repeated, staring at her.

She nodded. 'If you want me to stay.'

He looked down at their hands and she let go, as if a little embarrassed.

'I'd very much like you to stay and help us. Please.' He gulped. 'And help me too.'

She smiled at him. 'Thank you. I can't think of a more beautiful place to spend the winter.'

'What, stuck here in this boathouse?' he said, rolling his eyes.

She laughed. 'Well, I was thinking about the view of the lake, to be honest.'

He found that he liked it when she laughed and smiled. It lit up her pretty green eyes and he had to tear his thoughts back to the present problem.

'So I guess it's time for us both to be honest with everyone,' he told her.

'I guess so,' she replied, nodding.

The fact that he wasn't going through it alone any more took some of the pressure from him, he found. And the fact that it was Lily pleased him even more.

It was going to be tough, that much he knew. But even so,

confessing his ideas about the lodges made him feel as if his creative well was filling up again. He felt inspired. The hotel might just come together with her design ideas and a touch of his modernisation. There was hope at last.

Lily was right. The hotel was special. It always had been. And, if they worked together, it might just be enough to save it.

19

In a way, Lily was pleased that she had been stuck in the boathouse with Ben for the past hour as it had forced them to finally be honest with each other and perhaps move forward at last.

The fear of getting sacked was now in the past. They were going to work together to decorate the whole of the hotel and she was excited for the future.

Perhaps she would have to start opening up to Hannah and her best friends as well so as to avoid any further misunderstandings. Maybe it was time to put her trust in the Jackson family as they had done with her.

She looked at Ben as he tried to prise open the front door once more. In a funny way, she trusted him too. They had been entirely honest with each other and rather than being at odds, it felt as if they were becoming friends.

'So we've got a lot to do to get the hotel up and running,' said Lily, mulling over her now huge to-do list. There were all the bedrooms, the entrance hall, the lounge, dining room and perhaps even the snug as well.

'I'd still really like to get it open for the beginning of December,' Ben told her, turning around. 'That way perhaps we can capitalise on the Christmas holidays.'

Lily nodded, thinking how pretty the hotel would look decorated for the festive period. 'That's going to take a lot of work,' she told him.

'Yeah,' he replied. 'I'm going to have to call in a few favours.'

'But first we have to get out of this place,' she reminded him.

He glanced back at the door. 'That way out isn't an option so I guess the only way is down.'

He pointed at the opening in the far corner of the floor.

Lily followed him across the floor and peered through the square hole. Down through the gap she could see a boat bobbing up and down on the water.

'Is the ladder safe to use?' she asked, glancing around the rest of the boathouse which, whilst looking sturdy, was also in serious need of renovation.

'I guess there's only one way to find out,' he told her. 'Unless you'd rather spend the night here with me until someone misses us both.'

He shot her a cheeky grin and for a second, she found herself blushing. Was he actually flirting with her? Surely not, she decided and concentrated instead on watching him slowly descend the ladder. His foot slipped a couple of times on the rungs, causing her to take a sharp intake of breath, but he finally made it safely to the dock.

Once he reached the bottom, he stood next to the ladder and looked up at her.

'Your turn,' he called out. 'But be careful. There's a couple of rotten rungs. I'll watch you come down. Don't worry.'

Lily grimaced before swinging her leg around and tentatively taking her first step onto the ladder. With Ben's encouragement, she slowly went down step by step. A couple of times, he warned her to avoid the next step down as it was rotten but finally, and with immense relief, she was grateful to feel the wooden dock below her feet.

She turned around and for a second she was close to Ben as he hadn't stepped away yet. They locked eyes for a second before both moving away towards the boat at the same time.

It was a wooden rowing boat, obviously not used for a long time given the heavy staining and where the rain had accumulated inside in a few puddles.

They looked at each other.

'You're the expert,' she told him. 'What do you think?'

He laughed. 'I am in absolutely no way an expert with boats. But Dad and Grandad have definitely used this in the past to go fishing out in the centre of the lake. It appears to be all right.'

She bit her lip and looked around. The shore was a good twenty metres away. 'I suppose we'll have to take a chance. Otherwise we're going to have to swim for it.'

He nodded. 'I agree. At least this way, we'll stay dry and warm, apart from our feet.'

He carefully stepped inside the boat, grimacing as the water sloshed over his trainers. But once he had sat down and steadied it, he called for her to join him.

Tentatively, Lily stepped inside, taking his hand to steady herself before sitting down on the wooden seat next to him.

'Well, so far so good,' she said, watching him untether the rope and feeling the boat bob about a little bit more as it was unmoored. She clutched onto the seat as it wobbled.

He drew out the oars and moved them around in their rings.

'They don't seem too bad,' he told her, holding one out for her to take.

'What am I supposed to do with this?' she asked him.

'Row in time with me,' he replied with a grin.

'You make it sound so easy,' she told him, taking the oar and giving it a waggle. 'For the record, I've never rowed in my life.'

'Well, now seems like a good time to give it a go,' he said. 'Okay. Here we go.'

It took a little time for them to find their rhythm. At first Lily wasn't rowing in time with Ben, causing the boat to aim for the middle of the lake and not the shore.

But eventually they found their co-ordination and they ended up heading in a straight line.

However, Lily's earlier failure to steer had caused them to be quite far off from the shore.

'You know, it's probably about the same distance to the beach at this point,' said Ben, nodding at the sandy beach just to the side of the hotel.

'That still seems like a long way away,' Lily told him, with a grimace.

'It's a beautiful autumn afternoon,' he said. 'What else could we be doing?'

He seemed in a particularly cheerful mood, thought Lily. And she couldn't help but agree with him. The sun was shining on them and despite the exertion of the rowing, it was nice to be out in the fresh air.

She was just about to tell him that she agreed when she noticed that the water sloshing around the bottom of the boat was deeper than it had been initially.

'Is it me or is there more water inside the boat than there was earlier on?' she asked.

Ben looked down and gave a start. He looked back at her with wide eyes, full of alarm. 'You're right,' he said. 'We'd better get going a little quicker.'

She nodded in agreement and they picked up the pace of

their rowing. But the quicker pace seemed to cause even more water to flood into the bottom of the boat. And more water meant that the boat became heavier and less easy to move.

Soon, the water was over their ankles and up to their calves. It was becoming increasingly apparent that pretty soon it would be up and over the sides.

'Are we going to sink?' asked Lily, glancing at the beach which was still some distance away.

'I don't know,' said Ben.

But he wasn't meeting her eyes any more and she knew the truth.

Pretty soon, the boat began to sink under the weight of the water.

'We're going down,' he told her. 'Brace yourself.'

Lily just had time to take a deep breath before the boat capsized, pulling them both into the lake.

She gasped at the cold temperature of the water as it enveloped her. The only good news was that she could feel the bottom of the lake under her trainers, meaning that they were close to shore. Therefore, they were both able to stand up and keep their heads above the freezing cold water.

In unison, they both began to wade towards the beach, desperate to get out of the chilly water. Finally, they were on the sand. But a breeze across the lake made them feel even colder.

They shared a grimace and slopped their way in sodden clothes and trainers towards the hotel. Lily shivered in the cool air, aware of her clothes clinging to her and making her feel even colder.

Finally and somewhat gratefully, Ben held open the front door of the hotel and let her go inside first.

They squelched their way across the entrance hall but stopped as Frankie came out of the office.

She took a long look at them both, up and down before looking up into their faces in astonishment. 'Is it raining outside?' she asked.

Lily looked at Ben and they both burst into laughter at the same time.

20

After one long and very welcome hot shower, Lily joined Ben in the kitchen to regale the family with the story of their disastrous escape from the boathouse over dinner.

'And then the boat sank!' said Ben, finishing the story to huge roars of laughter.

'I should have taken a photo when Ben and Lily came into the reception,' said Frankie, laughing in memory. 'They looked like they had actually fallen into the lake.'

'That's because we had,' added Ben with another laugh.

'Have I taught you nothing about being on the water?' asked Walter, shaking his head but smiling.

'You've taught me that I shouldn't get into another boat without checking that it's actually able to float first,' replied Ben.

'Then you've learnt your lesson,' said Walter, with a nod.

After a delicious meal, Lily was enjoying the warmth both from the roaring fire and the congenial atmosphere around the table. For once, the awkward atmosphere between Ben and Walter was nowhere to be found.

She was also feeling warm on the inside as well, mostly from the extremely strong cocktail that Frankie had made them all.

'Wow,' muttered Hannah with a slight cough upon taking a sip of her drink. 'That's pretty strong.'

'Alcohol is the glue holding this place together,' said Frankie, with a wink.

'Not love?' asked Faye, with a soft smile.

'Oh, that's sweet,' said Frankie, giving her friend a nudge with her elbow. 'But no. You're wrong. It's definitely alcohol.'

Everyone laughed once more.

'Just what did you put in this?' asked Ben, staring at the cocktail glass he had just sipped from with wide eyes.

'Everything, from what I've just tasted,' replied Walter with a grimace, putting down his half-full glass carefully on the table as if it was about to detonate.

'Is this something you've made before?' asked Lily, taking another, much smaller tentative sip.

'It's an old recipe. I used to be a barmaid,' Frankie told her. 'Let me tell you, you never lose that magic touch.'

'Is that what we're calling it?' asked Ben, locking eyes with Lily briefly to share a smile.

He seemed like a different person, thought Lily. Was it the soaking in the lake that they had had? The earlier talk to clear the air? Or perhaps just the strong alcohol, she told herself.

Either way, she was enjoying the new, relaxed Ben who was sitting across the table from her that evening.

'What I don't understand is what you were both doing in the boathouse in the first place?' asked Frankie, looking from Ben to Lily.

'Lily was looking for artistic inspiration when I left her in there,' said Faye.

Lily glanced at Ben before taking a deep breath. 'Then when

Ben found me, I decided it was time to tell him the truth about my job.'

Hannah frowned. 'What are you talking about?' she asked, looking confused. 'What truth?'

'I lost my job,' announced Lily, with a small gulp. 'Two weeks ago. Just before you rang me, Hannah.'

She was about to carry on when Ben interrupted her. 'Redundancies,' he said.

The fierce look in his eyes made her not want to disagree with his small lie.

'I'm sorry to hear that,' said Faye. 'That must have been a real shock for you.'

Lily looked at Hannah. 'I'm sorry. I wanted to tell you but I was embarrassed. You were so keen for me to come here and I didn't want to let you down.'

Hannah shook her head. 'You should have told me,' she said in a quiet tone.

'She is telling you,' said Ben. 'Right now, in fact.'

Lily was grateful for his support but still felt bad about the hurt look in Hannah's eyes. Once more, she felt bad that she hadn't owned up before that moment and been truthful with her friend.

'The most important thing is that Lily is going to help us redecorate the whole hotel from top to bottom,' said Ben. 'In her own style.'

They shared a secret smile. She was grateful that he wasn't going to reveal her clandestine plan that had been at odds with his own ideas. They were finally on the same page, it felt.

'And then what?' asked Faye, looking at Lily.

'Well, after this job, I've big plans to set up my own business,' replied Lily. 'I've always wanted my own interior design company so hopefully that dream will finally become a reality.'

'Well, if we get this right you'll have the best recommendation from us,' said Walter.

'Where will you go?' asked Hannah, looking concerned.

'I've no idea,' Lily replied truthfully, with a sigh.

'You should stay on with us in the meantime,' said Dotty, smiling warmly. 'This place is beautiful in the summer.'

Lily shot Ben a quick glance. 'That's very kind,' she began.

'Perhaps Lily has other places she would like to go, Grandma,' said Ben.

Dotty frowned. 'But she just said that she had no plans,' replied his grandmother.

'Of course Lily is welcome to stay with us to help finish the hotel,' said Ben. 'And after that, it's up to her.'

Walter nodded thoughtfully. 'Well, we'll be glad to have you stay on, however long that's for.'

'And I've decided that the first thing I'm going to do tomorrow is hang a brand-new door on the boathouse,' said Ben, obviously trying to change the subject for which Lily was grateful. 'Preferably one that opens from both sides.'

'What for?' asked Frankie, looking confused, despite the laughter around the table. 'Who's going to be using it?'

'I don't know,' said Ben, his laugh fading. 'I thought perhaps that in the future we could use the boathouse for something. That's why I've made sure that the electrics and plumbing updates reached that far.'

'I've always loved that building,' said Dotty in a dreamy voice. 'The view is one of my favourites.'

'Mine too,' said Walter.

'So we'll see it renovated as well very soon?' asked Dotty in a hopeful tone.

'I think we'd better do the hotel first, Grandma,' Ben told her, looking a little pale. 'Before the money runs out.'

'Oh, we'll be fine with Lily in charge of the interiors,' said Dotty, looking not at all concerned. 'I guarantee that the place will be packed with guests as soon as she's finished making it look pretty.'

'I hope so,' said Lily, giving Dotty a warm smile.

She took heart from the fact that the family weren't concerned that she no longer worked for the interior design firm. In fact, they seemed more interested and excited by the fact that she was staying on for as long as the updates took.

She was excited too, she realised. It wasn't just about the job, whatever prospects it would bring her. She wasn't quite ready to leave this warm and loving family yet.

She looked at Ben once more. He really was quite handsome, she decided as she watched him chat to his mum and Frankie. But it must have been just the strong drink talking, she thought.

After dinner, when the family took their drinks into the lounge, Lily stayed behind in the kitchen with Hannah to clear the table and load the dishwasher.

Lily sensed that Hannah was still upset about her lie and wanted to clear the air. But it was Hannah who spoke first.

'I can't believe you didn't tell me about losing your job. Don't you trust me?' asked Hannah, once they were alone.

'Of course I do,' Lily told her. 'And it was wrong of me not to tell you as soon as I found out.'

'I should have known,' muttered Hannah. 'You've always been a little secretive with all of us.'

'Not deliberately,' said Lily quickly, anxious that she might have damaged their friendship forever.

She thought back to her conversation with Ben and decided that the time had come to be a little more honest with her best friend.

'The trouble is,' she carried on tentatively before hesitating.

Hannah watched her and said nothing, waiting for her to speak.

So Lily had to carry on. 'The trouble is,' she began once more, deciding to be brave, 'I'm rubbish at friends. I never really told you how lonely my childhood was growing up. Until I moved into that house and met the three of you, I had no friends at all. Not through school. Nobody.'

Hannah gasped. 'Truly?' she asked. 'You never said!'

Lily nodded. 'We moved around so much that we were never anywhere long enough for me to make friends. And since then I've been so busy concentrating on my career, trying to prove my parents wrong actually. I wanted to show them that I had chosen the right job. And it became all-encompassing, the need to be right.' Her throat became thick as she tried to hold back the tears. 'And that was wrong of me. Because you and Beth and Ella are more important than my job. Than anything. I love having you all as my friends. Truly, I do.'

Lily was about to carry on, when she found herself smothered by one of Hannah's warm hugs. She let herself lean against her friend briefly before taking a step backwards.

'We've always known that you're ambitious,' said Hannah. 'That's not a crime.'

'Yes, but I let it get bigger than everything else in my life,' said Lily, a tear escaping to roll down her cheek. 'I started concentrating on my deadlines and cancelling seeing you all. I even missed your birthday party!'

'It doesn't matter now,' said Hannah, reaching out to squeeze her hand. 'We can start again.'

Lily nodded. Perhaps it was time to start over. 'I want to stay, if that's OK with you. To help wherever I can.'

Hannah smiled. 'Of course it's OK. It's the best news I've heard for a long time. I want you here. And so do my family. They need you,' she carried on. 'We all do. If the hotel is going to be a success.'

'It will be,' said Lily, with a firm nod.

Because it turned out that she needed this job. This hotel. This family. Perhaps even more than they needed her.

21

Sitting down by the fireplace in the lounge, Ben could feel Frankie's strong cocktail seeping through his veins, relaxing him until the stress of the past few weeks and months finally went away.

At least temporarily, he thought, glancing at his grandad who was sitting opposite him. There was still no guarantee that Walter would agree to Lily's ideas for the whole hotel. Stress was replaced with nerves as to how he would react.

But the alcohol also gave him the strength to bring up the subject, especially when Lily came to sit down on the sofa next to Walter. Safety in numbers, he told himself.

'So Lily had some different ideas as to decorating the rest of the hotel,' began Ben. 'Not just the bedrooms.'

'I see.' Walter's grey eyebrows joined together in a frown.

Ben was a little pleased to see Lily take a nervous sip of her own cocktail before turning to face his grandad. 'You see, Walter,' she began. 'I've been thinking that it's all about adding textures. The wood is beautiful and natural, of course. But on the floor, it feels a bit cold and noisy, to be honest. I know rugs would work downstairs here, for instance in front of the fireplace, but upstairs in the bedrooms, we need carpets. You want it to feel soft and relaxing. Especially under bare feet.'

'Carpets?' repeated Walter, looking surprised.

'It's a bedroom,' she reminded him. 'And it would be a good noise excluder as well. On top of that, each room needs some texture and colour to make it more warm and inviting. Working with what we've got, for example. I mean, think of that amazing view of the lake. Plus the forest all around us. It's just enhancing what Mother Nature has already given us.'

There was a long silence before Walter finally gave a nod of his head. 'Sounds good. You know, those people you used to work for must be idiots to let you go.'

'Thanks,' said Lily.

Ben was flabbergasted. 'I've been trying to get you to agree to carpets for months!' he spluttered.

'Yes, but she said it better,' said Walter, giving Lily a nudge with his elbow. 'Besides, she understands about this place, don't you?'

'Well, I understand it a bit more having been actually in the lake this afternoon,' she replied, laughing.

'You wait until next summer,' Walter told her. 'When there's a heatwave and that water is cool, clear and delicious. There's nothing like it.'

'It can't have been any colder than today,' said Lily, still smiling.

'Come and join us, Lily,' called over Dotty, who was sitting at the table where a large jigsaw was spread out. 'We need all the help we can get over here.'

Ben watched her as she walked away, those long legs encased

in slim jeans, her red hair swinging around her shoulders. She really was one of the most attractive women he had ever met. He dragged his attention back to his grandad now it was just the two of them.

'So how bad is it?' asked Walter softly.

Ben gave a start, was his grandad implying that he had a crush on Lily?

'The books,' said Walter, a smile twitching on his mouth. 'How bad are our finances?'

It was the question that Ben had dreaded his grandad asking and yet, in a small way, it was a relief to finally meet Walter's eyes with the truth.

'That bad?' said Walter.

Ben glanced around but the rest of the family were all deep in conversation over the other side of the large room. So he felt safe enough to draw out the letter from the hotel chain from his pocket. He'd been carrying it around like an unexploded bomb for weeks now.

'I've been holding on to this for months,' he said, holding the letter out for his grandad to take. 'But I shouldn't have kept it from you. It was wrong of me.'

Walter took the envelope and opened it up. Ben waited for him to read it, wondering how his grandad would react.

But apart from noticing his grandad's trembling hand as he handed the letter back to Ben, Walter was calm.

'Well, thank you for finally telling me the truth,' said Walter.

'I'm sorry it isn't what you wanted to hear,' Ben told him.

'And you want to sell to them?'

Ben was aghast and looked at his grandad, feeling horrified. 'Of course not!' he said quickly. 'I haven't replied and hopefully will never need to. Maple Tree Lodge is not for sale.'

Walter sagged with relief. 'That's a lot of money to turn down,' he muttered.

'I know.' Ben grimaced. 'We can get by without it, I reckon. But we do need to make some changes around here because then I honestly think we might have a fighting chance now, whatever happens,' carried on Ben. 'With the renovations and Lily's ideas for decorating, it gives the hotel the best hope that I think we've had in ages.'

Walter nodded and then cleared his throat. 'I agree,' he said. 'I want to thank you, however this works out.'

Ben stared at his grandad in shock but couldn't find any words.

'But when all these updates are done then you must move on. It's time for you to live your life, not mine. Or your father's,' added Walter.

'You don't want me here?' Ben found himself asking. Was the distance between them so great now? he wondered.

'What I want is for you to carry on living just like you did before,' said Walter.

In the short silence that followed, only the creaking and cracking of the logs on the open fire filled the air.

'What if I don't want to leave?' asked Ben eventually.

'Why would you want to stay here?' said Walter, with a grunt of humour. 'All those fancy places you designed. You must be climbing the walls being stuck here. You've got a real gift,' he carried on. 'All that training, all those hours of studying you put in. I was so proud of you. We all were.'

Walter went to carry on but Ben held up his hand. 'I need to tell you something,' he began. 'That architects' firm in London? All those fancy places I designed? They didn't fill my soul, not like here. Not like home.' Ben sighed. 'The reality wasn't what I expected.'

Walter gave a sad smile. 'Life never is, son,' he replied.

'But Lily said something to me this afternoon,' said Ben, remembering her words. 'About how I could help redesign this place. Not the hotel,' he said quickly, at his grandad's alarmed expression. 'But perhaps we could put in planning permission for some lodges.'

'Lodges?' Walter's grey eyebrows shot up in surprise.

'Private places for people to stay in,' carried on Ben. 'Wood framed. Reflecting the look of the rest of the place. There's a real demand for this kind of thing from what I've heard.'

To his amazement, his grandad broke into a smile. 'You know, your father had the same idea, I seem to remember.'

'He did?' Ben was touched.

But his grandad's smile faded. 'You're never supposed to outlive your own children. That's not the way things should be. The guilt has weighed heavily on me that I couldn't see how ill the pressure of the business was making him. And I'm sorry I've taken out my frustrations on you. But I don't want you to become as stressed as your father was. I don't want this place to swallow you up either. And I don't want to lose you. I love you too much.'

Ben's throat grew thick with emotion. 'I love you too, Grandad,' he replied.

'What I'm saying is that I want you to follow your own path, not mine or your dad's,' carried on Walter. 'If that takes you away from us then so be it. We'll miss you, of course. But if you're happy, truly happy, then I can make my peace with that.' Walter's voice began to falter and Ben could hear the true emotion coming through. 'Because that's all I ever wanted for you. To be happy.'

'The trouble is that I wasn't,' Ben confessed. 'And, despite us not getting along so well recently, I've really enjoyed being home. I'm not saying that the hotel isn't worrying me but if we can work together, I think we can save it for all those future generations you were talking about.'

'What about your own dreams?' asked Walter. 'They're equally important.'

'What if saving Maple Tree Lodge is my dream too?' said Ben, suddenly filled with emotion.

The silence stretched out as they locked eyes, his grandad's tear-filled ones staring back at him.

'You need to be sure,' said Walter.

'This place is in my bones, my soul,' Ben told him. 'Perhaps I had to leave to discover that what I really wanted was to be at home.'

Walter's shoulders relaxed, as if the stress and worry that he had been hanging on to for so many months, even years, finally left him.

'I was talking with Lily about why I became an architect in the first place,' said Ben. 'About building great places that are here for generations to come. Like our hotel.'

Walter nodded. 'Longevity. Something we can both agree on.'

'I want to keep it for the future,' Ben told him in a fierce tone. 'Protect it. For our family's future.'

'You'll save this place,' said his grandad, nodding his head. 'I can feel it. You're a hard worker, you're bright, you're more than capable. You can do anything you set your mind to.'

'Even save our home?' asked Ben, suddenly feeling nervous.

'Even that,' said Walter. 'You won't be alone either. If you can let an old man help you out once in a while.'

'We'll save it together, Grandad,' said Ben. 'I promise.'

'Me too, lad.' Walter gave his hand a squeeze. 'Me too.'

Ben looked down at the letter he was still clutching in his other hand and made a decision. He reached forward and threw it into the flames, leaving a brief crackle and then it curled up into ashes.

Walter nodded his approval as they both looked at the fire.

Finally free of the letter, Ben could feel the tension leaving him. Change was coming to Maple Tree Lodge at last. And he was so grateful for Lily for being the catalyst for it all, he thought, glancing at her once more.

22

Despite her conversation with Hannah the previous evening, the following morning Lily was still feeling a little sheepish about not telling the Jackson family that that she no longer had a job with Hans Haubermann.

But they had been so kind about her redundancy that she couldn't help but feel enveloped by their kindness.

'Losing your job is never easy,' said Hannah over breakfast at the dining table. 'I've been through quite a few jobs already as well.'

'Mainly because they took advantage of you and worked you all hours until you couldn't take any more,' Lily reminded her.

Hannah gave her a sheepish grin. 'Perhaps,' she said.

'But you've always had your family around you,' said Lily. 'And I can see why you needed them. They're very supportive of each other.'

Hannah frowned. 'And you didn't have that?'

'Sort of,' Lily told her, with a small shrug. 'To a point, in any case. But it was always about their careers and then mine too. So I tried to emulate them. But I'm not sure it's quite me.'

'Maybe now you're staying, you can unpack everything you brought with you,' said Hannah. 'I'm not sure you've opened at least one of those boxes since the last move.'

Lily looked at her friend. 'Is that your subtle way of suggesting that I move around too much?'

Hannah gave her a wink. 'I didn't plan on being that subtle, to be honest.'

Frankie had just come into the kitchen and came over to stand at the end of the table. 'What's all this about moving about?' she asked.

Lily's initial reaction was to baulk about opening up. But then she remembered her conversation with Ben in the boathouse. About the problems she had caused herself by not being honest. And she decided to take a small tentative step forward.

'When I was growing up we moved around so often that I kind of got used to not having anywhere to call home,' she said. 'That didn't stop when I moved to London. But I didn't really enjoy it.'

'I understand,' said Frankie, for once looking serious. In a quiet tone, she carried on, 'I know what that's like. It's disruptive, isn't it? Lonely too because you never get to know anyone.'

Lily was startled and found herself nodding in agreement. 'It was,' she said. 'Really lonely.'

She looked at Frankie once more.

Frankie saw the question in Lily's eyes and sighed. 'My ex-husband never could keep a job. Or his fidelity either, the big cheat. And that's the polite version as you're a guest here.'

'I'm sorry,' said Lily.

'I'm not,' said Frankie, giving herself a little shake. 'I'm far happier and better off without him. Let me tell you something, ladies. Marriage is like a deck of cards. In the beginning all you need is two hearts and a diamond. But by the end, you just wish you had a club and a spade. To bury him, that is.'

Lily joined in with Hannah's laughter but she was beginning to realise that Frankie used her humour as her protective armour.

'You should join a dating app,' Hannah told her.

Frankie made a face. 'You first, sweetheart.'

Hannah shook her head. 'No way. I'm happily single. What about you, Lily?'

Ben had just entered the room and for some unexpected reason she found herself blushing as he overheard the conversation.

'I've been single for so long it's a way of life,' muttered Lily.

Frankie rolled her eyes. 'Youth is wasted on the young, as they say. Get out there and live life. Change things up a bit, why don't you?'

'There's been enough change in my life these past couple of weeks,' said Lily, still avoiding looking at Ben. 'Talking of which, and with regard to me being more open with you all, I'm going to tell Beth and Ella as well about my job,' Lily told Hannah.

Hannah looked surprised but pleased. 'Let's do a group call,' she said. 'So we can all chat together.'

Lily nodded. 'OK. You set it up. I'm going to ring my parents first.' She checked the time and headed into the lounge to make the call to Australia.

She had decided that it was time to tell them the truth about her job. She had been dreading admitting that she had lost her job but to her surprise they were very supportive.

'So what next?' asked her dad.

'Well, after I finish helping Hannah's family here, I want to set up my own business.' Lily still wasn't sure it was exactly what she wanted but, as expected, they were thrilled with her ambition.

'Our career girl,' said her mum. 'We're proud of you.'

Lily's smile grew a little rigid as she realised that she was still trying to be something else, something bigger, but at least being honest about losing her job was a tiny step forward in the right direction, wasn't it?

The conversation with Beth and Ella was thankfully a little more balanced.

'Listen, we've all lost jobs at one time or another,' said Ella. 'It's rubbish but you'll get another one. Especially with your skills.'

'In the meantime, she's staying put at Maple Tree Lodge to give us a hand,' Hannah told them.

'Excellent,' said Beth. 'Listen, I've got some holiday owing so I can come and help. Many hands make light work and all that.'

'Great,' said Lily.

'Me too,' added Ella. 'I'll come whenever I can.'

'I love you guys,' said Hannah, beaming.

'Me too,' Lily told them. 'And I'm sorry I couldn't be honest with you all before now.'

'It doesn't matter,' said Beth. 'We're your besties, OK?'

'Exactly,' added Ella. 'We've got your back, and your front too.'

Lily felt the tears prick at her eyes as she realised just how grateful she was for her friends' support.

Keeping the theme of transparency, Lily had decided to reveal her secret project to the family.

So later that morning, she asked everyone to follow her upstairs and showed them all the bedroom that she had been secretly updating.

She was relieved to see the family's enthusiasm over the new colourful décor.

'I like it,' said Walter, nodding his approval. 'Especially keeping that wall of wood.'

'So do I,' said Ben, with a smile.

'I love the colour,' said Hannah, reaching out to stroke the warm green of the painted walls.

'But this isn't finished, is it?' asked Faye, looking around.

'Not by a long shot,' replied Lily with a grin.

She looked at Ben to help her out.

'I'm getting in touch with the carpet fitters today so that we can get all the bedrooms kitted out,' he said.

'What colour carpets?' asked Dotty.

'A warm beige,' Lily told her. 'To match the wood in each room. Talking of which...' She took a deep breath and looked at Ben. 'There was another feature I wanted to talk to you about. Four-poster beds.'

Ben's eyes widened as he glanced down at the divan bed, still covered up with its plastic wrapping. 'The trouble is that I've just paid for all twenty new king-size beds,' he began, looking stressed.

Lily put up her hand. 'That's not what I meant,' she told him. 'The beds are great but just a little bland. Not romantic enough. So I was thinking that perhaps you could add an oak frame around the new beds to make them into four-posters.'

Ben looked at his grandad with raised eyebrows. 'What do you think?' he asked.

'I think we're going to be busy, lad,' said Walter. But Lily was grateful to see him smiling his approval.

'You're not the only ones,' said Lily, looking at everyone else. 'There's an awful lot of plain walls that need colour put on them in the rest of the bedrooms.'

'OK,' said Faye. 'Well, it's not like I've got anything else to do.'

'I'm at work at five,' said Hannah. 'But am around until then.'

'And my artistic talents are crying out to be used,' added Dotty with a warm smile.

They all looked at Frankie, who had remained quiet until then.

She made a face. 'Well, I've just checked my bank account. Unfortunately I've worked out that I've got just enough money in my savings to retire early and live comfortably for about two minutes. So I suppose I'd better help you!'

As everyone laughed, Lily found that she was grateful for her secret designs being out at last.

She glanced at Ben and found him smiling back at her. Perhaps, she thought, the fresh start for the hotel might just be a new beginning for her as well.

23

The decorating of the guest bedrooms continued apace but Ben had to admit to himself after a few days that the hard work was immensely rewarding. Because at the end of each day, he could finally see progress and it felt as if things were looking up for the hotel at last.

Lily was busy painting, ably aided by Hannah, Faye, Frankie and Dotty. The ceilings were now all completed and room by room, the walls of the bedrooms were beginning to come to life with colour. The part-painted, part-exposed wood of the walls gave a warmth to each room and Ben liked that each bedroom had its own individual decorating scheme, colour wise.

Whilst the bedrooms began to be transformed, Ben and Walter cut down a number of oak logs to create the four-poster beds. They carefully measured the lengths before Walter used his electric saw to cut them to size. Then they worked together to construct them around the modern beds.

Ben was enjoying getting his hands dirty again, as it had been so long since he had been in the workshop with his grandad. It took a while to get the fixing right so that the oak framed the bed perfectly but as they both stepped back to look at the first one that they had completed, Ben had to concede that the effect was very stylish.

'It looks good,' he said, turning to look at his grandad.

Walter was looking equally pleased. 'Knowing your grandmother, she'll want one as well!'

It was tiring work though, as each night they continued into the evening until Faye called a halt to the proceedings with the call for dinner which nobody was allowed to refuse.

However, one evening Ben found himself alone with Lily as the only two people left working on one of the guest bedrooms. Hannah was at work and his mum and Frankie had arranged to see a friend in Aldwych for dinner. Walter and Dotty had already been sent home early to rest up for another busy day tomorrow.

Ben's stomach rumbled in protest but they worked on, content to hum along to the music that was playing from Dotty's old radio.

'I think this green is my favourite,' said Ben, taking a step back to look at the wall he had just finished putting a second coat on.

'Mine too,' replied Lily, standing at the top of a short stepladder where she had just finished painting the very top of the wall above the window.

She looked over at him and smiled. Ben found himself mesmerised by her pretty face, despite being dressed in a pair of paint-splattered dungarees with a scarf around her hair.

A love song played on the radio and he was temporarily distracted by the words professing the lure of a beautiful pair of smiling eyes. Her green eyes were certainly the deepest shade of emerald that he had ever seen.

She broke their gaze to glance over at the bed. 'You'll be able to add the four-poster in here tomorrow,' she said.

However, she was still looking at the bed as she stepped down the ladder and Ben suddenly realised what was going to happen.

'Wait!' he called out, stepping towards her.

But it was too late. Lily wasn't watching where she was going and the foot she was about to place onto the floor went into a large pot of paint instead. Ben watched as she began to fall over in slow motion as she went off-balance.

Rushing over to stop Lily from hurting herself, he tripped on the large roller tray still full of paint and they both landed in a crumpled mess, almost on top of each other. Both the pot of paint that Lily had stepped into and the large roller tray had both flipped over and they were both now coated in paint.

They lay on the floor in shock for a moment before both bursting into laughter at the same time.

'Are you OK?' he asked, feeling a little bruised from his fall but nothing more.

'I'm fine,' she said, looking down at the paint that they were now both splattered in. 'Oh, my goodness! What a mess!'

She burst into peals of laughter once more as she slowly sat up.

Ben joined in as he too straightened up. 'We've got more on us than on the walls,' he said, also laughing.

'Shall we call it a night?' asked Lily, glancing down at herself once more. 'I think this is the universe's way of saying that we might be getting a bit tired.'

'Absolutely,' he replied, standing up and reaching out to help pull her up as well. There was an awkward silence as they stood so near to each other. 'Are you sure your foot's OK?' he asked.

She looked down as she slowly rotated her left foot. 'A little sore but it'll be fine,' she said. 'Oh! What a waste of good paint. I'm so sorry.'

'It doesn't matter,' said Ben. And he found that it really didn't.

'Gosh, I'm starving,' she told him. 'Your mum said that there were various options for our dinner in the fridge and freezer. Shall we get cleaned up and see what there is to eat?'

But for once, his mum's cooking didn't tempt Ben. And he found he had a much better idea. 'Let's go out,' he told her.

Lily looked at him in surprise. 'Out? Like this?' She glanced down at her splattered clothes once more and laughed.

'Well, maybe we'll get changed first,' he told her. 'Come on. There's a great Italian place nearby. My treat to say thank you for all your hard work.'

'I'm not finished yet,' she reminded him.

'Thank goodness,' he said to her. 'Because as you know, I'm useless at interior design.'

She laughed. 'OK, well, if you're paying for dinner then it's a date,' she replied with a soft smile. There was a short silence as her smile dropped and she blushed. 'I mean, well, you know what I mean,' she stammered.

'I do,' he told her. 'I'll see you downstairs in half an hour.'

As she wrapped a piece of plastic around her foot to stop spreading the paint across the remainder of the bedroom floor and hobbled out of the room to clean up, Ben smiled to himself at her gaffe.

So, it wasn't a date, he reminded himself. Of course it wasn't. But still, the thought of having Lily all to himself made him rush through his shower and choose his clothes afterwards with more care than he had done for a long while.

24

Lily sat down at the small table for two in Platform 1, the Italian restaurant in Cranfield. It was only a quarter of an hour's drive away from Maple Tree Lodge.

Ben had told her that it had been the waiting room of the old railway station and now she looked closely, she could see the memorabilia and posters that adorned the place. But in the dark evening, it felt warm and, dare she say it, even romantic. Fairy lights were strung all across the ceiling and along with the glow of the nearby fireplace, each table had a flickering candle as well.

She felt a little shy at sitting there alone with Ben, despite every other table being full.

'It's a good thing they had a cancellation,' said Ben, picking up a menu that had been left on the table. 'It's very popular because the food is so delicious.'

Lily glanced at the plates of food that had just been served on the next table. 'It looks amazing,' she told him.

She glanced down at the knee-length skirt that she was wearing. It was only Ben and a casual meal out and yet she had found herself selecting her black V-neck jumper and suede boots with care. As well as rushing to wear a full face of make-up for once. Her hair had only needed brushing but was still fluffy from the shower.

She looked across the table at Ben. There was no trace of the paint splattered t-shirt and jeans that he had been wearing only a short time ago. Now he was wearing a smart blue shirt and dark trousers, only his damp hair a reminder that he too had needed a shower before heading out.

He looked up at her from the menu suddenly and she was mildly embarrassed to have been caught looking at him.

'What are you going to have?' he asked.

'I don't know,' she told him, immediately glancing down the options. 'It all looks delicious.'

'Don't get your hopes up,' said a man in a chef's apron coming to stand next to their table. 'You haven't tasted it yet!'

'Ryan! How are you?' asked Ben, standing up to shake the man's hand.

'Good to see you, mate,' replied Ryan. 'It's been too long.' He then looked down at Lily. 'Hi. Nice to meet you. I'm the owner and chef here.'

'I'm Lily,' she replied. 'I'm helping out at Maple Tree Lodge.'

'Yeah, I heard from Del that the place was being done up,' said Ryan, nodding in approval before looking at Ben with a concerned look. 'How are the family bearing up?'

Ben nodded. 'They're OK, thanks,' he replied. 'Early days and all that but battling on, as Grandad says.'

Ryan smiled. 'Well, Walter was always a tough one,' he said. 'Send them my love, would you?'

'Of course,' replied Ben.

'So what'll it be?' asked Ryan, nodding at the menu.

'I was thinking about the risotto,' Lily told him.

Ryan nodded his approval. 'Good choice.'

'I just fancied a pizza, to be honest,' said Ben, with a grin.

Ryan rolled his eyes. 'Heathen,' he said, snatching the menus from the table. 'But seeing as my pizza is as fantastic as my risotto, I don't blame you. Let's get you some drinks and nibbles to get you started.'

Almost immediately, they were served with a non-alcoholic beer for Ben as he was driving and a large glass of white wine for Lily. Along with their drinks, Ryan's fiancée Katy placed a large sharing plate of olives, bruschetta and dips between them to whet their appetites.

'What an amazing place,' said Lily, once she had taken a sip of wine. 'So how do you know the owner?'

'I went to infant school with Ryan and his brother,' Ben told her. He leaned back in his chair and looked around the restaurant. 'I must say they've done wonders with the old place. It was in almost a worse state than the hotel was, if you can believe it.'

'Maybe you should have used their interior designer instead,' said Lily, glancing around. It really did feel like such a warm and inviting place, entirely suited to its environment.

She turned her attention back to Ben and found him studying her.

'I think we've hired just the right interior designer actually,' he said.

She found herself blushing. 'Let's hope so.'

'Tell me what made you interested in interior design,' he asked. 'From what you've told me, it wasn't a natural career choice.'

She hesitated and took another sip of wine. Not normally used to talking about herself, she found herself telling him about the gift of the doll's house and how it sparked the creativity that she still had to that day.

'So this doll's house is important to you?' he said.

She nodded. 'That's why it's all wrapped up safely in my room.' She rolled her eyes. 'It's got a bit bashed over the years. One of the front doors doesn't close properly and the roof is all askew.'

'Well, perhaps I can take a look at it,' said Ben. 'Or Grandad if you trust him more to fix it.'

'Thank you. And, for the record, I trust you,' she told him, feeling the heat spread across her cheeks.

And it was true, she realised.

'You haven't seen my detailed carpentry work yet,' he told her, with a grin.

She laughed. 'I've seen the four-poster beds and they're just great,' she replied.

'Glad you approve,' he said. He looked around once more. 'Maybe the old railway station is proof that even the worst of places can be brought back to life.'

'I think it shows me that there's more people out and about in this area than I had thought possible as well,' said Lily, glancing around the busy restaurant. 'I mean, it's a Tuesday evening and yet the place is full.'

'Shame I can't lure Ryan over to the hotel to serve his delicious food there instead,' said Ben. 'And believe me, I've tried. We're going to need a chef. I think it's getting too much for Mum, to be honest.'

Lily nodded. 'I understand. Have you thought about using Hannah instead?'

Ben drew in a sharp breath. 'Of course, but she'll never agree to it. You know how lacking in confidence she is. The only people she likes to cook for her are her family.'

'Hmm.' Lily knew that he was right. 'Perhaps we can work on her together.'

'That would be great if we could,' he told her. 'I think it would really help her come out of her shell at long last.'

She was touched by how supportive he was of his younger sister.

'In the meantime, perhaps we could plan a pizza evening for the guests one night a week,' she suggested. 'It would give whoever the chef is a break for the night. All we would need is to get the orders in advance and have them sent over.'

'Now that's a great idea,' said Ben, as Katy delivered their main course to the table. 'Especially if it's as delicious as this.'

He held out a slice of pizza for Lily to take a bite out of. A little embarrassed, she took a taste and couldn't help but nod her approval. 'Wow,' she muttered with a full mouth. She could taste rosemary, the freshest tomatoes, succulent artichokes and sweet Parma ham. 'That's amazing.'

In return, she held out a full fork for him to taste her chicken risotto. As he took it in his mouth, Lily realised that to all intents and purposes to the other tables, they looked like a couple.

As they began to eat their food, he asked, 'So when was the last time you went out on a date?'

She almost choked on her risotto. 'I can't remember,' she mumbled, blushing in the candlelight. 'I'm normally too busy working to have any kind of life. I worked most evenings. It made me neglect my home life. My work-life balance. And my friends too, I've realised. I should have been around for them more, especially Hannah this last year.'

He nodded. 'Dad's death hit her pretty hard.' He paused. 'All of us, of course.'

'How have you coped with it?' she asked.

'I haven't really,' he confessed, with a frown. 'I was so busy trying to save the hotel for the family that there's been no time to breathe.' He paused and took a sip of his beer. 'It's his birthday coming up later this month. I'm dreading it, to be honest. But it would be a shame if we didn't remember him in some way.'

'You need to grieve too,' she told him.

She hesitated before she reached out to take his hand. He turned it over in his and looked down at it.

'I can only try and tell you what I've learnt this year and that's to trust your friends and family and ask for help if you need it,' she told him.

'I'm not much good at that,' he replied.

'Then perhaps it's time we both learned to do so. To learn that we're not alone,' she said.

They held hands for a moment longer before he finally let go to raise up his beer bottle. She picked up her wine glass and chinked it against the bottle.

'To not being alone,' he said.

After a delicious dessert and coffee, they thanked Ryan and Katy for the meal and headed home. They parked the car and walked back across the car park under the full moon. That night it was so bright they didn't need the external light to see where they were going.

'Beth would love a night like this,' said Lily, her breath showing in the cold air as she glanced at the huge sky above them, dotted with stars.

'They're my favourites too,' said Ben. 'I always missed this when I was in the city.' He frowned. 'I never considered that I was homesick before but I definitely was, now I come to realise.'

She felt wistful suddenly. A longing to belong. Something she had missed out on for so long. 'If this were my home, I'd miss it too,' she found herself saying.

She gave a start as Ben stroked her face softly with his fingers. 'As you're pouring your heart and soul into the place then you're allowed to call it home for the time being as well.'

They smiled at each other in the semi-darkness, where the only sound for a moment was an owl hooting. They smiled at the noise but it broke the moment and he dropped his hand.

As they headed inside, Faye and Frankie were in the hallway, having just come home themselves.

'Where have you two been?' asked Faye.

As Ben filled them in on their disastrous paint accident, Lily watched him, smiling.

It had been an unexpected but lovely evening and she had really enjoyed his company.

But he was just Hannah's brother, she reminded herself. The manager of the hotel. Her employer.

That was all, wasn't it?

25

When Friday lunchtime arrived, it turned out to be a momentous occasion.

Ben puffed out a sigh of relief. 'We've finished painting the bedrooms!' he said, looking around the kitchen table.

A cheer went up and the buzz of excited conversation swept over him. He sagged back in the kitchen chair. It had been a rush to get all the four-poster beds done as well but, along with the carpets being fitted that week, the bedrooms had been transformed.

'Just all the finishing touches to go,' added Lily.

'So the rooms aren't quite ready for our first visitors this afternoon?' asked Faye, with a smile. 'Not that I'm sure they'll mind too much.'

'Visitors?' asked Lily, looking a little alarmed. 'We've got our first guests already?'

Ben laughed and shook his head. 'Definitely not,' he told her. 'My best friends are coming down for the weekend. Maple Tree Lodge has still got another month until 1 December when we finally open.'

'Thank goodness for that,' she said, leaning back in her chair and looking relieved.

He was relieved too because they would need the whole month to finish all the communal areas, such as the entrance hall, lounge and dining room. Plus the website needed updating and then there was the big marketing campaign which they so desperately needed but couldn't afford. There was still a lot to do and he was grateful that his best friends were arriving later that day.

He listened in as Hannah explained to Lily who they were.

'Jake and Alex went to college with Ben,' said Hannah. 'And they've been best buddies ever since.'

'Are they architects as well?' asked Lily, looking across the table at Ben.

He laughed. 'Absolutely not,' he told her. 'Jake is a chef and Alex is an accountant.'

'Alex is also a triathlete,' added Hannah. 'That's how he spends nearly all of his spare time. He's won all sorts of competitions.'

'And next spring he's aiming really high,' said Ben. 'He texted me last weekend to say that he's been entered into the Commonwealth Games.'

'How exciting,' said Faye.

Ben nodded. Only he and Jake knew how much pressure their friend was under to achieve a gold medal. Alex's father was relentless in his training and Ben was grateful that Alex had managed to find time in his hectic schedule to stay for the weekend.

In fact, he was eager to see both of his best friends' reactions to the makeover and found himself pacing up and down outside until they finally arrived in Jake's car later that afternoon.

They greeted each other with a hearty hug.

Ever since they had met in the college bar in freshers' week, there had been an instant connection between the three men. Which, given how different their circumstances were, was remarkable in itself.

'You're looking wrecked, mate,' said Jake, ever the jokey charmer as he clapped Ben on the back.

As usual, Jake was full of laid-back style, from his soft but ever so expensive leather jacket to his dark hair gelled into place.

'Cheers,' said Ben, rolling his eyes. 'And there was me thinking I looked OK.'

'You look great,' Alex told him.

Where Jake was the joker, Alex was the quiet, thoughtful one of the group. He was a gentle giant, over six feet tall with defined muscles from years of training and competing.

They all walked towards the new front door, now framed with two large bay trees dotted with fairy lights. In the darkening light of a November evening, they looked very pretty.

As they headed inside, Hannah rushed out of the kitchen to greet them.

'Hello!' she said, heading towards them.

'Hannah! Sweetheart, you're looking even more gorgeous than ever,' said Jake, always the charmer, as he gave her a hug.

Jake had spent most of his summer holidays during college hiding from his parents' vicious divorce. Ever since then, whenever he had any free time from his busy work life as a chef, he would spend it at Maple Tree Lodge and had grown to love Hannah as his little sister. He flirted with her, just like he flirted with everyone, but it didn't mean anything to him or to her. Ben wasn't sure if Jake would ever fall in love with anyone at all, given the toxic nature of his parents' divorce.

Contrary to Jake's huge hug and flirtatious manner, Alex was more refined in his manner. Years of athletic toning and conditioning meant that he was rarely out of control or even showed emotion. But he was equally fond of Hannah, giving her an awkward hug in greeting as he said, 'Hey.'

'Hey yourself,' she told him, with a warm smile.

'Don't remember the old place looking quite this, well, stylish,' said Jake, blowing out a low whistle as he looked around. 'No offence. I mean, it was always my favourite place in the world but now, it's even better.'

'I agree,' said Alex, nodding his head enthusiastically. 'You've done an amazing job.'

'And this is just the start of it,' said Hannah. 'Wait until you see the bedrooms.'

'I only did the rough stuff,' said Ben, not wanting to do Lily a disservice. 'Electrics, plumbing, all the boring bits. It was Lily's designs that made it work. It wasn't all me.'

'Some of it was,' said Hannah, as ever being fair. 'But yeah, you two make a good team.'

Ben was surprised. 'You think so?' he asked.

'I know so, dummy,' she said, nudging him with her elbow.

'Then I can't wait to meet her,' said Jake, with a waggle of his eyebrows.

Ben and Alex locked eyes as Jake wandered over to peer into the lounge.

'I hope she's got her sunglasses on so she won't be dazzled by our resident playboy,' said Alex, with a grin.

Ben smiled but found it grew rictus hard on his face. He was desperately hoping so too. The last thing he wanted was for Lily to fall for Jake's handsome charms. But why was the question that he didn't want to answer at that precise moment.

'When are you due to reopen?' asked Jake, wandering back to them.

'First of December,' Ben told him. 'Although I had an idea

that we could have a preview evening to show the place off to the locals. Then we'll open up properly the following day.'

Jake made a face. 'You do realise that it's only a month away, right?'

'Why do you think I invited you both down here this weekend to give us a hand?' Ben told him, with a grin.

His friends rolled their eyes but he knew that they were happy to help.

'Come and see the family,' said Hannah, taking Jake's hand and leading him away. 'They're desperate to see you both.'

As his friends headed into the kitchen, Ben looked around the entrance hall once more. There was still so much to do. But he had to admit that it felt like a tiny break in the relentless pressure to have his friends home once more.

However, as he went into the kitchen he was somewhat unsettled to find Jake already doing his best to flirt with Lily. She was smiling back at him, her usual dazzling smile lighting up her pretty face.

Ben found his good mood had instantly evaporated. Surely she wouldn't be interested in such a flirt like Jake? And why would it matter if she was?

Could it mean that he was beginning to care for Lily? He didn't want to admit that to himself.

They had grown closer day by day and they had opened up to each other when they had gone out to the restaurant for dinner. He enjoyed her company. But just as friends, he told himself.

But even so, he couldn't stop himself hoping that she didn't succumb to Jake's obvious charms. So where did that leave their own friendship?

26

Lily found that she was enjoying meeting Ben's best friends. It was like another piece of the Ben puzzle fitting into the overall picture, she thought, watching him laugh along with his friends at the other end of the dinner table.

'Faye, that meal was incredible, as always,' said Jake, leaning over to give her a kiss on the cheek.

Lily had sensed straight away that Jake was a born flirt but it was offset by a self-deprecating humour. She didn't think Jake could take anything seriously – that was her main impression of him.

Faye blushed. 'Oh, Jake, it's nothing like up to your standards,' she said.

'On the contrary, it's much better than the rubbish that I serve up in that ghastly trendy place,' Jake told her.

Jake had told Lily that he was a restaurant chef but from the sounds of it, he had travelled around even more than she had.

'Where are you working now?' asked Faye.

'Some upmarket Asian fusion place in Soho,' said Jake, before making a face. 'But it's so boring so I'll be out of there as soon as I find somewhere else.'

'I don't know which lasts shorter, your girlfriends or your jobs,' said Ben with a grin.

'At least I have girlfriends,' said Jake, in a pointed tone.

Ben shuffled in his seat, looking embarrassed. 'Well, at least I might keep my job,' he said.

'Thanks to Lily here,' said Jake, with a wink in her direction. 'I've seen our new bedrooms. She's got all the talent, not you.'

'It's a joint effort,' said Lily quickly, not wanting Ben's feelings to be hurt.

'I hope he's paying you extra for all that loyalty,' said Jake, with a cheeky grin.

Alex rolled his eyes. 'You wouldn't know what it means to be loyal to work,' he told his friend. 'Or your girlfriends, come to think of it.'

Alex was the quiet one of the three, thought Lily. Steady and reliable.

Jake shrugged his shoulders. 'Everyone and everything outside of Maple Tree Lodge is boring,' he announced. 'Why do you think I'm always desperate to come here?'

'Well, you're always welcome,' said Dotty.

Jake blew her a kiss across the table which Dotty caught with one hand, before giving him a wink.

'The bedrooms look great,' said Alex, turning to look at Lily. 'I can't believe how different they look.'

'Thanks,' said Lily. 'But they were already lovely rooms. I'm not sure I'll ever get over that view outside.'

'You never do,' said Alex with a soft smile.

Over dessert, Alex told them about his training. 'It's even more intense now that we're going for the Commonwealth

Games,' he said. 'Dad's hoping that with any success there, it might be a springboard on to the Olympics.'

There were murmurs of appreciation around the table.

'That would be a major achievement,' said Walter. 'If you and your dad get the training right. Sounds like a lot of hard work ahead.'

'Yup. I'm not sure there's too many early nights in your future,' said Jake, with a grimace.

Alex shrugged his shoulders. 'It'll be worth it,' he replied.

Only Dotty looked concerned rather than impressed. 'But there's more to life than training,' she said, looking across at Alex.

'Yes, there is,' he said, nodding his head in agreement. 'But try telling Dad that!'

Lily had already picked up on the fact that Alex's dad was his trainer and a hard task master at that, from the sounds of it.

'Anyway, there'll be no training this weekend,' said Faye, in a hopeful tone.

'Sorry to disappoint you, Faye, but I have to go for a short swim and run in the morning to keep on schedule,' said Alex, with a sheepish grin. 'Why do you think I brought my wetsuit with me?'

'I thought it was your attempt at fashion,' drawled Jake.

'Won't it be freezing cold?' asked Faye, looking concerned.

'I swim in wild water all the time, more often than not nowhere near as clean and beautiful as lovely Dragonfly Lake, of course,' said Alex. His handsome face creased into a grin as he turned to Lily. 'You can join me if you want.'

'To swim? Outside? In November?' Lily made a horrified face which made Ben laugh out loud.

'Coward,' he teased her.

'Oh, definitely. I mean, it's not exactly the Mediterranean, is it?' she said, still not convinced.

'Excuse me! It's even better,' said Walter, smiling at her. 'And cleaner.'

'Absolutely,' said Alex. 'You should see some of the places where I have to swim.' He shuddered. 'The water is disgusting sometimes.'

'That's not healthy,' muttered Dotty.

'Well, it's definitely clean here,' said Walter. 'The limestone rocks see to that. You can see almost through to the bottom, even in the deep bits.'

'I understand that it's lovely and clean.' However, Lily was still hesitating. 'But it must be too cold, surely?'

'Trust me, it'll be warmer out there than it will be in March or April after the winter,' Alex told her. 'Anyway, a few minutes is amazing for the circulation.'

Lily looked at Hannah.

'I'm game if you are,' said Hannah, with a laugh.

Alex looked delighted. 'Excellent! I'll meet you both out there at 7 a.m.'

Lily turned to look at Hannah. 'Now you've done it,' she muttered. 'What am I supposed to do now?'

'I'd pray for a heatwave, if I were you,' quipped Jake.

27

The following morning, Lily, dressed in leggings and a large sweatshirt over her swimsuit, hovered nervously on the beach with a similarly dressed Hannah.

Finally, Alex came out of the hotel wearing his wetsuit.

'Wow,' muttered Hannah under her breath.

Lily silently agreed. Alex had the body of an athlete, broad shoulders and muscles everywhere, all of which was shown off by the skintight wetsuit. It was pretty impressive and Hannah couldn't seem to take her eyes off him.

'Good morning,' said Alex.

'Good morning,' they chorused in return.

'Why haven't we got wetsuits?' asked Lily, slipping off her flip-flops and tentatively touching her toe into the water lapping beside them. She gave a squeal at the freezing cold temperature.

'Because it's too cold for you to withstand the water for any length of time, especially if you're not used to it,' said Alex. 'I know CPR but I don't want to have to perform it on either one of you so you'd better stay in for a short time. Five minutes maximum.'

Lily shivered. 'That's a shame, I was really hoping to be in there for at least an hour,' she joked.

'Only if you want chilblains,' said Hannah.

'I'll see you afterwards,' said Alex.

They both watched as he waded straight into the water before striking out with an impressive front crawl across the lake.

'He's a true athlete,' said Lily, awestruck at his athleticism.

'He's a true idiot if he thinks that's the right way to start any day,' said a male voice nearby.

Lily and Hannah spun around to find Ben standing behind them.

'I'd rather have one of Mum's pastries and a coffee, to be honest,' he carried on, with a grin.

Lily smiled at the joke but found herself agreeing with him.

'Are you joining us?' asked Hannah in a hopeful tone.

Ben laughed. 'Absolutely no way,' he said. 'But I promised Alex that I would keep an eye on you both in case your hearts go into some kind of arrhythmia with the shock of the cold.'

'Well, that's really encouraged me now,' muttered Lily, to which Ben shot her another grin.

Hannah shrugged off her sweatshirt. 'Come on,' she said. 'We can't let Alex get the better of us. Last one in is a frozen penguin.'

Hannah slipped off her leggings to reveal her swimming costume and quickly ran in, fully immersing herself in the lake water almost immediately with a shriek.

Lily groaned and looked at Ben.

'I'd get it over with if I were you,' he said. 'I'll time you both.'

Feeling self-conscious stripping off in front of Ben, Lily quickly undressed to her swimsuit. Then, with a wail of determination and mostly terror, she followed Hannah into the water. She wailed again at the shock of the cold water hitting her body and it almost took her breath away. She could see why Alex wanted someone to keep an eye on them as the cold would definitely cause some people problems.

Once her pulse had calmed down, they splashed around a bit in the water, doing a bit of half-hearted swimming. Lily's main problem was her limbs going numb from the extreme temperature. But she could at least appreciate the beautiful clarity of the water, crystal clear and a dark turquoise under the early-morning skies.

'Five minutes is up! Come in,' called out Ben, not a moment too soon as far as Lily was concerned. She could feel her whole body growing numb with the cold.

She and Hannah ran out of the lake and threw the towels they had brought with them around their shoulders.

Hannah shivered and she hopped from foot to foot. 'Oh my gosh, I'm so cold,' she wailed.

Ben headed over and rubbed his hands over her shoulders and arms to work the circulation back into her body.

'Better?' he asked.

'Better,' she nodded, still shivering. 'You'd better do Lily as well. She's just as cold as me.'

Ben seemed to hesitate before walking over to Lily.

'Do you mind?' he asked.

But Lily was so cold and beyond caring about anything other than growing warm again.

'Please,' she pleaded with him.

So, with a smile, he reached out and rubbed her upper arms and back with his hands. Instantly she could feel her skin beginning to wake up again.

'Oh! That's lovely,' she blurted out, with a satisfied sigh.

Then she realised that it sounded as if it were the feel of his hands on her that was lovely and gazed at his face in embarrassment.

'Oh, look, you've got the colour back in your cheeks at least,' said Hannah. 'Come on. Let's go grab a shower to warm up properly.'

Lily's cheeks were still glowing as she picked up her clothes. She just hoped Ben didn't notice, but thankfully, when she checked, he was looking out across the lake where Alex was still ploughing through the water.

28

After watching Alex swim around the lake for a while, Ben headed back indoors to warm up.

In the kitchen, he found Jake cooking everyone hearty breakfasts, telling Faye that it was his pleasure to treat her for once.

'And it has been a real treat,' she told him. 'That smoothie was delicious.'

Ben was glad to see his mum looking relaxed. She was a lot quieter these days and with his late father's birthday the following day, she appeared even more strained.

In recent weeks, however, she seemed to have begun to come out of her shell. He had often caught her and Frankie laughing with Lily as they helped her decorate the bedrooms. Lily seemed to have brought some much-needed light to the place, along with his best friends.

Lily came into the kitchen shortly afterwards, a few damp tendrils of red hair clinging to her neck. Seeing her in her swimsuit had almost rendered him speechless. Those long legs and the curves of her body. Well, he had tried not to stare but it had taken serious self-control not to do so and he felt his pulse quicken once more at the thought of it.

'Eggs?' asked Jake, tipping a delicious-looking omelette onto a plate for Lily.

She smiled at him and Ben found himself a little unsettled. Surely Lily was looking for someone more serious than Jake?

He loved Jake like a brother but the man had serious commitment issues, thanks to his parents' disastrous marriage. He would need someone as strong as he was to put up with it, even knowing how kind and generous his friend's heart was.

'So, how was the water?' asked Jake.

'Painfully cold,' Lily told him, laughing.

Jake shook his head. 'Think too much training has affected Alex's brain, to be honest. The man must be mad to go out in that cold water day after day.'

'He certainly trains very hard,' said Faye.

'Too hard,' said Jake, frowning. 'And I'm not sure how much of it is his choice.'

'What do you mean?' asked Lily, looking confused.

Ben replied on Jake's behalf. 'Alex's parents, well, his dad I guess, is desperate for Alex to achieve some kind of success,' he told her.

'I'm not sure a gold medal would even be enough to satisfy Alex's dad, unless it came with a world record as well,' added Jake, shaking his head before appearing to brighten himself up deliberately. 'Thankfully my parents don't give a damn about me so I don't have that kind of pressure.'

'They love you in their own way,' said Faye quietly.

Jake smiled at her. 'Because you're so kind and lovely, I won't contradict you on that.'

Faye smiled back at him. 'What was that about changing your job I heard you mention last night?' she asked.

'I'm bored,' he said.

Ben wasn't surprised. Jake frequently changed his job and relationships, citing boredom. Ben had always figured that Jake just hadn't found the right place or woman yet.

'Are the people at the restaurant that bad?' asked Faye.

Jake shook his head. 'Not really. But you know that the only people I really like are right here.'

He had often used Maple Tree Lodge as an escape whenever he could and seemed to regard Ben's family as his own. Something Ben was happy to let him do.

And Alex as well, he realised. His own family circumstances may have been strained from time to time, but the hotel had always been a welcome refuge for his friends.

And now Lily too, he thought, glancing over at her as she finished her omelette.

'I'm starving,' said Hannah, as she came through the door. 'I need a caffeine pick-me-up after that cold shock.'

Jake made a face. 'That stuff will rot your insides,' he said, with a grimace. 'I'll whizz you up an energising smoothie to start you off.'

'Is it chocolate flavoured?' asked Hannah, her eyes gleaming.

Jake rolled his eyes. 'Just sit down and let me do the cooking. You may be the master of all things cake but brunches are my speciality.' He frowned, glancing at Faye. 'Well, I'm the deputy to the master over there.'

He was obviously at pains not to upset Faye but she didn't seem to mind. In fact, she was nodding thoughtfully to herself.

'You know, I've been thinking about changing the breakfast menu when we reopen,' she said, looking across at Ben. 'Different choices, I mean.'

'Sounds good,' he said, surprised but pleased.

'Have you found a chef to cover the dinner shift yet?' asked Jake.

Ben shook his head. It was a constant problem, trying to lure someone out into the heart of the countryside to provide dinner for the guests. Thankfully he and his grandad had come across a solution. 'Not yet. But Grandad and I have agreed that we'll just offer bed and breakfast at first, until we find our feet.'

'OK. Well, we can work out the brunch menus this weekend, if you like, to keep the guests set up for the day,' said Jake.

'It would be great to get a young person's input,' replied Faye. 'We need to keep up with the latest ideas and fads, don't you think?'

'Sounds ghastly,' said Walter as he came into the kitchen. 'What's wrong with eggs on toast?'

'Nothing, Grandad,' said Ben. 'But not all changes are bad, are they? Lily's redecoration is a case in point.'

'Keep me out of this,' she said, with a sheepish grin.

Ben smiled back at her as they locked eyes.

Their moment, however, was interrupted by Walter placing something down on the table in front of them. It was a basket made of woven strands of willow, something he had been making for years.

'What's this?' asked Jake.

'A wicker basket,' Walter told him. 'Faye asked for one to replace the fruit bowl which was broken.'

'Oh, Walter, it's lovely,' said Faye, beaming as she picked it up. 'So light as well.'

'So light that it floats,' said Walter.

'It floats?' asked Lily, looking amazed.

Walter beamed. 'Just say the word and I can set it off across the lake after breakfast,' he said.

Coming Home to Maple Tree Lodge

'Maybe we can send a message to Alex if he's still out there,' said Jake, with a grin.

29

At the end of the day, Lily sank onto the sofa in the lounge with a sigh of relief. After her cold water shock first thing, she had worked non-stop and was grateful to finally be resting.

She had spent the day beginning work on the lounge which had meant painting the plain walls either side of the fireplace. The soft green worked well with the stone hearth but there was still so much to do, along with the entrance hall and dining room as well. Then there were all the final touches to add to all the areas. The work ahead still seemed to be vast.

Thankfully Alex and Jake had helped clear the huge number of empty boxes that had built up from all the televisions that Ben was beginning to install in the bedrooms, as well as helping to fill two large skips with all of the debris from the bathroom renovations.

Lily took a sip of the cocktail that Frankie had made them after dinner. This time it was a warming concoction of rum and spices and she could feel it dulling her senses and making everything just a little bit softer and more relaxed.

Ben sat down next to her and gave her a smile before he looked at the roaring fire next to them.

'I needed this,' he said. 'I've spent all day updating the reception desk computer and, despite my brain being ready to explode, you'll be glad to know that we now have an online booking system as well as a website where people can book at long last!' He raised a glass to her and she recognised Frankie's cocktail.

'Careful,' she told him. 'It's another strong one.'

He took a tentative sip before his eyes clicked wide open. 'Strong but pretty tasty. Glad I'm not doing any more work tonight. I'm not sure I should be operating any machinery after one of these.'

Lily smiled and sighed, closing her eyes briefly as she leant back against the sofa. There was a short silence before she opened them again and found him watching her with his dark brown eyes completely unreadable.

'You've had a busy day too,' he told her, moving his gaze to admire the paint colour either side of the fireplace. 'I like the colour.'

'Well, it's a start,' she replied.

'It certainly is.' He reached out his glass for her to chink with his. 'Cheers. To a job well started.'

They both spluttered after taking another sip of the drink before Ben took her glass and placed it on the coffee table in front of them.

'So what next?' he asked as he sat back.

She laughed and groaned at the same time. 'Give me at least one night off,' she told him. But all the same, she couldn't help but let her eyes wander around the lounge, imagining how it would look when it was finished.

'I would but I recognise that look in your eyes,' he said, laughing softly. 'So tell me, what are your plans for in here?'

'Similar vibe to the one I want in the bedrooms,' she told him. 'Luxe cushions, blankets, all-round cosiness. Lots of hurricane lamps and soft lighting. Luckily the wood adds so much comfort and decoration that we won't need to do too much painting in here.'

He nodded. 'Sounds great.'

'But you're going to be needing a long ladder because I'm thinking lots of fairy lights entwined around all those lovely oak beams up there,' she carried on.

He looked up and she heard him groan. But, to her pleasure, he didn't protest. Finally, they were both on the same side, she thought with a smile.

She looked down at the table and idly picked up the small wicker basket that Walter had brought in earlier. Faye had turned it into a fruit bowl and it was filled with apples and pears.

'This basket is so clever,' she said, admiring the neatness of the entwined tiny branches.

She wanted to talk further with him but they were interrupted by the rest of the family and friends joining them in a noisy fashion.

'That was an excellent dinner,' announced Alex, sitting down on the opposite sofa.

'I thought you only ate anything healthy and yet I'm sure you helped yourself to a second serving of Hannah's chocolate cake,' said Jake, sitting on a nearby armchair.

Alex glanced at Hannah as she sat down nearby with Frankie. 'Well, it was too delicious to resist,' he muttered.

As the conversation continued, Lily carried on watching Alex and saw the touch of rosiness in his cheeks. She guessed that it had nothing to do with the welcome heat of the fire and more to do with the look that he had just given Hannah, who had completely missed it as she laughed and joked around with Jake.

Lily smiled to herself. Alex's secret was safe with her. But she made a note to casually ask Hannah about him at some point in the future.

Walter sat down next to Alex and smiled at Lily when he saw the wicker basket in her hand.

'Still admiring my handiwork,' he said.

She nodded. 'Of course,' she told him. 'I still can't believe that they float.'

'You don't trust me?' asked Walter, raising his grey eyebrows in good humour.

'Of course I do,' she told him truthfully.

Later on, as the mood became more lively after Frankie's cocktails were all finished, a rousing game of Monopoly was taking place on the large table.

Lily took advantage of the family's laughter to talk quietly to Ben where they were sitting by themselves on the sofa.

She hesitated before speaking. 'Your mum told me that it's your dad's birthday tomorrow.'

Ben took a deep breath before blowing it out slowly and nodding. 'We're going to the graveyard in the morning,' he said. 'Put down some flowers. Don't like it there, to be honest. It's too cold and impersonal. This hotel is a better memorial to him, I always think.'

There was a short silence as he looked deep in thought.

'You know, when I was growing up, my dad was stationed in Vietnam for a year. We went to Hội An one weekend,' she told him, thinking back. 'They have a famous lantern festival at night there. Boats and everything else is decorated. It's so pretty. But what they do have is some floating candles that they set off down the river. It was supposed to pay respects to people's ancestors.' She looked at Ben. 'Perhaps we could do that tomorrow evening, if you'd like.'

He looked started. 'A lantern festival?' he asked, with a confused expression.

She smiled and shook her head. 'I mean, set off one of your grandad's floating baskets across the lake with a candle. We could light it as a way of paying our respects to your dad.'

For a second, he looked nonplussed and she expected him to laugh at her. But instead, he nodded slowly to himself. 'This place meant everything to him,' he finally said. 'And with Grandad having made the basket, I think it's a lovely idea.'

Lily felt pleased, hoping that the small ceremony might just take away the pain of the anniversary.

So they ran the idea past Faye and Hannah when they had the opportunity, both of whom approved of the gesture.

'I think it'll be lovely,' said Hannah, looking teary.

Ben brought her into a hug, enveloping her with both his arms.

'I agree but let's see what your grandad says,' added Faye, looking concerned.

But she needn't have worried. Walter was a little confused by the idea until Lily googled the lantern festival and showed him the floating candles.

'I see,' he said. 'Well, we know that they float. And I think it's quite symbolic.'

'Like something I saw in *Game of Thrones*,' added Dotty.

'Hopefully more poignant than that,' said Ben, with a soft laugh.

'You'll probably need to head out a little way on the boat,' Walter told him. 'Otherwise it might just end up bobbing around on the shoreline.'

'I agree,' said Ben, nodding. 'I'm happy to do that.'

'I can help,' said Lily quickly. After all, it had been her idea.

She didn't want it going awry and ruining what was supposed to be a poignant occasion.

She also found that she didn't want Ben to be out there all alone. That she wanted to help him. And be there for him. As a friend.

Except she was beginning to hope that they might just be so much more.

30

The following evening, Ben and Lily were joined by the rest of the family, as well as Jake and Alex, as they all walked out to the lake shore.

Ben was pleased that Lily had offered to come out in the boat with him. It had been a sad day but it had felt right to dedicate a few quieter moments in the graveyard earlier in the morning with his mum and sister. And yet he still felt as if it hadn't quite been enough to honour his dad and he was grateful for her company with the important task ahead.

Night had now fallen and it was dark enough for them to head out into the middle of the lake.

'This boat's not going to sink, is it?' asked Lily, as she swung a leg over to climb into the rowing boat.

Ben shot her a grin as he sat down. 'I've made triple sure,' he said.

They settled into their seats and then picked up the oars.

'I'm getting déjà vu,' he heard Lily mutter as they began to row their way away from the pier and out onto the water.

They nodded at the family and set off at a slow but steady

pace. It was cooler once they were on the open water, a gentle breeze wafting across the water which seemed darker without the warmth of the day. The overhead sky was clear and dotted with stars and the moon had just appeared above the trees to cast a light upon them as they made their journey to the centre of the lake.

Once they were in the middle of the water, they both stopped rowing and let the boat bob up and down for a while.

Glancing over to the pier, Ben could see his family waiting on the dock, huddled together with his friends. Jake had his arm around Faye whilst Alex was holding Hannah. His grandparents had locked arms together and their heads were close to each other's, along with Frankie who was next to them.

Ben then looked at Lily, who had picked up the wicker basket. It was only then that he noticed the short, coloured candle inside.

'I chose blue,' she told him.

'Dad's favourite colour,' he replied, looking up at her in surprise.

She nodded. 'That's what your mum told me.'

They locked eyes for a moment before he brought out the lighter that he had hidden inside his coat. Lily held out the wicker basket and he flicked the switch to light the long wick. The flame took hold and fluttered in the gentle breeze.

'Do you want to place it in the water?' she asked him.

Ben shook his head. He felt very emotional suddenly and didn't want his hands to shake and drown the candle before it had achieved its purpose.

So Lily gave him a small smile of understanding and leant over to place the basket on top of the water. Ben held on to the sides of the boat to steady it as she straightened up. And then, with a gentle push with her fingers, the basket began to drift away from them across the water.

Ben hadn't known what to expect with regard to his feelings. His main concern had been that he might not feel anything at all.

But there, on the lake, with the reflected lights from inside the hotel glinting across the rippled water, he felt almost overwhelmed with emotion. He would have loved to have seen his dad again in that moment. But perhaps the lantern was enough, he thought.

'It feels like he's with us again,' he found himself blurting out. 'Wishing us and the hotel on.'

Lily took his hand in hers and squeezed it gently. Without a second thought, he leant his head on her shoulder and she drew her arm around him to hold him.

He savoured her support and strength as they sat there, looking at the flickering light as it bobbed across the lake towards the other shore.

Then, just as the flame began to fade, Ben lifted his head to look at Lily. Her face was so close to his now and it seemed the most natural thing in the world in that moment to lean forward and kiss her gently on the cheek.

'Thank you,' he murmured.

It wasn't a kiss of passion. It was a kiss of friendship, of support and of family love. He knew deep down that she knew that because when he drew back her eyes were glistening with tears along with his.

'Are you OK?' she asked softly.

He nodded, glancing once more at the lantern. The light was almost out now and they watched it in silence as the flame flickered one more time before disappearing altogether.

They sat silently for a few more moments and he was grateful that she allowed him to mourn and grieve in his own time.

Finally, when he was ready, he looked at her. 'Shall we go back?' he asked.

She looked across to where the family were still waiting for them on the dock and nodded.

Ben glanced once more at the basket which had disappeared into the night. His grandad had reassured him that the temporary netting he had put up underneath the wooden bridge would catch the basket before it headed downstream.

He glanced at the heavens above, nodding at the moon and stars before turning the boat around to start rowing back to the dock.

When they had climbed back out of the boat, the family embraced, with Lily standing nearby with Frankie and his friends.

And yet Ben couldn't help but feel that it was because of her that he felt a little more at peace, a little more grateful for the moment of remembrance that evening. Once more, he was glad that she had stayed on with them at the hotel for the past few weeks.

The trouble was that he was beginning to secretly wish that she could stay on once the hotel was open again. He was getting used to having her around, needing both her support and craving her company.

But it wasn't as friends that he wanted. He realised in that moment that he was beginning to really care for her.

31

After the candle ceremony on the lake, everyone gathered in the lounge for a drink, clinking their glasses together as they all sat on the chairs and sofas in front of the fire to warm themselves up.

There was a feeling of peace and contentment, despite the sadness of the day that they had just endured.

'I must say, I liked that floating candle,' said Dotty, looking at Lily. 'Wherever did you get the idea from?'

Lily explained about the Hội An lantern festival in Vietnam that she had told Ben about.

'So there's more than one floating light?' asked Dotty, still a little confused.

Lily smiled and nodded. 'Oh, yes,' she said, drawing out her phone and showing Dotty the photographs she could find online.

'Oh, that's very pretty, especially when there's that many on the water,' said Faye, looking over Dotty's shoulder.

'The only thing they do on the water around here is the duck race on the river at Cranbridge,' said Frankie. 'Good fun but not as lovely to look at. Don't suppose we could have a race here, could we? Bring in the punters?'

'We can't have a duck race on here,' said Ben, laughing.

'No tide or fast current for a start,' added Walter, with a grin.

'Well, there's a very small current but it would be the slowest duck race in the world,' said Ben.

It was good to see him and his grandad getting along so much better, thought Lily. They were even able to share a joke these days.

Faye sat back next to her and they continued their conversation.

'So you think I should make a wreath for the front door?' asked Faye. 'When we open to guests, I mean.'

'Of course,' Lily told her. 'Given your passion for floristry, I think it's a great solution. We could wrap some holly over the fireplaces and beams. Even up the stairwell.'

'I think that sounds great, Mum,' said Hannah.

'Oh, she's not the only one I've got plans for,' said Lily, with a grin. 'I was thinking that when the lounge is ready, perhaps we could have a tea trolley where guests can help themselves to not only a hot drink but one of your delicious cakes as well.'

'If you think they'd want that,' muttered Hannah.

'Of course they will,' said Alex fiercely. 'Nobody could ever turn down one of your cakes.'

Hannah smiled gratefully at him but Lily knew that her friend would need more encouragement to bake her cakes for anyone beyond the family. Thankfully everyone else thought it was an inspired idea and would keep encouraging her.

Hannah was also going to help Faye with the breakfasts, using the recipes that Jake had given them for some more updated menu items.

'Evening, all,' said Dodgy Del, wandering into the lounge.

'Del! What on earth brings you here tonight?' asked Walter.

'I was just passing and thought I could drop off those strings of fairy lights that I promised Lily,' said Del.

'Talking of which,' said Lily, standing up and looking down at Ben. 'There was just one more thing, if you want to follow me.'

'Uh-oh,' she heard Ben mutter, as he too stood up.

She led him over to the far wall. 'What are we going to do with this place?' she asked Ben, opening the door to the snug.

'The snug?' he asked, looking surprised.

'It's hardly snug,' she told him, heading inside and switching on the lights. 'It's actually a really great size.'

She could now see that it was actually a large room, despite the many boxes in there. It didn't have any furniture but what it did have was a stone bar along one side and a couple of smaller tables piled up in a corner.

'Was this ever used as a bar?' she asked.

'A long time ago,' said Ben, blowing out a sigh. 'I could ask Grandad. But it hasn't been used for years, I reckon.'

Lily's mind was racing as she turned around the room once more. She could imagine leather sofas and darker walls, giving a warmth and maturity where the lounge could be sunny and light. Perhaps even a snooker table, she thought, next to the armchairs and coffee tables. It would be perfect in the summer with the view of the lake and the door open to the long veranda.

But she could also imagine the fire on in the winter, the sun low in the sky, cosy sofas and blankets and rugs softening it up.

'Oh, no,' she heard Ben mutter.

She turned quickly to face him. 'What's the matter?'

'I recognise that look on your face,' he told her, with a soft smile.

'What look?'

'The "this is going to cost me money" look,' he replied, raising his eyebrows at her.

She laughed. 'Listen, don't you think the bar is a good idea?'

'Yes, but...' he began.

However, Lily was on a roll and interrupted him. 'Imagine all our guests coming in here before dinner, spending lots of lovely money on drinks and then relaxing. Think of all that extra profit coming into the hotel.'

'You're just trying to tempt me with the thought of more money,' he said, laughing.

Then his smile faded and his look was replaced by something more searing as he carried on staring down at her. Their eyes still locked together, she held her breath, his eyes glinting in the overhead light as time began to stand still. Her pulse began to thump as she looked up at him.

Suddenly all the lights went out and they were left in the darkness.

'Del!' came the usual shout from the lounge as Frankie raged about the power being shorted out again.

'I'm going to have to sort out some kind of electric car charging system as well,' said Ben. 'If only for Del when he keeps coming over.'

They smiled at each other in the semi-darkness then took a step backwards, but all the time his eyes were dark and probing, as if asking her the question as to what happened next.

Then the lights flickered back on as Walter flipped the switch in the electrics cupboard and the moment was lost.

'So, a bar, eh?' said Ben, still looking at her.

Lily tried to cool her racing pulse. 'I think it's a great idea,' she said, in an overly bright tone, still trying to concentrate back on the hotel and not the thought of standing close to Ben.

'Staff is a problem though,' he reminded her. 'I'm not sure until we're up and running whether our funds will be able to stretch to a full-time barkeeper. And where on earth would we find one anyway?'

'Luckily I have just the solution to that particular problem,' she told him with a knowing smile.

32

Lily found that she had never worked so hard and yet never enjoyed any job quite as much before. Working on the hotel felt like the ultimate dream project.

Each day she would start early, fuelled by one of Faye's delicious breakfasts, and then carry on working.

First on the list to be finished were the bedrooms. Ben had put in a rush order for some neutral-coloured carpets and they arrived and were fitted as soon as the painting was finished.

Slowly, with each new layer of colour, such as the new bed linen, the textures that she had been wanting came to life in front of her eyes. Each room felt comfortable but fresh too.

'Everything's washable,' Lily told Ben when he looked at the large pile of cushion covers and blankets which had just been delivered. 'So it's not impractical.'

'I'm trying to believe you,' he told her, with a grin.

She was reminded once more how handsome he was when he relaxed and smiled.

'The four-poster frames look amazing,' she said. 'Very romantic.'

She blushed as she reminded herself that she didn't know too much about romance, given her love life in recent years.

'Now for the fun bit,' she said, swiftly changing the subject. 'Those all-important finishing touches.'

'And how much are they going to cost me?' he asked, with a grimace.

Lily broke into a winning smile. 'As it happens, almost nothing,' she told him.

She had been inspired one day when she had asked Dotty to show her some of her souvenirs that she had collected over the years. As Lily began to look through the boxes, she had to agree with Dotty that they were indeed treasures. There were vases and ornaments, glassware and candle holders. There was a vast number of different patterns and themes but once she broke everything down by colour scheme, she realised that it was going to work.

She looked at Ben. 'Follow me and I'll show you,' she said, leading him into the next bedroom.

She looked around at the room they were standing in. She had placed a distressed gold-framed mirror over the dressing table. Then she had added some leather-bound books she had found, alongside a small gold tray in the shape of a leaf, on top of which was a tall bud vase.

'I was aiming for sophisticated country instead of rustic,' she told him.

He nodded and smiled, as he looked around. 'And you've achieved it,' he said. 'This looks great. Amazing, in fact.'

'I'm glad you like it,' she replied, pleased with his reaction.

They walked into the next room which had been decorated in soft blues.

In this room she had added some blue coloured glasses and a vase which Dotty had told her she had bought in Marrakesh.

'Brilliant,' said Ben, looking around. 'Oh, and the coffee machines are arriving tomorrow.'

Lily followed his gaze. Whereas the new colour schemes had softened each bedroom, the new high-tech equipment such as the televisions and USB charging ports ensured that the rooms felt stylish and modern as well as comfortable.

'I must say these were a great idea,' said Ben, walking up to a large, framed photograph on the wall.

Lily agreed. She had been inspired when she had come across a number of Dotty's old photograph albums. They had spent a lovely evening going through some of her many photographs from around the world.

But best of all had been some of the early photographs she had taken when she had first arrived at Maple Tree Lodge. They were all different views and themes. Sometimes a close-up of a dragonfly on a reed bed, a streak of bright green or blue. Or a black and white photograph of the hotel on a winter's morning. The lake under a blue sky and the maple trees showing off their autumnal glory.

Lily had got them framed so that they could be hung in the bedrooms. Then she had tasked Dotty with taking current photographs, especially the hues of autumn, for the downstairs.

Dotty had taken up the idea with huge enthusiasm and it was great to see her a little more lively day by day.

Lily glanced at Ben once more. It wasn't just the rooms that were slowly being transformed, she thought. Since being stuck in the boathouse, her relationship with Ben had changed as well. From open hostility to a truce, now they were friends who were a little more honest with each other. They trusted each other. Friends who exchanged more than a healthy glance at each other perhaps. But that was only because he was good-looking, she reminded herself.

'I like the fact that we're reusing stuff from around the whole place,' said Ben.

She nodded in agreement. 'I've always been resourceful and tried to work to a budget,' she told him.

'Even a budget as tight as ours?' he asked, laughing.

'Even that,' she said, with a smile.

He looked around the room once more. 'I guess that's what I like most about you giving our old junk items a new purpose. And as the family has been here for over a hundred years, we've got a lot of junk!'

'And thank goodness,' she told him. 'Because we've got a lot of rooms to decorate.' She went over to move the vase slightly so it lined up properly on the table she had placed it on. 'I had no idea that staying in one place, one home, for so many years was normal,' she said, hearing the wistful sound in her own voice.

A place to call home. It had always been her dream but she hadn't imagined seeing somewhere like Maple Tree Lodge and realising that it was possible in real life.

Ben walked over to stand next to her. 'You think my family is normal?' he asked, raising an eyebrow at her in a humorous manner.

She smiled at his joke. 'I think your family is just lovely,' she told him truthfully. 'There's an underlying strength here, from what I've seen and felt. The strength of staying put in one place. Of having a home as a sort of fortress against the outside world. I like it.'

It was true, she realised. She was beginning to feel like she was part of a team. Having been on her own for so long, having battled by herself day after day, it was a nice feeling to be enveloped by the hotel but, more importantly, the people who lived there.

For a moment, their eyes locked. She couldn't read the look in his eyes before he turned away and headed towards the door.

But she found that she had been holding her breath when she was alone in the room once more as she exhaled, letting out a puff of air.

She could feel herself developing feelings for Ben. She had dated a few men over the years, of course. Mainly to stop her friends nagging her. But there had never been a depth of feeling before. Ben was different. She knew him. She was living in his home and with his family.

Still the old feelings surfaced. It was an anomaly for her to let someone break down those carefully erected barriers she had placed around her heart, trying to concentrate only on her career.

In contrast, she found that she wanted to talk with Ben. To be open with him.

But even more surprising was the fact that she didn't feel the need to shy away with him. That she could feel herself wanting to get even closer to him.

And the feeling both surprised and frightened her.

33

As they raced towards the hotel opening deadline of 1 December, Ben could hardly believe the transformation that occurred day after day.

In the entrance hall, the reception area was now warm and inviting with photos of the hotel and lake adorning every wall, thanks to Dotty's skills as a photographer. A comfortable chair had appeared, as well as an old desk that had been polished and smartened up by a jug of seasonal flowers, arranged by his mum.

The wall next to the staircase had been painted a dark green which made the double-height room seem much more cosy and the oak balustrade was now entwined with fairy lights which gave a soft romantic feel in the dark winter light.

He then went into the lounge, which was now inviting as well as comfortable. Lily had somehow managed to tone down the almost overwhelming feeling of leather and wood. Now there were lots of cushions along the sofas and armchairs, as well as blankets dotted about. There was no carpet downstairs but instead large, fluffy rugs had been placed, giving the sense of softness. Thick pillar candles and flowers on the tables added to the whole luxurious feel of the place.

Above the stone fireplace was an old mirror and candlesticks, entwined with fairy lights and various fake pumpkins and leaves in velvet and silk, giving the place an autumnal seasonal twist which matched the view outside.

Either side of the hearth there was more ironwork and hurricane lamps, gleaming in the reflection of the soft flames.

In addition, there were a couple of piles of old books which added to the comfortable, lived-in feel of the place. His mum and Dotty had dug out lots of spare items from their storage and eagerly donated them to the cause, which made him realise that it still felt like home. But one that he was proud to share with their guests, if they ever arrived.

He smiled to himself. Lily had done an amazing job. He could even see himself sitting down in the lounge on a winter's evening, sharing a bottle of wine with Lily, the Christmas tree lights twinkling and listening to the crackling of the logs. But, of course, she wouldn't be there, he realised, with a frown.

But at least she had been prepared to stay until the opening of the hotel, to ensure the smooth running of everything.

And besides, he thought, trying to cheer himself up, perhaps she could treat herself and come back when it was open to guests. If she wanted to, of course.

He looked up as his grandmother came into the lounge, holding a couple of newly framed photographs.

'All done,' said Dotty, placing them on the mantelpiece.

'I've just taken a peek in the bedrooms and they look tremendous,' said Walter, with a huge smile, from the doorway.

'Even the coffee machines?' asked Ben, raising his eyebrows in good humour.

Walter gave him a look. 'Actually I've been thinking that it will be nice for our guests to have some hot drinks in their room.'

There was a flurry of exchanged looks between Ben and Dotty which Walter picked up on.

'I'm not a dinosaur,' he told them. 'Some of the modern ideas do work. After all, I upgraded from that old lathe to that new precision one with a cutting edge, didn't I?'

'Welcome to the twenty-first century,' murmured Dotty, with a knowing smile.

Outside, his mother was arranging a couple of chrysanthemum bushes on the veranda and either side of the front door. Their autumnal hues matched the feel of the place perfectly, as well as the new wreath on the front door.

He was pleased to see his mother enjoying her gardening once more, encouraged by Lily.

What a difference she had made to everyone's lives, he thought.

He went into the snug, although he had been reminded over and over that they really should change the name when the guests arrived. But in actual fact, he liked the name. It suited the space entirely and besides, nobody seemed to be able to break the habit anyway.

He went through the door and the change in décor hit him once more. It was another mixture of earthy colour palette, rustic textures and vintage finds.

Here three of the walls had once more been covered up, leaving only the wall on the lake side wooden clad. The rest had been painted a deep and yet warm navy blue. The dark colour scheme was enlivened by touches of rich gold, such as the candlesticks, picture frames and mirror.

He had forked out for the additional expense of some leather armchairs and sofas but he had to concede that they looked great.

With soft rugs once more laid across the floorboards, it was a relaxed, welcoming space.

In the corner there was a dart board and they had even found an old snooker table which, once it had been re-covered, fitted in perfectly. In the corners of the room there were also soft lamps, giving off a comfortable warm ambiance.

Lily had discovered some old board games which were piled up on the new bookcase, along with yet more books and even some old LPs alongside his dad's record player. It touched Ben to see things that his dad had cherished. As if he were alongside them now, cheering them on. There was even an old chess set that had been polished up and made ready for a game.

But best of all was the bar which had been refitted by none other than Dodgy Del. Despite being a calamity in so many ways, his electrician skills had been spot on and he had fitted rows of LED lights behind the bar, in warm white. The oak bar itself had then been buffed and waxed many times until it gleamed under the soft spotlights.

Behind the bar was the drinks cabinet, once more softened with warm lighting. Fairy lights trailed across the ceiling, with a couple of brighter LED lights over the pool table.

It was a place for people to linger in, to relax and enjoy themselves. Ben was thrilled with the result.

So too was Frankie, who was currently behind the bar, polishing up the bottles of cider and gin which had just arrived. They gleamed and sparkled under the new lighting.

'Delivery from Willow Tree Hall,' announced Frankie. 'All locally brewed, which is great, don't you think?'

It had been an inspired idea by Lily that Frankie should become their new barkeeper. She had never been really suited to being a receptionist, that much they all knew.

He just hadn't worked up the courage to ask her yet if she

wanted the job. But now appeared to be the best time, he realised.

'The liquor licence has just been sent through,' said Ben.

'Great,' said Frankie. 'I've been looking up some cocktail recipes online for the preview evening next weekend.'

'Well, last night's concoction was certainly interesting,' he told her, before clearing his throat. 'Listen, I've got something to ask you. How does the idea of a sideways promotion strike you?'

'A what now?' she asked, frowning.

'Well, you used to work in a pub, right?'

She nodded.

'So how would you feel about being our barkeeper when the hotel reopens?' he asked, bracing himself for an acid reply.

'I'd love it,' she said, breaking into a smile.

Because she smiled so rarely, he realised how much softer and younger she looked when she did.

'I always did,' she carried on. 'But we're less likely to get the scumbags that I used to deal with in that hellhole of a pub. And if we do, I know just how to deal with them.'

Ben gulped. 'Great,' he said, with a small amount of trepidation. He'd need to ask his mum to have a word with Frankie about toning down her somewhat strident views on handling people.

'But what about the reception?' asked Frankie, frowning. 'We'll still need someone out there to handle the guests if I'm busy in here.'

Ben nodded. 'I guess I could do it,' he said.

'Better yet, what about Lily?' said Frankie.

Ben was delighted. It was an inspired idea, he thought. Much better that it was Lily, who was more discreet, softer and courteous.

'But then again, isn't she going to leave when the hotel is finished?' asked Frankie.

Ben frowned to himself. He hadn't actually thought about her actually leaving any time soon. He hadn't wanted to.

And suddenly he realised that he didn't want her to go. He was beginning to care for her too much.

'Perhaps if she likes the place, she might just carry on living and working here,' said Frankie, giving him a knowing look. 'You know, if there's something in the hotel that she really likes.'

Ben locked eyes with her but said nothing.

'In any case, she's a better idea on reception than you are,' carried on Frankie. 'She's more friendly than you and more organised. I see you as a behind-the-scenes kind of person. You know, so we can keep concealing your grumpiness.'

'I'm not grumpy,' protested Ben.

'Not when Lily's in the room, anyhow,' he heard Frankie say as she turned away.

But she'd already left the room and he was left wondering if he'd misheard what she had said.

Besides, he had to work out how to ask Lily to man the reception. He knew she had dreams of having her own design company and it had only ever been a temporary arrangement for her to stay at the hotel. But perhaps she might just remain a little bit longer to help out Hannah and the rest of the family. He knew in his heart that he really wanted her to stay on as well. So he would find the suitable time to ask her. And he was really hoping the answer would be yes.

34

Lily looked around the dining room with a satisfied nod. It looked great, she thought to herself with a smile.

In actual fact, the room hadn't needed too much work other than painting the walls a deep blue to add depth and warmth to the area. The wooden floorboards had also been polished and the oak beams hadn't needed anything other than more strings of fairy lights and long garlands of fake tiny flowers which added an ethereal effect to the whole room. It felt fresh in the morning sunshine for breakfast and, if dinner was ever served, it would be more intimate in the evenings.

While the budget didn't stretch to new furniture, it turned out that the dining-room chairs and tables, built by Walter many years ago, were sturdy enough that they didn't need replacing. But in order to soften the effect, and the seating as well, she had asked Dotty and Faye to make some new tablecloths, along with matching seat cushions.

To make the area a little more romantic in the evening, old jam jars had been repurposed with tea lights to be placed on each table. She had been impressed and pleased when Faye had come up with the idea to press flowers onto the outside of them, giving them a pretty and fresh appearance.

It looked so much better, she thought, pleased with all of their work.

She just had a few minor touches to add to the entrance hall and the hotel was finished. Her finest project to date and her favourite as well.

But along with her pride in a job well done, she couldn't stop herself feeling incredibly sad. Because once it was done, then she would have to leave. There was no reason for her to stay. And she was sadder about that than anything that she could ever remember.

With a heavy heart, Lily had quietly begun to search around online for both a new job and a new place to live. The rooms she had viewed to rent in London looked depressingly familiar, both in tiny size and bland decoration. Where was the warmth of the wood? The incredible view of the lake? The peace and tranquillity of the surrounding countryside?

But it wasn't just the four walls of the hotel that she would miss. It was the family as well. She had grown much closer to Hannah these past few weeks and would miss seeing her best friend on a daily basis.

The feeling was reciprocated and Hannah had pleaded and tried to reason with Lily at every moment.

'The project is finished,' Lily had told her. 'There's no need for me to stay. I have to find a job. What would I do here now it's all decorated?'

'I don't know,' replied Hannah. 'Can't you help out in the kitchen?'

Lily laughed. 'Have you seen my cooking skills? I can open a tin of soup and that's about it!'

Hannah hadn't laughed at the joke though and looked downcast. 'You're going to stay until after the preview evening, aren't you?'

'Of course,' Lily told her. 'But after that you'll be too busy as you're all going to be inundated with guests.'

She was trying to keep a brave face on it but the truth was that she desperately wanted to stay. But she knew that if she were truly honest with Hannah then her friend would be even more keen for her to remain at Maple Tree Lodge.

But how was it even possible? She needed to get on with her career, didn't she? However she was finding that the thought gave her no pleasure like it used to. Her mind was taken up with different things these days. The only deadlines were the hotel ones. But then there was the soft light of dawn and the amazing sunsets to enjoy. The way the view changed every passing day as the seasons moved on. Then there was the family. She loved being part of the family dinners and all their raucous laughter and gentle teasing.

'Wind's getting up,' said Walter, suddenly appearing next to her.

Lily glanced outside and saw the trees swaying from side to side, buffeted by the predicted gales that were due to arrive at any moment.

'I'm sure the hotel will be all right,' she told him.

'Of course it will,' he replied. 'This place has survived everything that Mother Nature has thrown at it.' He looked around the dining room. 'I must say, it's never looked quite so stylish as it does these days.'

'Did I do OK, Walter?' she asked, suddenly anxious to find out.

He nodded and gave her a smile. 'You did,' he told her.

'Thank you.'

'Thank you for letting me stay for so long.'

Walter looked at her with his fierce grey eyes. 'It's your home now. Whenever you want to come back, you'll always be welcome.'

Lily felt the emotion rise in her throat, suddenly unable to speak. So she nodded, furiously blinking away the tears. Home. It was a bewitching idea, that one true place that she had longed for so many years. And yet it wasn't hers. She had to work, didn't she? Continue her interior design career, which she had given up so much for. Surely that had to be her purpose, her singular idea going forward, no matter the less joy it gave her these days, she found.

Ben appeared at the doorway. 'There you are,' he said, with a smile.

Lily smiled back and the thought leapt into her head. I don't want to leave. I don't want to leave the lake or this lovely hotel without seeing its success. I love this family. I love living here. I don't want to leave Hannah.

And Ben. She especially didn't want to leave Ben.

As Walter wandered away, they were left alone in the dining room.

'There's something I've been meaning to ask you but it's all been a bit crazy what with getting everything ready in time,' he began, coming to stand in front of her.

'What is it?' she asked.

'So the preview is happening in a week's time and then we're open for business,' he began, looking a little nervous.

'I think we're ready,' she said, anxious to reassure him.

'So do I,' he replied. 'But now I'm wondering about the future. Specifically yours.'

She took a sharp intake of breath. 'What do you mean?' she asked.

'Do you have any work lined up yet?' he asked.

She made a face. 'I had a lovely rejection email this afternoon, in fact,' she replied. 'I'm wondering whether Hans has made me an untouchable in the interior design industry. I think I'm unemployable.'

'Not necessarily,' he told her. 'I have a great job for you. Free bed and board included!'

She looked at him, nonplussed.

He took a deep breath. 'If you don't yet have a job lined up, or anywhere to stay, then we were wondering if you would like to stay on for the winter? Or at least until you find a new job.'

'Here?' She could hardly breathe. It was a dream come true. A secret dream that she had harboured for so long.

'Here,' he told her, with a nod. 'With us.'

'What would I do though?' she wondered out loud. 'I mean, the redecoration is done.'

'How do you feel about being on reception?' he asked.

She was surprised and delighted. 'But what about Frankie?' she asked.

He grinned. 'You mean, our new barmaid?'

'You asked her?' Lily's face lit up. 'And she said yes?'

'Quicker than I've ever seen her move at any other time, to be honest. She even smiled briefly.' He looked down at her and she almost lost herself in his brown eyes. 'So what do you say?'

She didn't even hesitate. 'I'd love to stay, thank you.'

Then, before she could stop herself, she flung her arms around his neck and gave him a huge kiss on the lips.

She gasped at what she had done and immediately stepped back. 'Sorry,' she stammered, blushing. 'I'm just so happy.'

'Well now, so am I,' he murmured.

Her blushes grew deeper. 'We'd better tell the family the good news,' she said, rushing away from him.

As she headed into the entrance hall, she realised in that

accepting to stay, she was finally letting go of her long-held ambitions. Was she really ready to let go of owning her own design company? Perhaps, depending on what her parents would say, she thought, feeling nervous.

But as the Jackson family broke into joyful merriment at the news that she was staying and she was smothered in hugs and kisses, she felt truly touched. As if the future were brighter than it had ever felt.

As she was drawn into yet another hug, she couldn't help but look at Ben one more time. It was just a temporary arrangement, that was all, she reminded herself.

And yet her feelings for him were as real and permanent as anything that she had ever felt before.

35

Ben had felt quite positive when he had first had the idea of a preview evening to show off the hotel to the locals and generate some publicity in the surrounding areas.

Lily had agreed with the idea and so suddenly it was a mad rush to get everything finished for the, hopefully, many visitors from the local area. Invitations had been issued online on various local groups, as well as in the community hubs in Cranley, Cranbridge and Cranfield, and they were hoping for quite a crowd.

But with a week to go, he was beginning to feel quite nervous. He checked his emails once more. They had asked people to confirm if they were able to attend the preview evening but the numbers were looking pretty small and there hadn't been any new bookings since he had last checked ten minutes before.

'What's the frown for?' asked his grandad, suddenly materialising next to the front desk.

Ben grimaced. 'We've not had many replies yet for the preview evening. That's too slow a start, isn't it? Considering it's supposed to be our grand opening and only a week away.'

Walter shook his head. 'Patience, lad,' he said softly. 'They'll come. Just because they haven't replied doesn't mean they won't show up. Folks always leave these kinds of things to the last minute.'

'You're not concerned?' asked Ben.

'No,' replied Walter. 'You know why? Because you and Lily have thought of everything and I believe in you.'

Ben was surprised but comforted as his grandad placed a hand on his shoulder briefly before he walked away.

Buoyed up, at least temporarily, by Walter's words, Ben looked down at the long list of things to do for the preview evening that Lily had typed up and placed in front of him.

The most pressing concern was food. Without a full-time chef, and with Hannah absolutely refusing to get involved apart from serving the food despite their best efforts, what to feed the hopefully high numbers of locals coming to the preview evening was of utmost importance.

He decided to video call Jake to ask for help.

'Do you know of any decent chefs in the area?' he asked, once they had exchanged brief pleasantries.

'Only me when I'm visiting,' drawled Jake. 'What's going on?'

'We've decided to hold a preview evening to generate a bit of publicity locally,' Ben told him.

'Sounds like a good idea,' replied Jake, yawning. 'Sorry. Not you. Late night.'

'Anyone I know?' asked Ben.

Jake broke into a grin. 'No. Anyway, I thought you were already spoken for.'

Ben glanced around to check that the office door was definitely closed before returning to look at the screen. 'Not sure about that,' he said.

'She kissed you, didn't she?' said Jake, rolling his eyes. 'Perhaps you should take that as a sign that she does actually like you.'

'I guess,' said Ben. Although it had only been a brief peck on the lips during a moment of happiness. There had been no passion or desire behind Lily's gesture.

Despite that, he still couldn't get it out of his head and he had been kissed many times. But he had to forget about it for now, he reminded himself. There was lots to do.

'The great Ben Jackson lacking confidence?' carried on Jake. 'Wonders will never cease. Now, talk to me about the food situation.'

'It's in a week's time and I have no idea what we should serve,' said Ben. 'People will be coming through at various times to view everything so it's not like we can serve a sit-down meal.' He dragged his hand through his hair. 'And yes, I appreciate we've left it awfully late before you berate me about that.'

Jake frowned. 'You'll be lucky to get anyone decent at the moment, being so close to Christmas,' he said. 'Everyone I know is pretty busy. Thankfully I know just the person to help you out. Solid, reliable and startlingly handsome as well.'

Ben sat back in his chair in amazement. 'You?'

'Who else?' said Jake, with a grin.

Despite being delighted with the offer, Ben was still worried. 'It's next weekend. Can you afford the time off?' he asked. 'I don't want you to lose your job.'

'Oh, mate, I'm so bored with this restaurant that I'll be grateful to get away,' Jake told him. 'Besides, if the future of Maple Tree Lodge rests on a successful preview evening, then just try and keep me away!'

'But what about work?' asked Ben.

'I think I'm just about to come down with a very swift flu bug,' replied Jake with a wink. 'Don't worry, I'll start complaining about a sore throat tomorrow to sow the seeds of my imminent illness.'

'I seem to remember you doing the same just before your exams,' said Ben.

'Which is why I'm stuck working in a crummy restaurant like this one,' said Jake. 'Anyway, I'll be down early next week so I can get going then. OK?'

'OK.' Ben smiled gratefully at his best friend. 'Cheers. Thanks for this.'

Jake nodded. 'See you next week.'

True to his word, Jake arrived the following Tuesday and immediately began discussing the menu ideas with Ben and Lily as soon as he had arrived.

'I reckon bitesize is the way to go,' Jake told them over coffee in the kitchen. 'It'll be easier on the portions.'

But Ben frowned. 'Not sure tiny little appetisers are going to go down very well,' he said, looking at Lily for her to agree.

But she merely looked at Jake as if wanting more information.

'They won't be tiny,' he told her. 'They'll be filling and most importantly delicious. So what do you think?'

'I think I'd rather listen to the professional chef than the architect when it comes to delicious food,' she replied, with a grin.

Jake winked at her before turning to Ben with a mock glare. 'As always, the lady is quite right. And besides, I remember that you couldn't even cook beans on toast at university so you won't mind if I go ahead and ignore your cooking suggestions.'

Ben ignored their gentle teasing. 'But we need food that's filling,' he went on.

Jake rolled his eyes. 'It will be,' he assured his friend. 'I'm talking mini beef wellingtons and burgers. Halloumi fries and falafels. Brie and cranberry bites. Smoked salmon mousse and sushi.'

'Sounds amazing,' said Lily, standing up. 'Look, I've got a delivery of all the new crockery and utensils so I'll leave you to it. But, Jake, just ignore Ben and I'm sure it'll be wonderful,' she added, shooting Ben a brilliant smile that made his insides lurch before walking out of the office.

'I'm beginning to really warm to her,' said Jake, watching her leave the room. 'Amazing pair of legs as well.'

'Don't get too warm,' warned Ben, with a scowl.

Jake burst into laughter. 'Oh, you have got it bad! Rest assured, with my delicious food and maybe some of Frankie's wicked cocktails inside you as well, maybe you'll get that next kiss after all.'

Ben knew his friend was teasing but couldn't help but wonder and hoped that, as well as being a gifted chef, Jake was also good at predicting the future.

36

With Jake promising to cook up a storm, it was left to Lily and Ben to ensure that everything else was ready for the preview evening the following day.

Ben was still frantically finishing off the many odd jobs around the hotel, such as fixing light switches and hanging curtain rails. So Lily had to deal with the bulk of the party organising.

However, they were both concerned about low attendance as the number of RSVPs was still worryingly small. Walter kept telling them not to worry, that the word amongst the locals was positive, but still the doubts remained.

'Do you think we've got enough napkins?' Lily asked Ben, later that afternoon when he came into the dining room. 'Or shall I get a rush order for some more?'

He glanced at his phone once more before shoving it back in his pocket. 'Think we might have too many, to be honest,' he replied with a grimace.

Lily was aghast at his worried expression. 'They'll come, won't they?' she asked.

After all their hard work, it would be awful if the start of reopening the hotel was a disaster.

'Of course they will,' he told her, avoiding eye contact.

But neither of them believed his words.

'The trouble is, if they know the hotel, it's not like it's anything new,' said Ben. 'We need something else to draw them in. Something bigger. I just don't know what.'

'Surely a complete makeover is new enough,' said Lily, trying to think positively. 'Come on, let's get some fresh air. I haven't been outside all day. That always makes me feel better.'

It was true, despite having always lived in an urban environment, she really did feel healthier and happier out in the countryside, she was beginning to realise.

They wandered outside and stopped for a minute to breathe in the crisp air before wandering along to the sandy beach. It was colder now, and with only a month until Christmas, there was already a sense that the forest and the creatures that lived within its canopy were hunkering down for the long winter ahead.

Lily looked out across the lake, the bright blue of the wintry sky reflected in its water. She took a deeper breath of fresh air.

'The first time I came here, I thought it was in the middle of nowhere,' she said.

Ben laughed. 'It *is* in the middle of nowhere!' he reminded her.

She smiled at him and shook her head. 'You didn't let me finish. But the fact that it is so peaceful here has allowed me to breathe for the first time in a long time. To think. To revive. Even restore myself.'

She stopped, feeling a little embarrassed about revealing her innermost feelings to him, something that still didn't come naturally to her.

But he was looking at her intently. 'You know that motto that you wanted us to find? For the hotel? I think you've just come up with it,' he told her. 'Maple Tree Lodge. Rest. Revive. Restore.'

'Oh, Ben! That's great!' said Lily, nodding enthusiastically.

'I'll stick it on the website straight away.' His smile faded. 'Let's just hope everyone else agrees, if they actually bother to come here.'

She could read the concern on his face and was tempted to step forward to give him a reassuring hug. His pain was her pain at this point. They both loved the hotel so much and wanted it to be a success, so that the family future was secure.

But before she could say anything else, Walter appeared next to them, holding a wicker basket.

'What's that for?' asked Ben.

'Thought we could use a few about the place at the preview evening,' said Walter, with a shrug. 'Don't ask me what for. I just like making them.'

Suddenly Lily had an idea. 'I know,' she said. 'Walter, if you have some spare, we could place some candles in them and have them lit on the lake. It'll look very pretty.' She glanced at Ben. 'What do you think?'

He nodded. 'I like it.'

'So do I,' said Walter, looking pleased. 'Shows off the main feature of the place as well.'

'I thought that was the hotel!' said Ben, laughing. 'Not Dragonfly Lake!'

'Can't it be both?' Walter grinned at him before turning back to Lily. 'How many do you reckon we'll need?' he asked.

'As many as you've got,' replied Lily.

Walter's grey eyebrows shot up in surprise. 'I could probably rustle up twenty or so,' he said. 'I'll go and find them.'

But he was smiling as he headed back towards his workshop.

'He seems much happier these days,' said Lily, watching him go.

'He is.' Ben turned to look at her. 'We all are.'

'You mean that you're rested, revived and restored?' she asked him, with a soft laugh.

'Yes, that's exactly what I meant,' he replied, with a smile.

'Me too,' she told him.

She glanced back towards the hotel and knew in her heart that she was happier than she had ever been. It had only been two months but she felt transformed by her stay. Before then she had been rushing around, chasing her career. Or rather, building up everyone else's at her own expense. Had it been worth it? She knew the work experience had helped her prepare to use her skills at the hotel. But the days, nights and weekends where she had missed seeing her friends, putting her work first? No. She now knew that it was a sacrifice that hadn't been worth it.

There were more important things than work now in her life. Such as her friends. And Ben too, she thought turning to look back at him.

She found him watching her with his dark eyes.

'Are you?' he asked in a husky tone. 'Happy, I mean.'

She found that she couldn't look away from him. 'Yes,' she told him. 'Very much so.'

They both took a step forward at the same time so that their bodies were almost touching. She felt a little breathless as she stared up at him, their heads beginning to lean towards each other.

'There you are!' shouted a voice nearby.

Lily leapt back at the same time as Ben did, turning around to find Ella striding towards her.

'I've been looking everywhere for you,' she said, coming

across to give Lily a big hug. 'Never fear, your super social media whizz kid is here!' She shot Ben a grin.

'Glad to hear it,' he told her.

'Thought you'd both be rushing around inside getting ready for the big reveal tomorrow night,' carried on Ella.

'We just needed a breath of fresh air,' Lily told her. 'It's been so hectic.'

'Brrr. It's freezing out here,' said Ella, shivering in her long white coat. 'I must remember to start dressing for the country and not for the city.'

'Come on, I'll take you back inside,' said Lily.

As she linked arms with her friend and began to walk back to the hotel, Lily glanced back at Ben, who had turned to stare out across the lake, deep in thought.

She had thought for a moment that they had been about to kiss. Maybe she just imagined it, she told herself. Except she found herself wondering what might have happened had they not been interrupted. And she realised in that moment that she very much wanted to kiss Ben and was hoping that he felt the same way.

37

On the day of the preview evening, Lily lay in bed for a while, mentally running through everything on her checklist.

The hotel itself was ready for its grand unveiling to any locals that might yet decide to show up that night. She and Ben were still concerned about the lack of replies as to who was coming but the show had to go on, they had decided. If only for the family's sake.

Everyone had contributed to the evening and it felt very much like a family affair. Faye had designed some lovely flower arrangements that had been placed around the ground floor. After some persuading by everyone, Hannah was going to make some delicious cakes that would serve as desserts. Walter had made good on his promise to ensure that there were twenty or so floating wicker baskets with candles which would be cast onto the lake later that evening at sunset. Frankie had stocked the bar full of every conceivable drink. Even Dotty had shown an unexpected gift for calligraphy as she had drawn and painted the signs and menus to be placed around where needed. That just left the final checks to be done.

Lily leapt out of bed, threw on her jeans and sweater and headed downstairs.

The noise coming out of the kitchen sounded very lively, thanks to the addition of their friends who had come to support them.

She was about to join them when she heard movement in the snug and went to investigate.

Heading through the lounge, she reached out to plump up a few of the cushions as she went but she was so pleased with how it looked.

She went through the doorway into the snug and she thought that no matter how many times she went into that particular room, she would be thrilled by the difference.

It was a warm-feeling room, airy but cosy, thanks to the dark blue walls behind the bar. That was already lit with fairy lights, giving it a magical air. The snooker table was laid out ready for its first game and the whole room looked wonderful.

'Morning,' said Frankie from behind the bar. 'Couldn't sleep for nerves so I had to come in and triple check everything.'

'I know the feeling,' said Lily, slipping onto one of the leather stools in front of the bar. 'Do you think you're all set?'

'I reckon so,' replied Frankie, with a nod.

Lily cleared her throat, feeling a little nervous. 'About the strength of the cocktails later,' she began.

But Frankie held up a hand. 'Ben's already had a word. Quite a few. Far too many, in actual fact.'

'Oh.'

Frankie shrugged her shoulders. 'I'll get over it. I just need to be a drama queen for a bit. Look, I know some of the ones I've been making for the family have been a bit strong.'

'A bit?' murmured Lily.

Frankie grinned. 'Yeah, but it was fun, wasn't it?' She laughed.

'But listen, I get that this is a business so of course I'm not going to make them strong and use up all our lovely alcohol.'

'OK,' said Lily slowly.

'Look, if you don't believe me, here's the cocktail menu for tonight.'

Frankie held out a card onto which Lily could see Dotty's beautiful calligraphy had written about six different cocktails.

Lily took the card and skimmed the words. 'Half of these are non-alcoholic,' she said, in surprise.

Frankie folded her arms in front of her in a defensive manner. 'Yeah, well, sometimes I drink water, you know. Just to surprise my liver and keep it on its toes, obviously.'

'Obviously,' repeated Lily.

'And besides, quite a few of the locals will be driving and not everyone wants alcohol, the mad fools.' Frankie smiled at Lily before it faded into concern. 'You think it's going to be a success tonight?'

Lily held up her crossed fingers. 'Let's hope so.'

Frankie nodded. 'Too early for a drink, I suppose?' she said, with a grin. 'Just to settle the nerves, that is!'

'Think I'll stick to coffee just for now,' said Lily, giving her a wink.

She left Frankie in the snug to join the throng in the kitchen.

Jake had been staying with them for a few nights to organise the buffet whereas Alex, Beth and Ella had only arrived the evening before. It had been Ella's first time meeting Jake and suffice to say they hadn't exactly hit it off.

His smooth playboy charm had instantly rubbed Ella's cool control up the wrong way and when Lily joined them in the kitchen they appeared to be carrying on from the previous evening's bickering.

'I'm not arguing with you, Jake,' Ella was saying with her

hands on her hips in front of the breakfast bar. 'I'm merely explaining why I'm right and you're wrong.'

'Good morning,' said Lily in a bright tone of voice. 'How is everyone?'

'Loud,' muttered Alex as he poured himself a coffee. He held out a mug for Lily and offered her a drink as well.

'Yes, please,' she replied.

'Listen, it would take too long for me to explain to your dim little brain about how influencers work,' carried on Ella to Jake.

'The translation being that you have no idea how they work,' said Jake, before looking down at the tomatoes he had been chopping. 'All I know is that they seem lacking in substance.'

'Something you would know all about,' Ella told him in a triumphant tone before walking over to the table.

Lily joined her and the rest of the family who were all chatting excitedly about the evening ahead. Only Ben seemed quiet and she looked at him with raised eyebrows. He merely gave her a shrug and held up two crossed fingers. She nodded, feeling his nerves across the table.

After a quick breakfast, Lily headed into the dining room to start preparing the tables, helped by Hannah, Beth and Ella.

'What was all that about with Jake?' asked Lily.

Ella rolled her eyes. 'He overheard me saying that I was considering becoming a social influencer and it all went downhill from there.'

'You're serious then?' asked Hannah.

Ella nodded. 'I think I've had enough of working for other people. Anyway, I think I'd be really good at it.'

'Of course you would,' said Beth, ever positive. 'I think it's an amazing idea.'

Ella broke into a smile. 'Well, I'll need my besties' support when I get started, so thanks.'

'We'll be there cheering you on every step of the way,' promised Lily.

At that moment Ben passed by the doorway and Lily stopped to watch him briefly before turning her attention back to folding napkins.

However, Ella had spotted her looking.

'Hey,' she said. 'By the way, did I interrupt something last night when I found you and Ben by the shore?'

Lily instantly shook her head. 'No. It was nothing.'

'Nothing, huh?' Ella raised her eyebrows. 'Nothing was making you two stand awfully close to each other.'

Hannah sucked in a breath. 'Wow! Is something going on between you and my brother?'

'No!' began Lily before hesitating. She was still not comfortable with opening up with them but they were her best friends and she had promised that she would be more honest with them. So she forced herself to carry on. 'Well, maybe a little something. I don't know.'

'Aha!' said Ella, looking triumphant.

'This is so exciting,' said Hannah. 'My future sister-in-law!'

'It's so romantic,' said Beth with a sigh.

Lily rolled her eyes. 'I think you're all getting slightly ahead of the current situation. Nothing has happened yet.'

'So you haven't kissed?' asked Hannah.

Lily shook her head.

'But you want to, right?' asked Beth.

Lily hesitated before finally closing her eyes and nodding. It was the truth. She couldn't deny it to herself any longer.

'But please don't say anything,' she urged her friends. 'I mean, we're getting along really well, me and Ben. I just don't want to ruin whatever it is that we have.'

'Or what you might have in the future,' said Beth, still looking starry-eyed.

'Right,' said Ella in a firm tone. 'So no blabbing,' she added, looking at Hannah and Beth. 'Promise?'

'Promise,' they chorused in return.

Lily gulped, still blushing and feeling embarrassed about opening up about her tentative feelings for Ben.

She waited for the inevitable regret and yet, to her surprise, it didn't come. Instead, she felt a lightening of the burden that she had been carrying around for a while. Absolutely no regrets. Just the support and love that only true friends could provide.

And she found herself smiling and giggling with her best friends as they carried on working.

38

Ben tugged at his tie, which he had only just knotted over his shirt.

'Damn thing's strangling me,' he muttered, pulling at it as he checked his appearance in the large mirror in the entrance hall.

'Leave it alone,' said Hannah, reaching up to pat it back into place. 'I'll loosen it a little but we've all got to look smart this evening.'

He had to admit that even his sister had made an effort that evening, teaming high heels and black trousers with a silky blue top.

'Don't know why we have to be trussed up like this,' he moaned. 'I mean, these are local villagers. I went to school with some of them.'

'Not everyone will be,' she reminded him. 'Ella's put the word out and you've got local travel bloggers and influencers coming here as well, thanks to her. These professionals could make a real difference to our success.'

'Humph.' He looked at his sister. 'Since when did you get so wise all of a sudden?'

'I always was,' she told him, laughing. 'Now leave that tie alone.'

'Nobody's getting married tonight, are they?' he grumbled.

Hannah glanced over his shoulder and smiled. 'Well, I know at least one beautiful single woman that'll be here tonight, if you're thinking about proposing.'

Ben spun around to follow her gaze and found himself gulping. Lily was coming down the stairs. But it wasn't the same Lily who had headed up there only half an hour ago, dressed in jeans and jumper.

Now she was transformed and he couldn't stop himself staring.

She was wearing a grey jumper dress. It was classic and understated but there was nothing simple about the way it showed off her long legs as it only reached above her knees, nor the long suede boots which covered the bottom half of her legs. Her long red hair hung about her shoulders in soft waves and he had to mentally fix his arms to his sides to stop himself reaching out to stroke it as she walked up to them.

'I love that top,' she said to Hannah before turning to look Ben up and down. 'Nice suit,' she added.

'Uh-huh,' he managed to croak out.

Lily raised her eyebrows at him in surprise.

'He's a bag of nerves,' said Hannah quickly. 'About this evening.'

And Ben had never been more grateful for his sister than in that moment.

'You look lovely,' carried on Hannah.

'You think?' Lily glanced down at herself. 'It's a bit close fitting but all those walks around the lake mean that hopefully all your amazing cakes haven't done too much damage.'

Ben stared at her curves and found his brain almost disconnecting. Thankfully Lily didn't appear to notice.

'So is everyone ready?' asked Lily, glancing around.

'We're all set,' replied Hannah.

'Good job there's so many of us tonight,' said Lily.

Finally Ben's brain clicked back into place. 'At this point we might have more staff than guests,' he managed to say.

Lily looked at him, her dark emerald eyes smiling softly at him. 'It'll be fine,' she told him.

Ben blinked at her and, finding himself at a total loss for words, spun around to walk away before he did something crazy like take her into his arms and kiss her.

He had nearly done so the previous evening before Ella had interrupted them by the shore. He shook his head, trying to clear his thoughts. His crush on Lily aside, he had far too much to worry about that evening and tried to focus on his to-do list rather than Lily's curves.

He went into the lounge, checking that the fire was still roaring, that all the fairy lights were on and that the candles were lit as well. Outside, he could already see his grandad's floating wicker baskets bobbing on the water nearby, lighting up the lake in pretty blues, greens and pinks.

'We're all set, I reckon,' said Alex, coming out of the snug to smile at him. He was also smartened up in a dark shirt and tie which showed off his wide shoulders. 'Just bring on the guests.'

'If they come,' said Ben, his fears still bubbling near the surface.

Jake strode into the lounge, his chef's apron still firmly in place. 'Just give me the nod and I'll start bringing out the trays to tempt our many visitors.'

Ben groaned. This had been a crazy idea. What if nobody

came? What if it were a total failure and after all their hard work, the hotel was still doomed?

'What's his problem?' asked Jake, nodding at Ben.

'He thinks nobody's going to turn up,' Alex told him.

Jake laughed. 'Well, I've just seen three cars pull up in the car park so somebody's come, in any case.'

Ben gave a start. 'You did?'

He rushed out of the lounge and into the reception, just in time to watch Lily step forward to greet their first guests. When another group of people followed almost immediately behind, Ben went to meet them. At least this time he recognised the faces.

'Welcome to Maple Tree Lodge,' he said, with a warm smile.

He instantly relaxed. He knew the Connolly family already as he had gone to school with the two brothers standing in front of him. 'Ryan, Ethan, glad you could come,' he said, shaking their hands.

'Nice to see you, mate,' said Ryan, stepping forward. 'Thought I'd check out our competition.'

Ben had heard that there were now a couple of Airbnb railway carriages that Ryan and his fiancée Katy had renovated to hire out.

'Of course we were going to come,' added Ethan, Ryan's brother, before shaking his hand. 'We wanted to see what you've done with the old place.'

'Well, we took inspiration from what you've done with the Cranfield,' Ben told him with a grin.

After Ryan and Katy had updated the nearby railway station into a successful coffee shop and restaurant, Ethan had completed the family success story with overhauling the steam engine, making Cranfield a now much-visited local attraction.

'Then I know how much hard work and money this has taken,' said Ryan, looking around. 'This looks great.'

'Thanks,' said Ben. 'Look, come in and I'll show you around.'

But as he said that, he glanced over their shoulder and saw Dodgy Del.

'Del?' he said, surprised to see him.

'Our cousin tagged along,' drawled Ethan, rolling his eyes. 'Hope you don't mind but we can't seem to shake him off.'

'No need to be so mean after all I've done for you all,' said Del, looking almost insulted.

'Done?' said Ryan, laughing. 'You've nearly destroyed most of our hard work a number of times!'

'You too?' asked Ben, with a sigh. 'I thought it was just us.'

'No, Del's catastrophes are not just limited to Cranley,' said Ethan. 'He can cause chaos wherever he goes.'

'Charming,' muttered Del, before looking at Ben. 'And you owe me, mate.'

'How on earth do I owe you after all the electricity you've been stealing for your bloomin' taxi service?' asked Ben.

'Because I've put the word out for you all,' he said, glancing over his shoulder. 'Pulled in a few favours and, well, see the results for yourself.'

Ben peered over Del's shoulder and gasped in shock. There was a long stream of cars weaving their way through the woods towards the car park which was already over half-full. Masses of people were climbing out of their cars, all intent on seeing the hotel's renovation.

Ben turned to Del in awe.

'Looks like you owe me a nice big drink after all those insults,' said Del, with a wide grin. 'I'll be at the bar if anyone needs me.'

39

Lily found that the preview evening for the hotel rushed past in a blur.

She had only seen Ben briefly since the beginning of the night, looking particularly handsome in his suit and tie. He had been standing in the reception when she came down the stairs, watching her. For a brief moment he smiled at her and the world had closed in so it had felt as if it were just them. Then he was swallowed up by the arriving crowd and had vanished out of sight.

The crowd had grown bigger by the hour as more and more local people had arrived, to their relief. Wherever she went, there was a crush of people.

The lounge was popular as everyone took advantage of the roaring fires. They also braved the cold night air to stand on the veranda, taking in the floating lights and oohing and aahing at the view across the lake, lit from above by the full moon. The night was clear and crisp so the roaring fires in both the lounge and the snug made it feel cosy and warm back inside.

Everyone loved the relaxed vibe of the snug where Frankie's

delicious and thankfully not too strong cocktails went down a treat, alongside several spirited games of snooker and darts.

In the dining room, people helped themselves to the enormous amount of food that Jake had conjured up. They asked for the chef and Jake generously pointed them in the direction of Faye, giving them the breakfast menus that she would be serving to all the hotel guests. Hannah's cakes too were being wolfed down with yet more praise and Lily was pleased to see her smiling and soaking up the acclaim, for once.

Having found out from Hannah that Dodgy Del had managed to bring in most of the local villagers, Lily had been thrilled that so many people were sounding so positive about the hotel.

'It's charming,' they told her.

'Amazing.'

'So pretty.'

'When do you open?' she had heard someone ask.

'We're open as of now,' replied Walter, in his usual bombastic manner.

Lily grimaced and hoped Ben wasn't listening as they'd actually agreed that they wouldn't open the hotel officially until the following week. But, in the end, she had to agree with Walter. Why not open the hotel up now? The beds were made, everything was ready. She was just keeping everything crossed that the guests followed the villagers in their enthusiasm and numbers.

She had hardly seen Ben all night, such was the large number of visitors which had suddenly appeared.

And it wasn't until he had seen the last guest out and had finally closed the front door that he joined everyone in the lounge. Lily was sitting on the sofa, barely able to move from exhaustion. But even then she couldn't stop her eyes from straying to him when he came into the room. The man sure could fill out a suit very nicely, she thought.

'Well, that's that,' said Ben, sinking down next to Lily on the sofa.

'That was an unqualified success,' said Dotty from the opposite sofa.

'It really was,' agreed Lily.

'Never a doubt in my mind,' said Walter from his armchair. He and Ben exchanged a nod and a smile. 'And, Alex, you did a marvellous job highlighting all the health benefits of the place.'

'It was my pleasure,' Alex told him. 'I merely told them how pure the water is here to swim in.'

'And, Walter, everyone wants to know about your floating candle holders,' said Beth, taking off her high heels and rubbing her sore feet.

Walter nodded and yawned. 'I know what I'm going to be doing for the next few weeks then,' he said.

But Lily could see how pleased he was with the way the evening had gone.

'Those travel bloggers were all talking us up,' added Beth, giving Ella a nudge with her elbow. 'You really got the word out to the right people.'

'Thankfully I'm not as dumb as Jake looks,' said Ella in an imperious tone.

Jake merely laughed off the insult.

'Good job he cooks brilliantly then,' said Ben, with a grin.

'Everyone said that the food was delicious,' added Faye.

'I'll never top your breakfasts,' replied Jake, as ever refusing any praise. 'Nor Hannah's cakes.'

Hannah blushed before yawning as she leant against Alex's shoulder. She had spent the evening clearing the tables of plates and dashing back and forth and was looking exhausted. Lily secretly thought that Alex seemed pleased that she was using him for support.

'Frankie, your cocktails were delicious,' said Hannah, before yawning once more.

'Like I've always said,' Frankie told her. 'If you combine wine and dinner, you get winner.'

Everyone laughed.

Jake joined in with another of Hannah's yawns. 'Man, I'm shattered,' he declared.

'Well, I can't keep my eyes open either,' said Faye, standing up. 'We'll tidy up tomorrow. It's definitely time for bed.'

'I agree,' said Walter.

In fact, everyone stood up apart from Lily and Ben.

'We'll close up down here,' said Ben.

Hannah, Beth and Ella gave Lily a knowing smile and she could feel her cheeks beginning to grow pink.

'Goodnight,' they all said to each other and then it was just Lily and Ben alone in the lounge.

Someone, she suspected Hannah, had switched off the overhead lights as they left and now it was just them in the soft light of the fire, the candles which had begun to burn low and the fairy lights strung around the oak beams across the ceiling.

'How are you?' he asked, with a smile. 'I think I'm still in shock.'

Lily laughed softly. 'Actually, I'm half exhausted and the other half is totally buzzing about what a success it was. Did you get to talk to that hotel reviewer? The one with the red jacket that Ella managed to contact?'

Ben nodded. 'Briefly. What about you?'

'I showed her the bedrooms and she promised to come back for a proper stay very soon,' Lily told him. 'She seemed to have a lot of followers on Instagram.'

'That's great,' he said, leaning back on the sofa and closing his eyes. 'What a relief it went well.'

'Absolutely,' she murmured.

She allowed herself the luxury of looking at him, studying the dark eyelashes and handsome face as it relaxed.

She didn't know how long she looked at him until he suddenly opened his eyes and caught her staring at him.

'Well, we'd better start shutting everything down,' she began to say.

But he caught her hand and stopped her from getting up from the sofa. 'You look lovely tonight,' he said, reaching out his other hand towards her.

She found she was holding her breath as he held a long lock of hair in his fingertips.

'Thank you,' she managed to murmur in reply.

'I feel like we should somehow celebrate our success,' he said, sitting up so that they were much closer now.

Her pulse was racing as his hand moved from the lock of hair around to the back of her neck.

'We should,' she managed to say.

But she could barely think of anything other than the feeling of the touch on her skin as he stroked her neck.

'Perhaps we should have had one of Frankie's cocktails,' he said, leaning closer.

She shook her head. 'Too potent,' she whispered, unable to stop herself from leaning towards him.

'There's something to be said for intoxication though,' he murmured, his face within inches of hers now.

'There is,' she agreed.

And just when she couldn't bear it any longer and was about to pull him to her, he reached for her instead.

Their lips met instantly and she was lost. Powerless to stop herself from kissing him back as she wrapped her hands around his shoulders and pulled him even closer.

It began as a soft, gentle kiss. Then it grew deeper as her senses reeled with the touch of his lips and the blessed feeling of being in his arms at last. It was the kind of kiss that she had never had before. It was a kiss that she never wanted to end.

The kiss was all-encompassing, stronger and more passionate than any that they had shared so far. She didn't know how long she stayed in his arms until finally he drew back a little.

'I've waited a long time to do that,' he told her.

They stared at each other for a moment, both a little breathless and wide-eyed, trying to comprehend what had just happened.

'Me too,' she replied. She couldn't stop herself from being honest with him. She trusted him.

He leaned forward as if to kiss her once more but she put a hand on his chest to stop him.

'Perhaps we should say goodnight,' she found herself saying. 'It's been a long day.'

Despite the glorious kiss and how right it had felt in his arms, she couldn't stop her self-defence mechanism from kicking in.

He studied her for a moment. 'What's wrong?' he asked, still holding her in his arms.

'Nothing,' she told him. 'I'm sorry. I shouldn't have kissed you.'

'It didn't feel like you had any regrets,' he replied, pulling back from her. 'And I certainly haven't got any.'

She gulped. 'It's just that, well, I'm no good at this kind of thing.'

He raised his eyebrows. 'Kissing? I have to disagree with you. That was incredible.'

She was grateful for his gentle humour but felt that she had to press on. To tell him why this couldn't continue.

'It's just that I've managed to get this far on my own,' she told him. 'It's hard for me to let anyone get close.'

'You let the girls get close,' he reminded her, reaching out to take a lock of her red hair in his fingers once more.

'Yes and it took me fourteen years to start to open up and be honest with them,' she said. Her laugh was only half-hearted and she sighed heavily. How could she tell him that her fear of trusting someone with her whole heart would scupper any chance of a relationship that they might have?

Ben let go of her hair and looked at her for a moment. 'Come on,' he finally said. 'We're both shattered. But, for the record, this subject isn't closed.'

He studied her for a moment, his brown eyes almost black in the firelight. Then he got up from the sofa and she did the same.

It didn't take long to close down everything and soon she was lying in bed, staring up at the ceiling. But despite being exhausted, she couldn't get to sleep, yearning for more of his kisses despite the warning voice in her head.

40

'What a great evening,' declared Dotty over breakfast the following morning.

'Yes,' said Ben, nodding. 'It certainly was.'

He glanced at Lily, who was sitting on the opposite side of the table and smiled as her cheeks grew pink. She was clearly remembering their kiss and he had spent most of a sleepless night thinking of nothing else as well.

He knew that she had felt the connection between them as well. He knew from the way she had kissed him back, passionately. And yet he knew her so well these days that he also understood why she was holding back from him. Her fear of trusting that she had tried to explain to him.

He respected her wishes, of course. And yet he hadn't been able to stop thinking about the kiss all night, almost driven mad with the thought of her soft lips against hers.

'Everyone we knew came,' said Walter, who was looking very relaxed and basking in the success of the evening.

'And they brought along people we didn't know, thanks to

Del,' added Frankie. 'Well, he probably owed us a favour or two after everything.'

'Have you seen this?' piped up Ella, who had been staring at her phone. 'That travel blogger has posted her review already.'

She held out her phone and Ben took a nervous gulp before forcing himself to read aloud from the screen.

'Deep in the heart of the forest, historic Maple Tree Lodge makes for an idyllic lakeside escape. It has cosy bedrooms, wood-burning fireplaces and a luxurious and yet relaxing feel. The main lounge has comfortable sofas from which you'll not want to move away from the view. But if you can muster up the energy, a walk around the lake will pay dividends. The air is fresh, the walk sublime and the view will soothe away any stresses. Be warned – there's no mobile signal away from the wi-fi in the hotel so prepare for a much-needed digital detox.

'Once back in the hotel, make time to have a delicious cocktail in the snug, where the bar shimmers among the many fairy lights and there's even time for a game of snooker, if you can tear yourself away from the amazing view, that is. Book a stay at Maple Tree Lodge and you'll come away relaxed, revived and restored. And probably wanting to book a second stay as well.'

There was a short silence before everyone started talking and laughing at once.

'This is tremendous,' said Ben, feeling instantly buoyed up. He couldn't stop himself from looking across at Lily. 'What a review!'

'That's amazing!' she said, beaming from ear to ear. 'Isn't it great? We need to upload it to the website with some quotes ASAP.'

'I agree,' he replied, checking his own phone. 'And I've just had even better news. We've got a couple of bookings for next weekend! We're off and running!'

A huge cheer went up around the table and everyone was in high spirits.

'Well, I'm glad to be leaving you all with everything going so well,' announced Alex, standing up. 'But I've got to get back home as I've got a plane to catch later.'

'Where are you off to this time?' asked Faye.

'Australia,' Alex told her. 'A bit of climate training before the Commonwealth Games.' He gave a nervous grimace.

'You'll be fine,' said Faye, stepping forward to give him a hug.

'Wish I was going with you instead,' Jake told him, looking gloomy that he had to return to his normal restaurant job and leave the family once more.

With Beth and Ella leaving as well to get back to their day jobs, the hotel felt a little quieter despite everyone being in high spirits that day.

Walter was whistling to himself as he brought in some more logs for the fires.

Hannah was also looking pleased with herself, buoyed up by the positive feedback from so many visitors who had complimented her on her cakes.

But best of all was their grandmother. Dotty was fizzing with energy as she buzzed around the hotel.

'What's got into you today?' asked Frankie over dinner that evening. 'Have you been helping yourself to my bar?'

Dotty laughed and shook her head. 'Not yet! I don't know what I feel today. I saw so many friends last night who I haven't seen in a long time.' Her smile faded a little as she reached out to squeeze Faye's hand. 'And we all know why I hid myself away for so long, grieving. I mean, I loved Tony. We all did. And we always will. But I have to carry on, for his sake and for mine, to be honest.'

'He would have wanted all of us to do that,' murmured Faye, squeezing her mother-in-law's hand.

'Well, last night was certainly a great first step,' said Ben.

'It was,' replied his grandmother. 'The only thing missing was some music.'

'Oh, yes, that's what I thought,' said Lily, nodding.

'I love to dance,' said Dotty in a dreamy voice. 'It's been too long.' She suddenly gave a start and looked down at her husband at the other end of the table. 'Walter,' she said. 'Are you thinking what I'm thinking?'

He broke into a wide smile. 'Well, why not?' he replied.

Ben looked between his grandparents, somewhat bemused. 'Could someone enlighten the rest of us who don't have telepathic communication?' he asked.

'The Dragonfly Dance,' announced Walter, with a wink.

'The what?' asked Ben, nonplussed.

'Oh, I remember!' said Hannah, her eyes lighting up. 'It was some kind of party, wasn't it?'

Dotty nodded. 'We used to have a dance every year on Valentine's Day,' she replied.

'When did you last hold one?' asked Lily.

Walter blew out a sigh as he thought. 'Probably twenty years ago,' he said.

'Longer than that,' Faye told him. 'The kids were only little when we had the last one, I think.'

'I just remember peeking through the bannisters and seeing everyone all dressed up,' said Hannah, in a dreamy voice.

'So it's a party?' asked Lily.

'It's a celebration,' Walter told her.

'Of what?' asked Ben, still unable to recall any kind of party. 'And why did I think it happened at Christmas time?'

'That was a different party,' said Dotty, waving her hand as if it were unimportant. 'This is better. This is unique. Dragonflies symbolise new beginnings, rejuvenation, if you will.'

'It's said that they symbolise a stripping away of negativity, enabling us to achieve all our hopes and dreams,' added Walter.

'Well, if that's not an excuse for a party then I don't know what is!' said Lily, laughing.

'They remind us that anything is possible,' said Dotty, with a soft smile.

Even saving a hotel? Ben wondered whether it was true. He hoped the dance would make all of their hopes and dreams come true, even the ones only he dreamt about, he thought as he looked once more at Lily.

He wondered whether they could ever be anything but just friends, despite him wanting so much more.

41

The opening weekend for the hotel came around and after lunch everyone was to be found pacing nervously up and down the reception area, waiting for the arrival of their first guests.

Once Lily had bumped into Frankie for the third time, she found her path blocked.

'Right,' said Frankie, to the family. 'Either we work out some kind of one-way system or most of you are going to have to leave.'

'Why can't *you* leave?' asked Hannah, with a grin.

'Because I'm the glue that binds this madness together,' said Frankie.

'Look,' said Lily. 'I'm the receptionist so I can't leave.'

'Yes, but everyone else can,' said Ben. 'It'll look ridiculous if we're all gathered in here when our first guests arrive.'

'Then we'd better scarper because look out,' muttered Frankie, nodding at the glass by the front door.

Lily could see a car pulling up and a young couple got out, looking across the lake and admiring the view.

'Here we go,' said Ben, looking nervous.

'Maple Tree Lodge is open for business,' said Lily in an overly bright tone of voice that she knew came from nerves.

Pretty soon, they were welcoming their first guests. About ten people were booked in for the weekend. Despite the lack of a chef, everyone seemed unconcerned that dinner wasn't provided and that they could either receive takeaway pizzas from nearby Cranfield or go out to the many local restaurants.

Lily had made sure that there were snacks and nibbles in the bar though, just in case anyone was still hungry. There was also Hannah's delicious cake to share, displayed under a glass dome in the lounge. It was an apple and cinnamon cake, the apples cut and spread out like rose petals around the cake.

'It's amazing. You've such a talent,' Lily had told her when she saw it.

As always, Hannah brushed off any praise almost immediately. But Lily could tell that she was pleased with the feedback. Slowly she was beginning to come out of her shell and relish baking for people other than the family. In fact, she had also made spiced biscuits shaped like leaves. They were buttery with just a hint of nutmeg and mixed spice to make them autumnal.

Then there was the huge choice of breakfasts that Faye served up each morning over the weekend. All tastes and preferences were catered for, from healthy options to a fully cooked breakfast.

'All the ingredients come from local farms,' Faye told one couple. 'We like to help out everyone in the local area.'

All the guests seemed extremely happy with their stay. Lily helped Frankie with the housekeeping and cleaning of the rooms and main area, whilst Ben ensured that the fires were permanently lit as the temperature outside began to cool down.

The forest looked spectacular that weekend, as if winter had been waiting for the first guests before bursting into a frosty winter wonderland. Everything outside sparkled under the deep blue sky.

Most guests took a walk around the lake before settling down on the comfortable sofas to relax. Lily's idea for a help-yourself trolley in the corner, with a coffee and tea machine that also served hot chocolate, and some of Hannah's delicious bakes, had worked out really well.

When Tuesday morning came, Lily showed Ben the guest book. All the guests had left glowing praise for the hotel and had told them that they were going to recommend the hotel to all their friends.

'It looks as if we might have a success on our hands,' said Lily, with a gleeful smile.

Ben's face, though, didn't look quite as certain.

He had told her that the hotel needed to be full for each weekend for them to meet their financial goals. But at least it had been a good start to their opening weekend.

'And now we've got Christmas to look forward to,' said Dotty later. 'My favourite time of the year.'

Lily smiled at her in return but she had to admit that it had always been quite a lonely time for her. In the past, sometimes she had flown out to join her parents wherever they were in the world at that time and celebrate Christmas together. But the rest of the time, she had spent Christmas alone. With each of her friends with their families, she hadn't wanted to invade their special time together so had always made an excuse.

But this year, she wouldn't be alone. She would be with the Jackson family at the hotel and secretly she couldn't wait to celebrate with them.

Her parents, though, were still asking about her future, every time she spoke to them.

'So when are you moving on from this place?' asked her dad.

'I mean, it looks lovely from everything that you've shown us,' said her mum. 'But we're a little concerned about your current role as a hotel receptionist.'

'Well, it's a bit more than that,' Lily tried to explain. 'There's always a new season for me to decorate the place. And we're having a Christmas party as well so that will need totally new décor...'

'Yes,' interrupted her mum. 'But this isn't your chosen career. You're an interior designer, aren't you? Everything you've achieved and trained for has led you forward.'

'It just seems as if you've taken a backward step,' added her dad. 'I mean, it's nice that you're spending time with Hannah but don't you think you should be pushing yourself to actively seek out a new job?'

But the truth was that Lily didn't want a new job for a while, she realised. The truth was that she was truly happy at Maple Tree Lodge and for the first time ever, she didn't feel a great need to move on.

The Jackson family had welcomed her into their home and their hearts and it was wonderful to get closer to Hannah too.

However, she knew deep down that the main reason that she didn't want to leave was Ben.

She regretted pushing him away after their first kiss. She flip-flopped between desperately wanting him and more of his kisses and the fear that he would eventually finish the relationship anyway.

There was a chemistry between them that she couldn't deny and she knew that he felt something for her as well.

Her best friends had tried to urge her on but her trust issues kept getting in the way of speaking to him about any of this.

So she concentrated on work and tried hard not to think about Ben in that way.

It was also hard to stay settled when her parents were encouraging her to get back on her career path. She was still applying for interior design jobs and yet she wasn't checking her phone every day, desperate for news about any offers.

The truth was that she felt settled at Maple Tree Lodge. And despite all of her inner reservations, she wanted to see where her relationship with Ben might go. It felt far too important to leave before it had even begun.

Soon she would move on, she told herself. But not yet.

42

As December whirled by in a flurry of festive cheer, Lily found she was waking up each morning with a new sense of purpose. She would bound downstairs to join the family for breakfast, eager to discover what the day ahead would bring.

The bookings had begun to trickle in for the hotel and day by day they were all getting in their routine of the hotel being open to guests once more.

December also brought about the need for further decorations around the hotel. Ben had cut down a large Christmas tree which had been erected in the hallway, ably assisted by Walter and Del. It was then decorated with many fairy lights and decorations until Ben announced it would keel over if they added anything else to it.

Faye created some lovely Christmas wreaths for all the doors and windows, along with mini pots of poinsettias that had been placed in each room to bring a splash of red to every corner.

Lily strung wreaths of holly and ivy swags across the many mantelpieces, as well as hanging stockings either side of the large fireplace in the lounge.

As she wandered from room to room, she was enveloped in either the sweet smell of pine or the aroma of Hannah's delicious gingerbread cookies and cinnamon buns.

Certainly the guests continue to agree that Hannah's baking was delicious.

'It's sooo good,' said one lady, her mouth full of an iced bun.

'What's winter for if not to load up on carbs topped with sugar?' replied Frankie, with a large grin.

Frankie had created a couple of Christmas-themed cocktails which had also gone down well with the guests, as well as the family. The Holly Jolly Christmas cocktail was a particular favourite with everyone who tasted it.

But despite all the positivity around the arrival of the festive season, there was no denying that the hotel bookings since reopening were a little slow.

'It's the holidays,' said Walter over dinner the week before Christmas. 'Folks want to be with their families, not stay at a hotel.'

'I disagree,' replied Ben, with a frown. 'I mean, surely our bookings should be better than they've been.'

Walter sighed as he looked at his grandson. 'We've had lots of people stay in the three weeks since we opened,' he said. 'And every one has told us how much they love it here. Just take heart from that, son.'

Ben nodded but Lily could tell that he was still seriously worried about their finances.

It was a concern, certainly, but everyone was able to brush off their worries when the last of the guests had left and they could celebrate Christmas alone in their home.

They had an extra visitor with Jake who declared he had no desire whatsoever to stay with either of his parents that Christmas.

'Dad's new girlfriend isn't even as old as me,' he told Lily, rolling his eyes in despair. 'And Mum's new husband is an absolute bore. So I eagerly accepted the kind invitation to come here.'

'I think you invited yourself,' murmured Ben.

But everyone was happy to have Jake stay with them, especially when he announced that he would be cooking Christmas dinner to give Faye a much-needed rest.

Christmas morning brought great excitement as they all sat around the tree in the lounge to open their presents. Lily's parents had wired her money as usual. But the Jackson family presents felt more personal. Especially because most of them were homemade.

They had all been on a strict budget, given the state of their finances, so had agreed on only one present each but that had meant that they had to be a little more creative with their gifts.

Dotty was first up and delighted to find her old Nikon camera inside. 'We got it repaired,' Faye told her. 'Now that you're taking photographs again it was time to bring it out of storage.'

'It's wonderful,' said Dotty, hugging it to her chest. 'This was my first camera and my favourite. I can't wait to get outside and take some pictures later.'

Faye was equally pleased with the three-tiered ribbon holder that Ben had carved out of wood for her. Hannah had filled each tier with different colours and styles of ribbons.

'This is perfect for my flower arranging,' beamed Faye, looking a little teary. 'I absolutely love it.'

Hannah received two homemade wooden chopping boards, one for herbs and one for bread. 'Grandad and I doubled up by mistake,' said Ben, laughing.

'But we'd figure you'd use them both anyway,' added Walter.

'I shall use nothing else,' Hannah told them.

Ben had taken great care to carve Walter a wooden stool for him to sit on whilst he was busy in the workshop.

Walter's eyes were a little misty as he looked at his grandson. 'That'll come in very handy,' he said, before proudly showing Lily the skills that Ben had used to make it.

Frankie received a bar apron made out of leopard-print material and declared it, 'Sexy and perfect. Just like me!'

Lily hadn't expected anything as she knew that she wasn't family. And yet Jake had received a carved gentleman's tray to hold his watch and cufflinks, which he was chuffed to bits with.

Then Ben went behind the tree to bring out the largest wrapped present of all which he placed in front of Lily.

'For me?' she said, looking down at the present in wonder.

She carefully tore the paper aside and was stunned to find a wooden doll's house inside. Except this one was a perfect replica of the hotel.

'Ben and Grandad made it,' Hannah told her. 'We left the walls blank so that you could decorate them yourself.'

'It's perfect,' Lily stammered, feeling choked up. 'I love it.'

She stared down at the small version of the hotel. As well as all the rooms that she knew so well being in proportion, it had tiny fireplaces and even a miniature bar in the Snug, complete with fairy lights.

'You'll always have Maple Tree Lodge wherever you go,' she heard Ben tell her.

She looked up at him, her eyes filling with tears so that she could only nod and smile in response.

Christmas dinner was a cheery time. It had originally been suggested that they hold it in the dining room but everyone was far happier to eat in the kitchen at the long table. So it was a relaxed meal, complete with many helpings of food and groan-inducing jokes in the crackers.

'Jake, that dinner was delicious,' said Faye, sitting back in her chair after they had all finished.

'Definitely,' agreed Lily. 'It was incredible.' She held her stomach after eating far too much. 'But I'm not sure I'll ever be able to move again.'

'A walk around the lake will help with that,' announced Walter from the head of the table.

Most of the family groaned in response.

'I was promised that there would be no aerobic activity on this festive day,' grumbled Jake. 'It's not like Alex is here to make us all feel guilty.'

'It's a tradition,' said Dotty. 'We always go for a walk before the sun sets on Christmas day.'

'And we moan all the way around the lake as we go,' added Hannah, with a smile.

'Good,' said Frankie. 'At least that sounds like my kind of tradition.'

But in the end, the walk around the lake was a jolly affair. They all wrapped up against the biting cold wind that whistled across the water. But as the sun sank low in the sky, leaving behind a blaze of pinks and oranges in its place for a short while, everyone stopped complaining and agreed that it had been a great idea.

On the walk, Lily fell behind a little, joined by Ben.

He had been quiet that day and she had guessed the reason why.

'How are you?' she asked softly so that nobody else could hear.

'It's been a bit strange,' he replied, also keeping his voice low. 'You know, without Dad being here.'

It was their first Christmas without his dad and she was sure that everyone was quietly feeling the sorrow that day.

'I'm sure,' she said.

Before she could help herself, she slipped her gloved hand into his and gave it a squeeze.

Ben gave her a small smile and they held hands all the way back to the hotel.

He hadn't mentioned anything about the kiss since it had happened. She loved him for being patient and waiting for her to be ready. That he respected her feelings.

And yet, as they reached the oak-framed porch long after everyone else, she found herself hesitating and not wanting to go inside just yet.

Ben turned to look at her, raising his eyebrows at her in question.

'Well, it is Christmas,' she told him, pointing to the bough of mistletoe that had been hung there a few weeks before.

He smiled and drew her into his arms, bending his head towards hers.

'It's like an extra Christmas present, just for me,' he murmured before closing the gap between them.

At the touch of his lips, she surrendered to the feelings that she had been trying to bury for the past month. The yearning she had had for another kiss.

She forced herself not to run, despite her inner voice telling her to flee. So she relaxed into his arms and they kissed again before finally heading indoors.

43

In the new year, after the Christmas decorations had been taken down, Faye replaced all the red berries and holly with pristine whites and dark greens.

'This looks great, Mum,' said Ben, admiring the new floral centrepiece in the entrance hall.

'Glad you like it,' she replied. 'I was going for a fresh new look to match the new year.'

As she tied a dark green ribbon into a bow on the wreath, Ben thought how much happier she was keeping busy with her flower arranging these days.

He was also trying to stay positive after so many good things had happened to the hotel but the truth was that the bookings had died right down after Christmas and remained low.

But where he could lie to the family and pretend that all was OK, he found that he couldn't make anything up in front of Lily.

One evening, halfway through January, she sat down next to him on the sofa hugging a hot chocolate.

'Are you OK?' she asked. 'You were pretty quiet during dinner.'

He blew out a sigh and leaned against the back of the sofa. 'Just business,' he told her. 'I know that January's always a terrible time for retail. Nobody's got any money after Christmas. But we're still not even at half occupancy every weekend.'

'It'll turn around for the better, I'm sure of it,' she told him.

Ben wasn't so sure. 'I just don't know what else we can do to get people here,' he replied.

'How about a different marketing campaign?' she asked.

'We're doing pretty much everything that Ella has told us to do and I trust her judgement,' he told her. 'We've reached out to everyone that we can think of. We can't spend any more money on advertising or else we'll have no profits at all.'

'We'll think of something,' she told him.

To his surprise and pleasure, she snuggled in closer and drew him into a hug. They hadn't kissed since Christmas Day. He had talked to Hannah, who had urged him to be patient and that Lily's feelings for him were real no matter how much she held back from him. Hannah had also told him a little more about Lily's parents and her lonely upbringing and he understood her reservations about getting into any relationship.

The silence stretched out, filled only with the sound of the logs crackling in the hearth, as they held each other in their embrace. He relished the feeling of strength that he got from her as she held him close.

When she finally pulled back, Lily searched his face anxiously, making sure that he was all right.

'We're getting great reviews,' he told her.

She nodded. 'Yes, we are,' she replied. 'Everyone says that they'll recommend us to all their friends.'

'It's just, I don't know, we're missing something to get the word out there that we even exist,' he carried on.

'What about the Dragonfly Dance?' she asked, with a soft smile.

But Ben's humour had gone missing. 'Valentine's Day is almost a month away.' He shook his head. 'I don't know if we can survive until then.'

'There must be something we can do,' she told him, frowning.

'I just don't know what,' he said, as the rest of the family joined them in the lounge.

'You look tired,' said Faye, as she sat down on the sofa opposite to him and Lily.

'I'd be glad to be tired,' muttered Ben. 'That would mean that at least I'd be rushed off my feet every day.'

'I have a whole list of things that need building in my workshop if you're bored,' said Walter, sitting down on an armchair.

But he knew that his grandad understood. That everyone understood. They needed guests to stay at the hotel in order to make a profit. It was too wretched a thought that after everything they might still lose their family home.

Frankie went across to the fireplace and lit the large pillar candles along the mantelpiece.

'Candles are so cheery,' said Faye, as Frankie sat down next to her.

They all were quiet for a while, sitting and hugging their drinks as they watched the flames lick higher and higher, keeping them all warm.

'I must say, I liked those floating candles that we had on the preview evening,' said Dotty, looking at Lily. 'Show me your photo again.'

So Lily leant forward, going through her phone until she found the one to show Dotty.

'Lovely but I think our lanterns were even prettier,' said Dotty,

Coming Home to Maple Tree Lodge

handing the phone back to Lily. 'You know, we should do it again but with more of them.'

'What are you talking about?' asked Walter, looking bewildered at his wife.

'Our very own light festival,' replied Dotty. 'Like that!' She pointed at Lily's mobile phone.

Lily looked down at the picture on her mobile before looking at Ben. 'Our own light festival?' she repeated.

He looked straight back at her, nodding thoughtfully. 'Our own light festival,' he replied, his mind racing with the possibilities.

'What's going on?' asked Walter. 'Why is everyone saying the same thing over and over?'

Ben laughed. 'Sorry, Grandad, to be so vague. It's just that I think Grandma's had a brilliant idea.'

'Of course I have,' said Dotty, with a flourish. 'I always do.'

'Can we do this?' asked Hannah, looking around at everyone. 'I mean, just create our own festival?'

'Why on earth not?' said Walter. 'It's our land, after all.'

Ben looked across at Lily for reassurance. 'We could do it,' she said slowly, staring back at him. 'I mean, it's a simple idea but very effective. We could add a bit of music over some speakers.'

'It could be the USP that we've been looking for,' said Ben.

'And it doesn't hurt the wildlife,' added Walter. 'The baskets are all made from our own trees.'

'But who would it be for?' asked Faye, looking concerned. 'I mean, who's going to actually see it?'

'Anyone who's staying or visiting locally,' said Ben, his brain now buzzing with ideas. 'We could throw it open to the locals, get the word out. And it advertises the hotel at the same time.'

'Especially if they want a drink to warm themselves up with afterwards in the snug,' added Frankie.

Ben's eyes gleamed with possibilities for more profits. 'Absolutely.'

'Or a warm bed to sleep in that night,' said Lily. 'You know, people love this kind of thing, if we get it right. A show for those on Instagram.'

'Free advertising too,' said Ben, nodding. He was beginning to feel excited at the idea that this might actually work.

'I've got about forty baskets in the workshop,' said Walter.

'We'll need a few more than that, Grandad,' Ben told him.

'Then you'll have to give me a hand, lad.' Walter looked at him. 'When's the deadline?'

Ben looked at Lily.

'No time like the present,' she told him, with a shrug. 'So let's start on Saturday night. That gives us three days to organise ourselves and get the word out.'

'Done,' he agreed, with a nod.

It was a frantic three days to get the inaugural Dragonfly Lake Light Festival up and running. Music had to be found and speakers set up. Thanks to Dodgy Del, the sound system was soon organised. Advertising was the main thing but once an announcement had been placed on the *Cranbridge Times* website, which covered the whole area, they were inundated with requests and bookings. In fact, they even brought in extra provisions for the bar in preparation.

'This doesn't mean that everyone will turn up,' Ben told Lily, as she unpacked some more gin. 'I'm still trying not to get my hopes up.'

'You've always got to have hope,' she told him softly.

And he was delighted when she reached up to kiss him on the cheek.

'Yes, you do,' he murmured, still feeling her soft lips on his skin.

If the light festival was a success, he was beginning to think that perhaps there was a future at the hotel after all. For everyone, including Lily.

44

The first visitors to the inaugural Dragonfly Lake Light Festival turned up at five o'clock. As it was the darkest time of the year, they had arranged for an earlier start as it meant that some preschoolers were able to come along on the Saturday night before their bedtime.

'It really is a family event,' said Lily, looking at the throng of families standing along the beach as she and Ben headed towards the boat underneath the boathouse.

She was so pleased that it was a good turnout.

'I just hope they're not disappointed,' said Ben, looking nervous.

'I just hope they don't all drink Frankie's newest cocktail,' said Lily, shuddering in memory of the taste test. 'I think it was the strongest one yet!'

Ben laughed and they climbed into the boat.

This time they had seventy or so candles to light up and so, once they were in the middle of the lake, they both brought out separate lighters.

'Ready?' said Ben, into his walkie-talkie, which they'd had to buy in deference to the complete lack of signal away from the hotel.

'Ready,' replied Hannah after a short pause.

They could both hear the soft music begin and that was their cue to get lighting the wicks of the candles. They then worked as quickly as they could, gently placing each light into the water and letting it drift away.

Just before Lily lit the last of the lanterns, she looked at Ben. 'You know, they say that you should make a silent wish when you send one out across the water,' she told him.

He glanced down at the lantern in his hand for a moment before nodding. 'OK then,' he said. 'Together?'

'Together,' she agreed.

So they placed their lanterns on the water at the same time and gave them a gentle push away from the boat. In silence, they watched the steady stream of lights drifting across the lake. The only sound was the oohs and aahs as the audience enjoyed the view from the beach.

'It's so pretty,' said Lily, with a smile, looking across at the baskets floating away.

The reflections of each coloured light appeared to double the effect which was very pleasing and added to the magic of the spectacle.

'Hannah says she'll take some photos from the beach for the website,' said Ben.

'You know,' said Lily, looking at the lights drifting away, 'we could use some different colours. Maybe even have themed nights.'

'That's an idea,' said Ben.

As the lights floated away from them, they were enveloped back in the soft darkness of the winter evening. The stars peeped down on them through the holes in the clouds as they drifted along on the water in the boat. Lily looked across the water and thought it was like being in a dream, both of them surrounded by fireflies.

In the soft light of the inky black, she could just make out Ben sitting opposite her. He was watching and smiling at her.

'What?' she asked.

'You,' he murmured. 'I never knew...'

His voice trailed off. But it didn't matter. Lily knew what he was trying to say because she was feeling the same thing.

They both leant forward at the same time. However, the boat suddenly rocked a little, throwing them both off-balance so that Lily began to slip off her seat. Ben went to hold her and slipped off his own bench, causing them both to fall onto the bottom of the narrow rowing boat.

They both laughed.

'Are you hurt?' he asked.

She shook her head. 'Just a bit damp,' she said, feeling a puddle of lake water seeping into her jeans.

'Everything OK over there?' came Hannah's voice a short while later from the walkie-talkie. 'I can't see you all of a sudden.'

Ben looked at Lily and smiled as he picked up his handset. 'We're just fine,' he replied, his voice a little husky. 'Just enjoying the view.'

She smiled back at him before they began to carefully get up from the wet bottom of the boat.

Some time later and back on dry land, Lily had managed to quickly get changed out of her wet jeans in time to help out with all the visitors. The hotel bar and lounge were full of people chatting and enjoying their evening. The bar till had been ringing all evening with the many orders for drinks.

Even better, where Lily was concerned, was the fact that Hannah had been persuaded to make some of her puff pastry canapés in case the visitors were hungry. To nobody's surprise, the Mediterranean pinwheels, sausage rolls and spinach puffs had gone down a storm with everyone and had quickly sold out. She had caught Hannah blushing when surrounded by the admiring guests but was delighted to see her friend chatting about her recipes and beginning to come out of her shell at last.

Finally, when the last of the visitors had gone home, the family gathered in the entrance hall.

'That was a huge success,' said Faye, smiling.

'Of course it was,' said Walter. 'There was never any doubt.'

'I shall have sweet dreams tonight of those pretty lights,' said Dotty, wrapping her arm through Walter's before they both wished the family goodnight.

'I think I'll tidy up the bar in the morning,' said Frankie, with a yawn. 'I'm dead on my feet.'

'Me too,' said Faye. 'Goodnight, all.'

'I'll come up as well,' said Hannah, her eyes flicking between her brother and Lily with a soft smile. 'Sweet dreams,' she added with a knowing smile before going upstairs.

Ben and Lily headed into the lounge to close up. They shut the French doors and switched off the lights but remained in the lounge to watch the dying embers in the fireplace.

As they sat down on the sofa, it was the most natural thing in the world for them both to move into each other's arms and begin to kiss.

'My sister's not the only one who'll be having sweet dreams tonight,' he murmured against her lips.

Lily automatically drew back. 'Just remember that I'm only here for a while. Everything is temporary,' she told him. 'It always is.'

'Are you telling me that our kisses meant nothing to you?' he asked, still holding her close. 'That you feel nothing when we're together?'

'Of course not.' The heat rose in her cheeks. 'I can't fake that. I never would with you.'

'And I don't want you to,' he told her.

He brushed her lips with his thumb and Lily tried to stay focused but the fact was that she wanted to kiss him so much over and over. 'But don't you see that this can't last?' she told him, despite drawing near to him. 'That it won't last?'

'Then we'd better make the most of the time we have, hadn't we?' he whispered.

'Absolutely,' she told him, closing the gap to kiss him once more.

As they lay on the sofa wrapped in each other's arms, she had one thought. Despite all her protests, all of her trying not to get too close to him, she was beginning to fall in love with Ben.

45

Ben was delighted with the success of the lantern festival. So much so that they were inundated with requests for it to be held again the following weekend, especially from locals who had been unable to make the previous night.

'The word's got out,' he told Lily. 'Especially after all the photographs that were circulating online afterwards.'

'We should make it every Saturday night,' replied Lily. 'That would appeal to those staying overnight and the locals will begin to think of it as a weekly event that they can come along to.'

'I agree,' said Ben, smiling at her.

He couldn't stop himself from looking at her, sharing a secret look with her before she blushed and turned away from him as Walter joined them in the kitchen.

It was still a secret love. Each night, after the family had gone to bed, they would wrap their arms around each other and kiss until the dawn finally moved them apart. During the day, there were silent looks and snatched kisses when nobody was around.

Ben was falling in love with her day by day. He knew that she was still holding back a little, that she still didn't wholly trust him not to hurt her. But he would spend the rest of his life proving it to her, if she would let him.

The Saturday night lantern festival became a huge draw for visitors during the remainder of January. They planned to change the lighting and music each month to update it for any frequent visitors.

'We can theme it to the seasons,' said Lily. 'So January it can be greens, blues and pinks like the Northern Lights but on the water instead. Maybe there's a way we can add some stars here and there as well.'

'I'll ask Grandad,' replied Ben.

With Walter's help, plastic stars were fixed upright on the floating baskets and added to the theme perfectly, along with many more baskets of candles to add to the spectacle.

Ben had also added lights along the jetty and around the veranda to add to the sparkle and ensure that the hotel was looking its best.

With the bar becoming busy with visitors each Saturday night, that added to the profits as well. Frankie had blossomed under stewardship of the bar and her banter and wit meant that there was always laughter and a festive atmosphere in the snug.

Hannah had gradually gotten used to baking for people other than the family and, after discussing recipes with Jake over the phone, had begun to create a different food menu for the bar each week. Ben loved to see his little sister slowly growing in confidence day by day.

When February began, Lily changed the lights to different shades of red to celebrate the month of Valentine's Day and replaced the stars with hearts for a romantic theme.

'Not that we need too much reminding of that,' Ben told her, drawing her into his arms after they had lit the candles the first Saturday night of the month.

It had been almost four weeks of having her in his arms. Four weeks of a happiness that he never knew could exist. Four weeks of falling in love with Lily.

But best of all, as far as Ben was concerned, each Saturday night he got to watch the light festival from the best seat in the whole place. Next to Lily, on the boat in the middle of the dark lake. There they could kiss each other under the stars, wrapped up in their world of romance, surrounded by the candles shimmering on the surface and the reflected soft lights on the water.

With the light festival being so successful, they began to get more bookings for Saturday nights at the hotel with guests then adding Friday night to make a weekend of it.

Gradually the word began to spread across the area and beyond and it felt as if the hotel might just make it through the most challenging time of the year profit wise.

The icing on the cake would be the Dragonfly Dance, just around the corner on Valentine's Day, thought Ben. The tickets had now almost sold out with local visitors, but there was also a number of bloggers and influencers who had heard about the light show and wanted to come and stay for the weekend as well. Consequently, they were almost full that weekend, which was unheard of so far.

Out on the water the weekend before the Dragonfly Lake dance, Ben checked his watch and groaned, pulling Lily ever tighter into his arms.

'We have to go back soon,' he murmured, bending his head to press his lips against her neck.

'Mmm,' he heard her say. 'So soon?'

His reply was muffled by her soft skin. 'Otherwise my family will start talking about us.'

Lily's soft laugh made her neck vibrate and Ben sit up to look at her. 'What?' he asked.

She shook her head and reached up to stroke his face. 'They might not be saying anything to you but there's plenty being said to me behind the scenes.'

He was astonished. 'Like what?' he asked.

'Like the fact that you're so happy,' she told him. 'Like the fact that we spend far too long in this cold leaky boat when all the candles are already lit.'

'Both of which have entirely plausible explanations,' he replied, with a wink. 'Good. I'm glad everyone knows.'

Lily's smile dropped a little.

'Don't you want them to be happy for us?' he asked her gently.

'Of course, but I don't know if I'm ready for all that attention yet,' she replied, snuggling in tighter to him. 'I like it being just me and you for the time being.'

'That won't change,' he whispered, dropping his head down to hers and kissing her until he forgot all about his family, the hotel, profits and anything else.

46

Lily was delighted that the idea for the Dragonfly Dance had taken hold and many of the local people who had seen the light festival on a Saturday night were equally excited about the event.

'I remember it from many moons ago,' said one elderly lady to Lily one evening after the light show. 'My late husband proposed to me at the dance.'

Not only did the original partygoers book their places but also newcomers to the event as well. And once the momentum had taken hold, the whole event had become the place to be in Cranley on Valentine's Day.

'We're fully booked!' announced Ben, rushing out of the office a few days before the dance.

Lily looked at him in astonishment and delight. 'We are?'

He picked her up in his excitement and swung her round. 'We are!' he shouted. 'Every single bedroom is booked! Wheee!'

Once he had settled her back down on the floor, he bent his head towards hers but they were interrupted by Dotty coming into the entrance hall.

'What's all the commotion?' asked Dotty.

'We're fully booked, Grandma!' shouted Ben, picking Dotty and carefully spinning her around once.

'Hurrah!' she said, laughing.

Lily was equally excited. Success was finally coming to Maple Tree Lodge and the whole family was buzzing with excitement for the Dragonfly Dance.

Not only was the hotel fully booked, every party ticket was sold too. Which begged the question, what on earth were they going to feed them all?

Once more, Jake came up trumps by creating a fork buffet menu that allowed people to wander around and see the lights without the rigidity of timings for a sit-down meal.

'And we won't need too many servers who will want paying either,' said Ben, looking relieved.

'But we'll still need candles on all the tables in here, as well as fairy lights to make it romantic,' said Lily, looking around the dining room.

'Hearts,' added Hannah, with a nod. 'Lots of hearts.'

'Definitely,' replied Lily.

So tiny paper hearts were scattered all over the tables, along with rose petals and the odd string of red heart fairy lights as well. Only a third of the dining room had been laid out though. The remainder of the floor was to be left free for a dance floor.

Meanwhile, Frankie was busy experimenting with new cocktail ideas, both alcoholic and non-alcoholic.

'This is delicious,' Lily told her, after tasting one such new red concoction. 'What's it called again?'

'Love Heart,' said Frankie, rolling her eyes. 'What has happened to cynical old me?'

'It's definitely my new favourite,' said Hannah, who was sitting next to her at the bar and licking her lips.

Coming Home to Maple Tree Lodge

Frankie leaned on the counter. 'So who are you both bringing as a date to the dance?' she asked.

'Are you kidding?' laughed Hannah. 'I'm helping Jake in the kitchen and making sure that the food doesn't run out.'

'We'll be working flat out all night,' said Lily.

'I'm sure Ben will find five minutes to dance with you,' said Hannah, with a knowing smile.

'Maybe even ten minutes if you're lucky,' added Frankie, with a wink.

Lily blushed and giggled.

'After all, it is supposed to be a dance,' Frankie reminded them. 'Now what about music?'

'It's all sorted,' said Lily. 'We've got a local band coming in. They play everything to cater for all tastes.'

'I'm hoping for a spin around the dance floor as well,' announced Walter, as he came into the room.

They all laughed as he tried to teach Hannah how to do the Hustle. Admitting defeat after a while, Walter shook his head and declared that there was no hope for the younger generations.

'Your grandma and I will show you how it's done on the night,' he told them.

Later on, when Lily had finished her cocktail and was about to head out of the room, Walter caught her arm. 'By the way, young lady,' he said in a soft tone that only she could hear. 'If my grandson asks you to dance on Saturday night, please just say yes, will you?'

Lily looked at him with a smile. 'Are you meddling, Walter?' she asked him, giving his hand a squeeze.

He laughed. 'Of course I am, my dear. But I love you both and just want to see you happy.'

So much for Ben thinking that their relationship was secret, she thought with a smile.

She was trying not to get swept up in the romance of the evening. After all, it was a major event for the hotel and the most important thing was that it would run smoothly and be a huge advertisement for the hotel and bring in more bookings.

But even so, the thought of dancing in Ben's arms was certainly appealing.

She knew that she wasn't being fair on Ben by letting the relationship continue. She told him over and over that she must leave eventually and yet as soon as he took her in his arms, she lost her train of thought. He said he didn't care but she knew that he did. And she hated herself all the more for it.

She would still leave when she got another job, something which she was beginning to look for with more eagerness these days. The stronger her feelings for him grew, the more she felt the need to run away. That way she wouldn't get hurt and more importantly nor would he.

But perhaps there would be time for just one dance before she left, she thought, unable to deny herself the feelings in her heart.

47

To everyone's relief, the Dragonfly Dance was a huge success.

Jake's food was delicious as were Hannah's desserts and both had received rave reviews, along with Frankie's Valentines-themed cocktails. The band had encouraged many people to get up and dance. Many more had stood on the veranda as the floating red candle and heart show had slowly made its way across the lake, under the watchful eye of the full moon above.

Lily had had such a busy evening she had barely had time to stop but as the night wore on, she finally began to relax and sought out her friends.

'I love that dress,' Hannah told her, as she joined them in the dining room.

Lily had chosen a full-length dark red dress with tiny glittery pieces on the spaghetti straps.

'And that colour is incredible on you,' said Lily, looking at her friend's long royal-blue dress. 'It matches your eyes perfectly.'

'That's why I chose it for her,' said Ella, coming to stand with them. 'Otherwise she was going to wear black again.'

Ella looked stunning in a long pale silver dress.

'Are we going to have this argument again?' asked Beth as she joined them. 'Black is vintage, classy and will never ever go out of fashion.'

Beth gestured at her fabulous vintage black ballgown with yards of bright red net underneath to match her red heels.

'Ladies, you all look wonderful,' said Jake, wandering up to join them. 'Ella, I'm surprised to see you wear silver. I thought that killed off witches, am I right?'

'Oh, Jake,' sighed Ella. 'Never let your mind wander. It's too little to be let out alone.'

She smiled at a man who had come towards her to ask her to dance and, taking his hand, shot Jake a glare before going onto the dance floor with the stranger.

'It's all so romantic,' cooed Hannah, watching her friend dance.

Lily saw Alex take a step forward from where he had been hovering nearby, a hopeful look on his face.

However at that moment, Dodgy Del came up and asked them for a dance.

'Why, Del, I've been waiting for someone to ask me,' said Hannah, taking his hand in hers with a soft smile.

Del looked as delighted as Alex looked wretched.

Lily watched as Jake placed a hand on his friend's shoulder and shook his head. 'Missed your chance again, mate,' Lily heard him mutter.

So she hadn't been imagining that Alex liked Hannah, she thought.

However, Alex seemed to brush off his misery and asked Beth to dance instead. But once on the dance floor, he still seemed to be unable to take his eyes off Hannah.

Lily didn't have too long to dwell on anyone else once she saw Ben heading across the room towards her. Her breath checked at how handsome he looked in his tuxedo. It had been such a busy evening that she had barely seen him.

She looked at him expectantly as he headed over.

'Crisis?' she murmured.

But he merely looked at her and smiled. 'There will be if I don't get a dance with you this evening.'

And with that, he took her hand and led her to the dance floor.

'We haven't got time for this,' she murmured, but nestled closer into his arms nevertheless.

'Everyone's enjoying themselves,' he replied. 'The party can carry on for a few minutes whilst I hold you in my arms and dance with you. Besides, Grandad's put himself in charge for the time being,' he told her, his breath soft on her ear as he bent his head down towards hers. 'He told me to ask you to dance and I never disagree with him.'

She laughed softly. 'That would be a first,' she told him.

'On the most important matters, we always agree,' he replied.

'Of course, if you didn't want to dance with me...' she teased him.

'Right at this moment, I can't think of anything that I want more,' he said, drawing her even closer so that every part of their bodies touched.

On and on they danced and suddenly she realised that they were close to the open veranda doors. Together they stopped and walked outside where, for a moment, it was just them alone on the veranda.

She shivered in the cool air.

'Cold?' he asked her, drawing her close. 'I thought you were a country girl at long last.'

'Hey, you're the one in the shirt and jacket,' she told him, relishing the warmth from his body as he held her against him. 'I'm in a sleeveless dress here.'

'Yes, you are,' he said, his eyes gleaming as he ran a finger up her bare arm.

Suddenly it wasn't the cool air making her shiver.

'Could the night be even more perfect?' she asked.

Then just after the moon came out from behind a cloud and lit up the starry sky overhead, she drew his head down towards hers. As their lips met, she was lost once more.

And then it was perfect.

48

The following morning, everyone gathered in the kitchen in high spirits, despite the enormous amount of tidying up that needed to be done in the aftermath of the Dragonfly Dance.

'It was a huge success,' said Hannah, pouring herself a much-needed second coffee.

'It was,' said Walter, with a proud look on his face. 'I'm very much looking forward to it becoming an annual event once more.'

'Can we recover from the first one please, Grandad?' asked Ben, with a groan.

'Oooh, I shall have to get a different dress for next year,' said Hannah. 'And if Lily's not wearing red again, I could always borrow hers.'

'I'll buy you both a new dress,' Ben told them, which made everyone look surprised. 'Because we are now fully booked every weekend for the next three weeks!'

There was a huge cheer from around the breakfast table. Everyone was thrilled with the success of the dance but more than that, the hotel was beginning to get a reputation as a relaxing place to stay and the future was looking healthy for the business at last.

Lily looked at Ben once more with a smile. They had danced together in front of everyone. Their secret relationship was not a secret any more. And she was filled with more joy than she ever thought possible. He made her feel cocooned in love, as if the cares and desires of chasing her career had been a mad game. But this? This was the most real thing she had ever felt. Life was sweeter, easier, happier and more fulfilled because she had become closer to her friends and was true to herself now.

Lily was just daydreaming about what colour dress she might choose for the following year's dance, and also about the kisses that she had shared with Ben the previous evening, when her mobile rang.

She picked up and headed out into the entrance hall, thinking that it was a guest who had somehow got the wrong telephone number.

But it wasn't about the hotel at all. It was a previous colleague of hers from the interior design firm, full of news.

'Where are you working these days?' asked Maisie, once she had told all her gossip.

'In the countryside,' Lily told her, looking out at the view across the lake.

'Poor you! Well, it might be time for you to discard your wellies because have I got big plans!' announced Maisie.

She then went on to tell Lily that she was creating her very own interior design firm.

'That's great,' said Lily, wondering whether Maisie had merely rung her up to brag about her career.

'But I'm not good enough to accomplish much by myself, which is why I've been thinking about a partnership,' carried on Maisie. 'And you're the perfect person for the job.'

'Me?' Lily was stunned.

'Your work is amazing,' said Maisie. 'I know how hard you work and plus I know it's always been your dream. We can share the stress and the profits too, if there are any. What do you think?'

Lily was so gobsmacked that she agreed to head into London the following day to discuss the matter further with Maisie.

They arranged a time and place to meet up before Lily hung up. She stared across the lake in shock, trying to take it all in, before she jumped as a hand came around her waist and spun her around.

'Hey,' said Ben, dropping his head to kiss her on the lips. 'Turns out I just can't keep away from you. Was it Frankie's cocktails?'

'It must have been,' she told him in a stilted tone.

Suddenly she was worried. Having her own design firm had been her dream for so long. For a long time it had been all she had thought about.

And then everything had changed over the past couple of months. Suddenly she had been consumed with the hotel. And the family. And Ben, of course. Was she willing to give all of that up for a partnership? She just didn't know.

'Are you all right?' he asked, studying her face with his dark brown eyes.

'I might have to go into London tomorrow,' she said slowly, a feeling of dread beginning to wash over her.

'London?' He looked astonished. 'What on earth for?'

She hesitated before speaking. 'One of my ex-work colleagues is starting up an interior design company and she wants me to be her business partner. She wants to discuss it face to face tomorrow when she'll have more details.'

Silence followed until she finally dared herself to look into Ben's eyes. He looked as shocked as she felt.

'Right,' he said, stepping back out of their embrace.

She instantly wrapped her arms around herself, feeling cold all of a sudden.

'I'm not sure I'll take the position,' she told him.

And she wasn't. The conflict of emotions that she felt was overwhelming her, crowding her thoughts and confusing everything.

'But it's what you've dreamed of, isn't it?' he asked her.

He knew her dreams almost as well as she did, she realised.

She could almost hear the relief in her parents' voices when she told them that she finally had her own interior design business. That she had made something of her career at last and made them proud.

But it would come at a cost, she knew. A heavy cost.

'Well, you must do what is right for you,' he told her. But his smile didn't reach his eyes. 'Right. I'd better start clearing up the dining room.'

He then spun around on his heel and walked away.

Lily went to call out to him, to try and explain how she was feeling, but what was the use? He knew her dreams and desires. He'd always known them.

She'd given herself and her heart to Maple Tree Lodge these past few months and it was destined for success. That would carry on without her.

Her career had always been there in the background on temporary hold. And now, after all the sacrifices, she might just be about to get her dream job.

So why did she want nothing more than to rush after Ben and throw herself back into his arms?

49

'Is that everything?'

Lily looked at Hannah's miserable expression and inwardly sighed, desperately trying not to show her own shaky emotion in return.

It had been three days since her meeting with Maisie. Three days of realising that her ultimate dream was coming true. Three days of packing up her own stuff and facing up to the fact that she was going to leave Maple Tree Lodge.

'I think so,' said Lily, handing the last bag to Dodgy Del, who was taking her into London.

She should be excited, she reminded herself. Her career was turning out just as she had always wanted. She would get the partnership she had always dreamed of, based in the capital where the majority of Maisie's contacts were.

Lily would be staying with Maisie temporarily until she set up her own place. They were going to search for an office to base themselves in. The future was looking bright. So why wasn't she feeling happy?

It was just nerves, she told herself.

She looked at Hannah and gave her a warm hug. 'I'm going to come back at the weekends when I can,' she promised her. 'Although I'll be busy for the first couple of weeks setting everything up...'

Hannah nodded, still looking upset.

'It won't be like it was before,' Lily told her. 'I promise.'

She had her best friends now and they were closer than ever. She wasn't going to lose all that she had built up with them over the winter.

'And I will come back to see you,' she carried on. 'All of you.'

Her voice broke a little on the last word as she glanced around once more but Ben was nowhere to be seen.

There had been no more kisses since she had told him about her trip to London. No more of the joy of being wrapped in his arms. Just stilted conversation about work and long silences. It had been wretched and she hadn't slept well for the past three nights.

She couldn't blame him. He needed to protect himself from hurt, something she knew all about. And yet she missed him so much already that she ached inside.

Dotty was looking tearful as she hugged Lily goodbye.

'We shall miss you,' said Dotty, in a tremulous voice.

'She's coming back to visit us, isn't she?' said Walter. But even his usual bluster couldn't hide the emotion in his voice. 'Hannah says she's invited her for Easter.'

'Of course I'm coming back to visit,' Lily assured them, nodding. 'Just try and keep me away!'

But the truth was that she wasn't sure that she could handle coming back on an infrequent basis. The goodbyes were much harder than anything she had ever endured. And then there was Ben to face over and over.

This was why she had never allowed anyone to get too close

to her, she reminded herself. This was what she had been avoiding all these years. The hurt and pain that she felt in her heart at that moment.

'You've got your hotel, haven't you?' asked Walter, sounding gruff.

Lily nodded. 'The doll's house is safely wrapped up on the back seat.'

Walter gave a shrug. 'Something for you to remember us by,' he muttered.

'I'll never forget you, Walter.' She stepped forward to give him a hug.

As she stepped back, he told her, 'Remember, we made it together, me and Ben.' He fixed her with fierce grey eyes and she nodded in understanding. It was Ben's gift to her as well.

She gulped away the tears as Faye gave her an enormous bear hug.

'Don't work too hard and please come back and see us,' she whispered.

'Of course,' replied Lily, holding her close.

Last, there was only Ben, who had finally appeared to head over towards the taxi. They stood awkwardly in silence for a few moments as the rest of the family discreetly stepped away.

Not known for his tact, Dodgy Del looked between them and, with a small shake of his head, got into the driving seat of the taxi to wait for her.

'Well, I'll let you know my new address just as soon as I've got the full details,' said Lily, in a bright tone. 'In case there's any problems back here there's a checklist under the counter of the reception desk.'

'I saw it, thanks. But I'm sure we'll be fine,' he told her.

'Well, just in case, I'm always happy to help with any queries.' Lily avoided his eyes and glanced up at the hotel. But even that didn't make her feel better. If anything, it just reminded her how lovely the place was and how much she would miss it.

But she was being foolish, she reminded herself. It was all about following her dream career.

Ben suddenly spoke again. 'Thank you.'

'For what?' she asked, as she turned her gaze back onto him.

'For doing this all of this for my family,' he told her.

She found she was shaking her head. 'I did it for me, to be honest.' She hesitated before adding, 'And I did it for you too.'

He took a sharp intake of breath before they allowed themselves the luxury of one last hug. With a shaky sigh, she finally drew back.

'I'll miss you,' she blurted out.

His eyes widened a little before becoming dark once more. 'Me too,' he replied. 'But you're planning on coming back soon, right?'

She accepted the lie gratefully even though neither of them believed it.

'Just as soon as I'm settled. Well, I'll see you soon,' she said, her voice husky with emotion.

'See you soon,' he told her.

She glanced up at him, hating that she was the cause of the pain in his eyes. She wanted to say more, much more, but what was the point? She had to go. It was what she had always wanted, after all.

With a heavy sigh, she turned away and got into the passenger seat next to Del.

'Ready?' Del asked, looking at her.

The emotions bubbled up in her throat, leaving it feeling thick so she merely nodded her head before buckling up her seat belt. Then the car moved forward.

She saw the others waving at her then, with one last glance at

Ben, the car swung around and she could only see him in the door mirror getting smaller and smaller.

A tear trickled down her cheek which she immediately brushed away.

'It's your dream,' she remembered Ben saying. 'I understand. I really do.'

It *was* her dream, she reminded herself as the tears pricked her eyes. So why didn't it feel right? Why did it feel so horribly wrong instead?

50

As Ben watched the taxi drive away, he had a sick feeling deep in his stomach.

He had known it would be painful saying goodbye to Lily but nothing like on this level of hurt. It was pure love. Forever love, he had thought. But maybe only for him.

After all, it was because he loved her that he had to let her go. Together they had saved Maple Tree Lodge for future generations. It was safe after all the stress and worry.

So now it was only fair that it was time for Lily to follow her own dreams. Her own life. Without him. No matter the pain that it would cost him.

He continued to look at the forest but Del's taxi had long since disappeared.

He felt his family leave him to go back inside but he carried on looking away. His eyes ran through the forest. He knew every tree, he realised. Which ones were the best to climb. Which ones he had decided to make into a treehouse for his children to play in. He frowned to himself. Children that he wanted with Lily. He wanted a wife, a family. He wanted multi-generational, messy living with her at the heart of it all.

The thought of carrying on without her seemed impossible for a moment. How would he even get out of bed in the mornings? How would he smile at all the guests who came to stay in the beautiful interiors that she had created? How would he enjoy the festival of lights as they drifted across the lake without having her with him on the boat out on the water?

He would miss everything about her, from her skills and help around the hotel, to her arms wrapped around him and those sweet lips.

So what on earth was he doing letting her leave when the past few months had been the happiest he had ever known? Because he loved her. But the thought only made him feel worse, not better.

A moan escaped his mouth as the pain bubbled up inside him once more.

'I thought you were supposed to be bright, lad.'

Ben spun around and found his grandad a few steps away, looking at him.

'All that money, education and talent and you've turned out to be a real dummy,' carried on Walter, shaking his head. 'I can't believe it.'

Ben rolled his eyes. 'Thanks for the support, Grandad,' he said with a heavy sigh. 'You've cheered me right up.'

'Lily's got this place in her blood,' said Walter in a fierce tone, stepping towards him. 'I can tell. I've always known from the first time I met her. She gets it, the magic of it. She gets our family in all of our messy madness.' He waved his arm back at the hotel. 'This right here is her home. Only a fool would let her leave when she clearly belongs here.'

Ben looked at his grandad. 'She wants her own design

company. It's what she's always wanted for her career,' he told Walter in a dull tone.

'So, work around it!' snapped Walter. 'Can't she here work part time? Make it work for the both of you! Are you honestly going to let the love of your life just leave without a fight?' Walter shook his head. 'Come on, son. I thought I taught you better than that.'

Ben stared at his grandad, realising that he was speaking the truth. Perhaps there was another way that didn't mean Lily leaving forever. Why was he letting her go? He must have lost his mind!

Suddenly galvanised into action, Ben automatically patted the pockets of his jeans. 'Where are my car keys?' he said in a panic.

He was about to rush indoors to find them when Walter threw something at him. Ben automatically caught the object with his hand and realised it was his keys.

He looked up at his grandad.

'Get going,' said Walter softly. 'Del's not known for hanging around in that damn taxi of his.'

They exchanged a determined nod before Ben turned to run towards his car, anxious to track down the best thing that had ever happened to him. He just hoped it wasn't too late.

51

Lily barely took in the glorious view out of the car window. In a way, it made her feel even worse.

All along the lane there were early daffodils pushing up. Spring was just about to burst into life in the countryside. And she would miss it, she reminded herself. She would be back in the urban sprawl. Away from the amazing colours and change that every day brought being so close to nature. Away from Hannah changing her seasonal flavours to spring-themed cakes covered with edible flowers. Away from Dotty with her sharp intellect. Away from Faye with her soft hugs. Away from Frankie with her fierce wit. And away from Walter with his stubborn shell under which lay a heart of gold.

And, worst of all, away from Ben.

Everything to do with Ben was tied up with the outside world. Drifting across the water in the boat with the endless sky twinkling with stars above them. Laughing as they sank into the middle of the freezing cold lake that first time. Enjoying their walks through the forest on hard ground underfoot when the frosts came. Cuddling up in front of a roaring log fire afterwards.

Now she would miss summer with its long evenings full of dreamy skies. The different sounds of the new seasons. She would miss all of it. But most of all, she would miss Ben.

It felt as if she had left her heart behind at Maple Tree Lodge. Outwardly she looked the same, but on the inside, everything had changed. She had changed. She trusted people now. Let them into her heart and soul. She had friends, warmth, laughter and support.

It was everything that she had ever wanted, her secret dream. To belong somewhere. She belonged at Maple Tree Lodge. She belonged with the Jackson family. Her biggest dream hadn't been about having her own business. That wasn't what she had dreamed of growing up. Back then it had been about security. A permanent home. A life in one place. A place where she could finally belong forever.

Somewhere along the way it had gotten mixed up with business. In her career and an ambition that had never been hers to begin with. But when she had designed the interiors of the hotel, it had given her more satisfaction than any other job. Not just because she had been given carte blanche. But because it meant something to her. Not someone else's home or office. It was her home. Hers. And Ben's too.

All those years of living alone. All that loneliness and longing. And she had finally found it. At Maple Tree Lodge she had finally gotten everything that she had ever wanted. For the last five months, she had been surrounded by love, so much love from her friends, from everyone.

Most especially Ben. She trusted him. She believed him. She loved him.

Lily suddenly sat upright in her seat. So why on earth would she throw away anything that precious on something as unimportant as work? Work wasn't the be all and end all, was it? That wasn't her dream. Her dream was back at the hotel, a life spent with Ben.

She glanced at the back seat where Ben and Walter's doll's house was alongside her own. It was like the hotel in almost every detail. But why have the miniature version when she could have the real thing every day? For the rest of her life?

She finally focused on the world outside of the taxi and realised that it was the wrong view entirely.

'Stop the car!' she blurted out. 'Del! Stop this car right now!'

Del jumped in his seat and slammed on the breaks, almost veering the car into a gate at the edge of the field.

'Wassup?' he said, his eyes wild and fearful. 'What's the matter? What have I run over?'

'Nothing! Turn the car around!' she told him.

'Why?' asked Del, looking confused. 'You forget something important?'

'Yes,' said Lily, with a small almost hysterical laugh. 'I forgot that I was already home! Take me back to the hotel, Del. I want to go home.'

Del's face creased into a delighted grin. 'Yes, ma'am!' he replied, before slamming the car into gear and executing a speedy three-point turn.

The return journey seemed to take far longer for Lily than it had when she had left. She drummed her fingers impatiently on her leg, anxious to get back to Ben and apologise. She just hoped he would believe her.

Del seemed equally anxious and drove at breakneck speed along the narrow country lanes to reach their destination.

Finally, he took a sharp left at the sign for Maple Tree Lodge and they were bouncing down the track, still at an accelerated pace.

Lily was so busy looking through the trees, desperate to catch that first view of the hotel, that she didn't see the car coming the other way until it was almost too late.

Del didn't appear to have seen it either and had yet to slow down, she realised in horror.

'Watch out!' she shouted.

Del finally saw the car and slammed on the brakes.

However, Ben's car, which had been heading towards them, had to swerve to avoid Del's taxi and Lily watched in slow motion as Ben veered the car off the track and went straight into the muddy pond.

52

Lily immediately leapt out of Del's taxi and ran towards Ben's car which was now stricken in the middle of the pond.

She hoped he hadn't been hurt in the accident and was grateful to see him push open the driver's door and jump out of the car.

He leapt straight into the mud but didn't seem at all concerned nor thankfully hurt either.

'Are you OK?' she said, rushing across to stand on the bank in front of him. 'Are you hurt?'

'I'm fine,' he replied, staring up at her with a confused look. 'I thought you'd left!'

'I came back,' she told him, with a tremulous smile.

'Why?' he asked, his look filled with nerves and uncertainty.

'Because I can't leave you,' she told him, with a sob. 'Because I love you.'

Finally he broke into a relieved smile. 'And I love you too. Does this mean you're staying?'

She nodded. 'Definitely,' she replied.

'Good because I think my feet are really stuck,' he told her, glancing down at his bogged-down trainers.

Lily couldn't help but laugh. 'That's great news,' she told him.

'It is?' He looked bemused at her happy expression.

'Because it means I can do this,' she said.

She stepped back and took a leap across the pond where, thankfully, she felt his arms reach out to catch her.

Somewhere in the background, she thought she heard Del whoop with joy and then the sound of running getting further away.

She looked up into Ben's face, his brown eyes so close that she could see the love in them staring back at her.

'You know, I have a confession to make,' she told him. 'I think I really did need saving all those months ago when we met. You know, when I was the one stuck in the pond.'

'Perhaps we saved each other,' he replied, in a soft tone.

'For what?' she murmured as he kissed her gently on the lips.

'For the future,' he whispered against her lips. 'Our future. Together.'

There was no talking for quite some time after that as he kissed her and she forgot everything else but him. Finally they drew apart.

'Thank God you came back,' he said. 'I'm not sure that I could have dared to imagine a life without you.'

'I was so stupid,' she said, rolling her eyes at herself.

'Just ambitious,' he said, shaking his head. 'And there's nothing wrong with that. You've still got dreams that you want to fulfil.'

'But they were different ones to what I had said out loud. Anyway, I had to come back,' she told him. 'I realised everything I ever wanted was right here. With you. I've travelled the world over but nowhere has ever felt more like home. This place is magical.'

'Yes, it is,' he replied. 'But it's you that makes it special for me. It's you that gives it the magic.'

'And you're the magic right here for me too,' she told him, reaching out to stroke his face. 'And I want to stay here. In this hotel. With you. I want to grow old here. Have our family here. Everything. All of it. All that life can offer.'

'This place is yours now as well,' he said, holding her close. 'I can see it everywhere, in each room, in the whole feel of the place. It's yours.'

'Ours,' she reminded him.

'Ours,' he repeated with a loving smile. 'You know, when I sent out my lantern across the lake, I wished for you.'

'And I wished for you right back,' she told him.

'So the magic really does work,' he said, with a soft laugh.

'It truly does,' she said, drawing his head down to hers once more.

As they kissed, she could hear the Jackson family in the background growing closer, a joyful throng as they realised that she had returned to them and what it meant for the future.

When Lily drew back, she looked up at Ben.

'I love you,' she told him. 'And I will never ever stop loving you.'

'I love you too. Welcome home,' he said, bending his head to close the distance between them once more.

And she knew that she was home. Forever.

53

The spring sunlight shone down on Ben as he walked back from his grandad's workshop.

April had arrived in a flurry of sunshine and everywhere he looked nature was bursting forth.

There were already ducklings on the shallows of the lake, scurrying along in and out of the reeds, trying to keep up with their parents. Fresh green grass and flowers were bursting into life everywhere, with pink and white apple blossom floating down from the trees to land on the surface of the water. Best of all was the cacophony of birdsong and chatter as the nesting season came into full swing as the eggs began to hatch and new life began once more.

Ben sighed a happy sigh. He too felt as if he had a new life, reborn this spring out of the misery of the past.

He looked up at the hotel in front of him. Thanks to his grandmother's inspired idea of the Dragonfly Lake Light Festival each Saturday night, the whole place had also burst into life.

Every weekend, visitors poured in from everywhere to enjoy the light show. They had even planned a special Easter-themed one for the following weekend where there would be decorated eggs, flowers and rabbits lit up on the water as well.

With so many evening visitors, the snug was doing a roaring trade in drinks and snacks. Even better, he had managed to secure a part-time chef to cater for the dinner service every weekend and the restaurant was full each Friday and Saturday night.

The hotel reopening had been above and beyond all of their expectations. Word was beginning to spread and at least half their bookings were recommendations from other guests.

Best of all, the hotel was fully booked every weekend. Such was the popularity that they had even had to open up a waiting list, something he would never have expected only a few short months ago.

It felt as if everything had changed for the better. The hotel, like the lake, was steeped in history, his family's history. But now they were all looking to the future too. The fresh growth of spring felt as if it were reflected on the inside walls of the hotel now as well.

Whilst still grieving, the family were finding hope with each new day as the hotel's success reflected on their personal lives as well. Ben glanced back at the workshop, where his grandad was busy making Easter baskets out of willow. Finally able to step away from the pressures of helping to run the hotel, Walter too had blossomed these past couple of months. At least twice a month he was asked to conduct a nature trail walk around the lake, and, with Lily's gentle persuasion, he had printed up some notes to place in the lounge and snug, alongside binoculars for nature watching. His wealth of knowledge was to be passed onto future generations, a subject which had always been close to his heart.

Hannah had also become more confident in her baking skills

after all the positive feedback from their hotel guests. Each day, she created delicious cakes and desserts that showed her growing expertise. With gentle encouragement from all the family, Ben relished watching his little sister finally beginning to believe in her own abilities.

Faye was busy providing wildflower bouquets in each of the bedrooms, as well as in the communal areas. She had also signed up for a local flower-arranging class and, day by day, was beginning to find her way in the world once more. Dotty was the life and soul of the snug on a Monday night, when her friends came to visit and gossip over a drink. She had already expressed plans to start up a games night in the future. And there was even talk that she would start up a wild swimming club when the warmer months arrived.

Frankie was a firm fixture in the snug, holding the fort and becoming hugely popular for her dry wit and delicious cocktails. In turn, she was enjoying the varied company of the guests and slowly the loneliness that had been surrounding her for so many years had begun to fade.

Everything had changed once more but this time for the better, thought Ben. Including himself.

He was so much happier these days. He felt as if his architectural skills were being used properly and the idea for both the new lodges and the boathouse renovations excited him more than any bland office block had ever done. He was far closer to his grandad these days too, enjoying his company but also feeling grateful that his grandad could finally relax and enjoy the place without the burden of responsibility around his neck.

Best of all, he got to enjoy each and every day with Lily. They were partners in both the running of the hotel and in their private life as well. She was the love of his life and he couldn't wait to see what the future held for them together.

* * *

Lily unlocked the patio doors and stepped onto the veranda of the hotel, relishing the ever-changing view.

With the arrival of spring, the air was warmed by the sun growing ever higher in the cobalt-blue sky. The stillness of the lake, where there was barely a whisper of a breeze, was in stark contrast to the air as nature enjoyed its busiest month of the year so far. The birds flitted from tree to tree, busy nesting and looking after their new flock. The trees were all wearing the bright green of the fresh growth as the new leaves unfurled. A carpet of bluebells brought a glorious purple haze to the ground surrounding the tree trunks. And there on the reeds, the dragonflies were beginning to emerge into the warmth of the day.

Dotty had been right all those months ago. Spring really did bring a magic all of its own. But then again, Lily found every day magical these days.

Waking up to the best view in the world helped, she reminded herself. But it wasn't just about the view. It was waking up to the excitement of another busy day in the hotel. The joy of working alongside the Jackson family, who treated her like one of their own. And, best of all, waking up beside Ben and starting the day with one of his sweet kisses. The hotel was a success and they couldn't be more thrilled. There had been much change in the inside of the hotel since she had arrived the previous autumn. The interiors had drastically altered, of course. But best of all were the guests that continued to arrive. Every weekend was fully booked and the hotel was at least half-full during the week as well.

Her phone buzzed with an email and as she read it, she smiled to herself. Ben's plans had been approved to begin work on the individual private lodges that would be built around the lake. Ben's skill as an architect had meant a swift approval by the local council as he had created them with such skill in deference to the hotel and boathouse designs that were already there.

In turn, Lily would design the interiors of both the boathouse and the lodges. She still enjoyed interior design but it wasn't the be all and end all to her life now. Sophie had understood when Lily had rung her to say that she could no longer accept the partnership in the new business and they had parted amicably. In fact, she had even contacted Lily to ask for some designs for a nearby job in the area. In addition, Lily had received some private commissions from hotel guests who had been delighted with the subtle colours and feel of both the bedrooms and communal areas. So it meant that she could still use her design skills as well as working alongside Ben, taking on the running of the hotel.

It was the best of both worlds, she had found. And her design skills kept getting renewed by the changing of the seasons outside so she was constantly inspired.

The recognition for her work was something she now received from herself. Her parents finally seemed content with her life choices and were even promising a visit to stay at the hotel over the summer. She didn't need their approval or crave it like in the past. But it was nice to have it, all the same, she thought, grateful for their support.

The hotel gave her more job satisfaction as well than she'd ever experienced. She loved the excitement of new guests, never knowing who she was going to meet coming through the door.

Her life would never revolve around work again though. There were too many important other things in it now.

The biggest success she now felt was in her private life. Determined to right the wrongs of her past, she made a concerted effort with her friends to always be there, no matter the time of day or night. She was the always the first one to organise the next meet-up and loved seeing them more often and being a part of their lives. She wanted to be there for Hannah, Beth and Ella to celebrate their successes and hold them close when they needed strength and support. She would make sure that they never felt second best in her life again.

She took one last look at the lake. Summer was just around the corner and Lily couldn't wait to enjoy the hot days with a dip in the lake or just to enjoy a picnic by the edge, hopefully encased in Ben's strong arms as they watched the sunset. They were a team now and she relished every moment spent with him. She loved him body and soul and told him so every single day.

'There you are,' said a familiar voice.

Ben's hand slipped around her waist and she leant back against him for a moment, so that they could both enjoy the glorious view across the lake.

She trusted him wholeheartedly. It had taken time but she now believed in him and their shared love. Best of all, she could always be herself around him. She didn't need to pretend to be anything else other than her own person. Whatever life threw at them in the future, they would face it together. She had moved into his bedroom in the family's private quarters and knew in her heart that after so many moves and different addresses, she was home at last.

Despite the beautiful view across the water, Ben seemed distracted and pretty soon she could feel his lips nibbling the side of her jaw and down her neck.

'Mmm,' she murmured, lifting her hand up to press his lips further against her skin. 'I don't have time for this.'

'We will always make time for this,' came his whispered promise against her neck.

'What about your meeting?' she asked, trying to keep her mind on the hotel and not on Ben's lips. But it was hard work to think about anything but him when he kissed her.

With a muttered oath under his breath, Ben finally drew back. 'I'd forgotten,' he said, spinning her around so that they faced each other. 'How am I supposed to concentrate when you're around?'

'You'll just have to try harder,' she told him, smiling as she reached up to kiss him on the lips.

'Now you're just deliberately teasing me,' he said, his eyes gleaming. 'I'd better go and see this guy. How else are we going to provide electric off-road bikes if I don't?'

'Off you go then,' she told him, reluctantly letting her arms fall from his shoulders.

'This is to be continued later,' he murmured, sneaking one more kiss before heading back indoors.

Lily took a deep and satisfied breath before turning to look once more at the view before following him inside.

Her eyes swept around the lounge and she automatically straightened the cushions and the rugs so that it all looked perfect. The fire in the hearth wasn't lit until the evenings now that the days were growing so much warmer. Summer would bring new possibilities as well. She and Ben had so many ideas for the future with how to grow the business even further. But for now she was just enjoying being there each and every day.

The replica of the hotel that Ben and Walter had made her was in pride of place in a glass box on display. The guests loved looking at it and Walter had even received a few commissions to make some others for the guests. The doll's house was special but it would never be as spectacular as the real thing, she knew. Because it was her home, now and forever.

Seeing a couple of visitors in the entrance hall, Lily quickly headed out of the lounge to greet them.

'Welcome to Maple Tree Lodge!' she said, with a smile.

* * *

MORE FROM ALISON SHERLOCK

Another book from Alison Sherlock, *Heading Home to Lavender Cottage*, is available to order now here:
https://mybook.to/HeadingBackAd

ACKNOWLEDGEMENTS

A huge thank you to my lovely editor Caroline Ridding for her continuing patience and encouragement as we embark on our fourth series together.

Thank you to everyone at Boldwood Books for all their hard work behind the scenes on all my books.

Thank you to all the readers and bloggers for their enthusiasm and reviews, which are important to so many authors, myself included.

Thank you to my lovely author friends, most especially my fellow Team Boldwood authors and the wonderful Surrey Buddies, especially Jennifer Bibby, Jenny Worstall, Sally Harris, Cara Cooper, Nina Barclay and Linda Corbett whose good cheer has kept me going this past year.

Some years are harder than others so thank you to all my friends for being there.

Best friends are the people that make your life better just by being in it and for me that's Jo Botelle whom I want to thank for the tea, cake and for her endless support.

Huge thanks to my wonderful family for all their continued support, especially Gill, Simon, Louise, Ross, Lee, Cara and Sian.

Special thanks to my husband Dave for finding the campsite next to beautiful Lake Annecy where inspiration struck for this new series of books set around a hotel with a lakeside setting. As always, this book could have never been written without your love, support and the many cups of tea you make for me.

ABOUT THE AUTHOR

Alison Sherlock is the author of the bestselling *Willow Tree Hall* books. Alison enjoyed reading and writing stories from an early age and gave up office life to follow her dream. Her series for Boldwood is set in a fictional Cotswold village.

Sign up to Alison Sherlock's mailing list for news, competitions and updates on future books.

Follow Alison on social media:

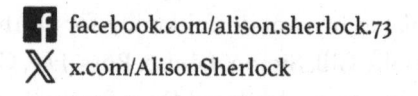

facebook.com/alison.sherlock.73
x.com/AlisonSherlock

ALSO BY ALISON SHERLOCK

The Riverside Lane Series
The Village Shop for Lonely Hearts
The Village of Lost and Found
The Village Inn of Secret Dreams
The Village of Happy Ever Afters

The Railway Lane Series
Heading Home to Lavender Cottage
New Beginnings on Railway Lane
Sunrise over Strawberry Hill Farm
Winter Magic on Railway Lane

Standalone Novels
Coming Home to Maple Tree Lodge

Boldwood EVER AFTER

xoxo

JOIN BOLDWOOD'S **ROMANCE COMMUNITY** FOR SWEET AND SPICY BOOK RECS WITH ALL YOUR FAVOURITE TROPES!

SIGN UP TO OUR NEWSLETTER

HTTPS://BIT.LY/BOLDWOODEVERAFTER

Boldwood

Boldwood Books is an award-winning fiction publishing company seeking out the best stories from around the world.

Find out more at www.boldwoodbooks.com

Join our reader community for brilliant books, competitions and offers!

**Follow us
@BoldwoodBooks
@TheBoldBookClub**

Sign up to our weekly deals newsletter

https://bit.ly/BoldwoodBNewsletter